_A_
TRUTH REVEALED

# TRACIE PETERSON

BETHANYHOUSE

*a division of Baker Publishing Group*
Minneapolis, Minnesota

© 2024 by Peterson Ink, Inc.

Published by Bethany House Publishers
Minneapolis, Minnesota
BethanyHouse.com

Bethany House Publishers is a division of
Baker Publishing Group, Grand Rapids, Michigan

Printed in the United States of America

Library of Congress Cataloging-in-Publication Data
Names: Peterson, Tracie, author
Title: A truth revealed / Tracie Peterson.
Description: Minneapolis, Minnesota : Bethany House, a division of Baker
    Publishing Group, 2024. | Series: Heart of Cheyenne ; 3
Identifiers: LCCN 2024012127 | ISBN 9780764241093 (paperback) | ISBN
    9780764244100 (cloth) | ISBN 9780764244117 (large print) | ISBN
    9781493448135 (e-book)
Subjects: LCGFT: Christian fiction. | Romance fiction. | Novels.
Classification: LCC PS3566.E7717 T78 2024 | DDC 813/.54—dc23/eng/20240325
LC record available at https://lccn.loc.gov/2024012127

Scripture quotations are from the King James Version of the Bible.

This is a work of historical reconstruction; the appearances of certain historical figures
are therefore inevitable. All other characters, however, are products of the author's
imagination, and any resemblance to actual persons, living or dead, is coincidental.

Cover design by Peter Gloege, LOOK Design Studio
Cover image of woman by Lee Avison, Arcangel

Baker Publishing Group publications use paper produced from sustainable forestry
practices and postconsumer waste whenever possible.

24  25  26  27  28  29  30      7  6  5  4  3  2  1

# 1

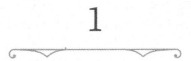

Laura Evans looked out the window at the snow-covered landscape as the train pulled into the Cheyenne station. After ten years living apart, she was about to be reunited with her father. At thoughts of Father, her fascination with the Western frontier faded, even as she surveyed the cowboy town that was to become her home.

Ten years.

Mama died in November of 1858. Consumption, the doctor said. A debilitating depletion of her body for which he had no understanding. And just a week after they buried her, Father sent Laura to boarding school over fifty miles away. Where he had gotten the money for such an endeavor was beyond Laura, but it had been her fate for the next decade.

In all those years, she'd only seen her father a handful of times. He had visited her at the boarding schools on several occasions and once during her college years. It had been six years since the latter visit. It came on the occasion of

Father settling her into the Tennessee women's college he'd chosen for her. Even with the war raging, he had figured her to be safe there. When that proved otherwise, and the college closed, Father had arranged for her to go abroad with a teacher to escape the ugliness of war. Now, the world was set right again—or at least it was no longer pitting brother against brother in a war that Laura still found difficult to understand—and she would soon be with her beloved father once more.

Granite Evans was the light of her life. He was her hero. Despite having sent her away, Father had always meant the world to Laura. He was generous and kind, making sure she had everything she needed. His absence had been difficult, but Laura had reminded herself that Father hurt just as much, perhaps more, in losing Mama than she did. She respected that he had needed time alone to grieve and mourn. It hadn't been easy for her, but Laura had been determined to be strong. She owed him that much.

"Cheyenne!" the conductor announced as he moved through the car. "All out for Cheyenne!"

Laura stood, adjusted her cloak, then brushed down the skirt of her burgundy traveling suit with her gloved hand. She wanted to look her best when she met her father again. She hoped—prayed—that he would be proud of her.

With the help of the porter, Laura stepped from the train, her travel bag clutched tight and her heavy wool cloak pulled close against her body. Father had told her that it would be cold in Cheyenne and to buy an appropriate wardrobe. She had taken the money he'd sent and did as instructed. As the December winds whipped at the hem of her cloak and skirt, Laura was glad she had listened.

She looked up and down the depot platform for some sign

of her father but found no one who resembled him. Six years was a long time, but she was certain he would look like he had when last he visited her.

Wouldn't he?

Making her way inside the depot, Laura shifted her bag from one gloved hand to the other. Quite a few people crowded into the building alongside her, and she allowed herself to be caught up in the flow of their movements. All the while she kept looking for the stocky, mustached man she knew would be there. And he was.

She spied him across the room talking with a couple of other men. She called out to get her father's attention. "Father!"

He looked up and caught her gaze. He smiled and quickly dismissed the two younger men. Crossing the room to greet her, he held open his arms.

"Laura!"

She dropped her bag and rushed to him. A sigh escaped her as his arms closed tightly around her. It was here she felt the safest and happiest. She thought of how few times she had known his tender embrace over the years, but she refused to let such thoughts discourage her. The fact that they'd had so little time together only served to make this moment all the more precious.

"Father, I'm so happy to see you again." She breathed in deeply of his cologne and the unmistakable scent of cigars and coffee.

"I thought you'd never get here. Welcome home."

*Home.* The word touched a place deep in her heart. She hadn't had a home since Mama died. Oh, but Laura had longed for one. She had enjoyed very little consistency as a child attending boarding school. Year after year, her father moved her to a better, more stately and expensive school. As he was able to improve his own situation, he improved hers, never realizing that consistency would have been a bigger blessing than larger, more elegantly appointed rooms and educational halls.

Laura stepped back and studied her father from head to toe. He looked well and happy. "How wonderful it is to see you," she told him. "I worried that I might not recognize you, but then I chided myself for such doubt. Nothing about you could ever seem foreign or strange to me."

"And you." He shook his head. "I had no idea you'd grow into such a beauty. You always favored your mother, but the last time I saw you, there were still remnants of childhood in your face and figure. That, alas, is gone for good. You are no more a child."

"I was full grown last you saw me, or nearly so. Sixteen years old, in fact. Most of my fellow students were engaged to be married. I can't imagine there being any remnants of childhood remaining then."

"Well, there were. You were more gangly and awkward. Now you're full grown and a lovely young woman."

"Oh, Father, you do go on. Six years could not have made such a difference. You look the same as I remember you."

"I'm an old man, and change is slower."

She laughed. "You aren't that old. Not even yet fifty." She wrapped her arm around his. "I'm just so glad to see you again. I want to know everything that has happened to you in the last six years."

He shook his head. "It's more important we plan a future than lose ourselves in the past. That was the reason for our separation in the first place. A separation that has been difficult but necessary."

She sobered. "And do you feel that time has healed your heart?"

"I will always have a place of emptiness where your mother once resided. She meant everything to me. You both did, but when she died, something in me died as well, and I knew I'd be no good to you. My poor precious girl." He frowned, looking very close to tears.

Laura hadn't meant to make him so uncomfortable, and in a public place. What was she thinking?

"Forgive me. This is a talk better suited to a private parlor." She stepped back to where she'd dropped her bag and picked it up. Rejoining him, she gave her father a smile. "I have claim tickets for my trunks. Goodness, but I brought so much stuff. I got rid of as much as possible, but some keepsakes and pieces of memorabilia were impossible to part with."

"It's of no worry, as I told you in my letter. We are well-off now. I have a large home for you and staff to wait on your every need. I'll give these tickets to my driver, and he'll see to it that the trunks are delivered. For now, I'll take that bag you're carrying, and we'll be on our way."

She handed over her valise, then took hold of his arm. "I have dreamed of this day for so long."

He led her through the station and outside, where the wind again whipped at her cloak from every side. Father approached an enclosed carriage as the driver jumped down from his seat in front.

"You have a landau," Laura observed as the driver opened the door. "What a treat. I came fully expecting buckboards or buggies at best."

Father assisted her into the carriage, and the scent of leather enveloped her.

Laura took a seat, and her father quickly joined her. He put her bag on the opposite seat and took up a blanket.

"I just had the landau delivered. It is a Christmas gift to us. As we rise to the top, it is only fitting that we travel in style."

"It's lovely." She ran her gloved hand along the leather upholstery. "I'm sure no one has a finer one."

"I have another smaller conveyance you can handle when you decide to move about town to see friends."

"You sound as though you are very rich, Father."

"I am. We are. It's for you that I've labored so long and hard. If we'd had proper money, your mother might not have died. Destitute patients get very little attention, in either the hospital or the church."

Laura hated to believe that her mother had died purely for lack of money, but Father had always insisted it was so.

"I've worked hard this last decade, bettering myself as I could. I invested heavily in the railroad, and it has done me well to be sure. There are, of course, other investments, and the ladies' store. I think you'll be impressed with what I've created there. I have items brought in from all over the world. Shipped right here to Cheyenne and made available to the women as if they lived in New York City or Paris."

Pride was evident in his voice. Laura smiled but refrained from telling him that luxury meant very little as far as she was concerned. Many of her friends at school also had money, but even those of lesser means had been far better off than Laura. They had family. Mothers and fathers who came and took them away for holidays and summers. Laura had been left to travel with old-maid teachers or matronly facilitators whose children were grown. More than once she'd remained with the headmistress at the school all summer doing little more than reading and taking long walks. She used to dream of her father showing up with a train ticket to take her away on some grand adventure. But he never came.

The carriage finally stopped, and the driver opened the door. Father was first to debark, then he turned for Laura.

She gripped his hand and stepped from the landau to gaze up at a flat-faced white house. Snow lay all about the yard, where there wasn't a single tree or shrub.

The house wasn't anything elaborate on the outside. It was two-stories tall with a large square frame of white clapboard and multiple windows to break the lack of ornamentation. To one side there was a carriage house, but Laura couldn't see beyond that.

"This is only a temporary home," her father explained as they moved toward the front door. "I have property over on Ferguson and plan to build us a mansion. You can see, however, the beautiful windows. Those cost a pretty penny."

"I know they must have, but they're lovely, Father. I'm sure you've made it a wonderful place."

"Well, it will be a home now for sure, what with having you here. There's so much I want you to know about me, Cheyenne, and this territory. I intend to do big things here, Laura. Big things."

She'd gathered from bits and pieces in his letters that her father had taken a strong interest in politics. He had left more than one hint at hoping to get involved rather than just be a sideline supporter.

"I've no doubt you will, Father. How could you not? You've done so well in just one decade. Imagine what you'll accomplish in another."

He fixed her with a proud look. "Exactly so. Now come. I'll show you the house and staff." He opened the door and ushered her inside out of the cold.

Laura was glad to find the house quite warm. She'd never much cared for cold weather. Mother often said the blood of Alabama women was much too thin for the colder climates. Laura didn't know if that was true or not, but she always suffered during her travels in Europe when they ventured where it was cold. She supposed she would just have to get used to it now.

"This is my housekeeper, Mrs. Duffy," Father said as three strangers entered the foyer. "She's agreed to act as your lady's maid until you can find someone else. She doesn't live with us, as she has two teenage boys, but she comes every day from six in the morning to nine at night. Her days off vary."

Laura smiled at the dark-haired woman. "I'm pleased to meet you, Mrs. Duffy."

"The pleasure is mine, Miss Evans." She had a small frame, but there was an edge in her voice that betrayed strength.

"This is our cook, Mrs. Murphy."

Mrs. Murphy was a stocky woman with a serious expression. Laura had often heard it said that she should never trust a skinny cook. There was no concern of that here.

Mrs. Murphy looked to be somewhere in her late fifties or early sixties. She gave Laura a nod, then looked her up and down as though trying to assess how much she would eat. The thought made Laura smile once again.

"I'm sure you are a blessing, Mrs. Murphy. Good food makes all the difference in a household." Laura saw her comment caused the older woman's expression to relax just a bit.

"And this young man is Curtis. Curtis does whatever needs to be done with the yard and stables. He often works with Mr. Grayson, my driver and stableman."

It was clear that Curtis was uncomfortable. He couldn't have been more than sixteen or seventeen. Laura took pity on him and offered him her best smile. "It's a pleasure to meet you, Curtis." The young man blushed and looked away after a brief glance.

Her father gave the trio a nod, and they all hurried away as quickly as they'd come. Laura untied her cloak, since the warmth of the room proved more than enough. Father put aside his hat and gloves, then doffed his coat and hung it on a nearby coat-tree.

"Not a very elegant approach to outdoor garments," he said, reaching for Laura's cloak. "But as I said, next year I intend to begin building a new and luxurious place for us. We'll have a full staff to take care of everything."

Laura pulled the pin from her hat and set both aside on a nearby table. Last of all, she drew off her gloves. "This looks like a lovely house, Father." She could see to his right that the pocket doors had been pushed back partway to reveal a large comfortable-looking room, complete with a hearth on the far wall. A fire blazed in welcome.

"It is sufficient for the time being, but I intend to better myself further. Many of us here feel the same. There are a great many quality families who have settled this growing community, and we intend to see that the elite make a clear and present mark on society."

Laura had never heard her father talk in this snobbish manner. She didn't feel it was proper to approach him on the matter her first day home and so gave a simple nod and followed him as he took her bag and led her upstairs.

"I'll show you to your room first. I hope you'll like it."

"I'm sure I will," Laura replied. "Everything seems perfect."

"I run a well-ordered house. Mrs. Duffy understands that and follows my instructions to the letter. I brook no nonsense, as I have a great many important people who come here from time to time."

She noted the highly polished oak banister and stairs. Mrs. Duffy apparently kept a very neat house. The upstairs hall was papered in a print of gold, beige, and green stripes, with prominent gold fleur-de-lis running down wide panels of powder blue. It wasn't something Laura would have chosen, but it gave the hall a touch of elegance.

A beige hallway runner covered the oak floors nearly wall to wall. A few decorative tables were placed between the multiple closed doors.

"My room is to the right," Father announced, pointing. "If you should need me for any reason in the middle of the night, do not hesitate to knock on my door."

"Thank you, I will." Laura turned as he drew her to the left.

"The door to your right is a bedroom that has been appointed for sewing and storage. The next door is a bathing room. I had a copper tub brought in from Boston. It's situated beside a stove that can be used to heat the water and keep the room warm when in use. I find a hot bath to be one of those things I cannot live without."

"How very nice." Laura had wondered what kinds of things would be available for their personal needs.

"And this door on the left is your room. It's actually two rooms. They seemed rather perfect to join together, so I had a doorway created when I knew for sure you'd be coming home." He smiled. "One can be used as your sitting room and the other your bedroom."

He opened the door, and Laura stepped inside. The room had been furnished with a large wardrobe and desk of matching white oak. Dark rose-colored draperies were hanging at the windows, and a delicate print of pink roses on white paper trimmed the walls. It had been designed with a young woman in mind. On the wall to the right was a small but efficient fireplace trimmed in white tiles with the same rose pattern as the papered walls. A fire had been built up, and it, along with the lamps, gave the room a beautiful glow. A large chintz-covered chair waited in welcome.

"I shall be quite comfortable here." She turned to her father and kissed his cheek. "Thank you so much." She ran her hand along the back of the chair. "It's just perfect."

"Nothing is too good for you, my dear Laura." He patted her shoulder. "Now come see the bedroom."

Turning away from the fireplace, Laura found the bedroom door already open. Inside was a beautiful four-poster bed and dressing table in the same white oak as the wardrobe and desk. The draperies and paper matched the sitting room.

"This is certainly everything a girl could want," she said, touched at all the details her father had put into the setting.

She went to the dressing table and found all sorts of bottles of perfume and lotions for her skin and a delicate silver hairbrush, comb, and mirror set. A large framed mirror was attached to the dressing table so that she could simply sit and survey her appearance at will.

"It's all so very nice, Father, thank you. I'm quite surprised by all of this. I read almost everything I could get my hands on about Cheyenne and Wyoming Territory, and I must admit, I wasn't hopeful of finding much, but I am pleased to be mistaken."

He chuckled. "We have worked hard to improve the situation in our little town. Mark my words, Cheyenne will one day be as fine a city as any other. Important people are making their mark here, and incredible things will be accomplished. You are to be a part of all that, my dear."

She could see the excitement in his eyes. This was significant to him, and she intended to join in as much as she could. If only to please him.

Granite Evans settled into the leather chair behind his desk and considered the young woman upstairs. His daughter. His only child. He'd hardly seen her in the last ten years, and now she would be his constant companion. Could he still manage to accomplish all that he had planned with her under his roof?

All of Cheyenne's society would adore her. The men would line up to court her. He could probably arrange a lucrative betrothal. It was something he hadn't given much thought to, but now that she was here, he could see she was a valuable prize. There weren't that many women in Cheyenne, and certainly none as beautiful as Laura. She favored her mother more than he liked to admit.

When he'd first seen her in the depot, she had startled him. For just a moment, he thought Meredith had returned in all her youth and beauty. Cinnamon-red hair framing a lovely oval face. Dark brown eyes and full lips. Laura was the spitting image of her deceased mother.

Then again, Laura had always reminded him of her mother. It was the reason he had sent her away. He couldn't bear the constant reminder of what he had lost. Meredith had been his entire world. He had been nothing of value prior to meeting her. She had transformed him with her love, and her death had forever changed him. Even now, remembering her and what she went through stirred undiluted anger, as though he'd lost her only yesterday.

Granite would never forget the attitude of the doctors and

hospital staff when he'd sought help for Meredith. With no money to pay up front for the needed treatment, they had been given nothing more than the smallest bit of attention and then sent on their way. Knowing his wife's faith, he had gone to the church, as well, but found them equally callous.

With nothing left to do, he had contacted her well-to-do parents in Birmingham. Meredith had defied them and run away to marry Granite. They denounced her as their child and refused to even listen when he begged for help. They told him she'd be better off dead than married to a low-life gambler. Rejections from the doctors, church, and family had left Granite hard and angry, and when his beloved wife died, he vowed to make a success of himself in such a way that he could get back at those who had denied her help.

Her parents died before he could do anything to them, and their wealth passed on to a distant cousin. But then the war had come, and opportunities arose on every side. Granite had never been afraid to step over the line where laws were concerned. As the South's needs grew, he found ways to accommodate, using the persona of an Irishman named Marcus O'Brien, while Granite Evans kept his hands and name clean. Eventually, Granite had a team of men working for him. They smuggled goods, robbed warehouses and shipments of supplies, and did whatever it took to put money in their pockets.

Granite didn't care about the outcome of the war. He wasn't a patriot in any sense of the word. Let there be slaves or none. Let the states be in control or not. The only things he cared about were himself, Laura, and getting back at the people who had failed him.

Already he'd had some of his revenge on the hospital back in Alabama. After the war, he had pledged to give them an endowment and help rebuild and expand their facilities.

There had been a front-page photograph showing Granite with the smug-faced hospital board members to announce his decision. He felt a great sense of satisfaction in knowing they were confident of good things to come. But that satisfaction could not equal the feeling of accomplishment that came when he denied them the gift based on trumped-up charges. His accomplices had been able to create quite an ordeal for the board with declarations of moral lacking and scandals too great to mention in mixed company.

It had satisfied Granite's sense of revenge—to a point. They had no idea of the real crime he held against them. But he had no intention of reminding anyone of where he'd come from. Instead, Granite let them think what they would and suffer his decision as the reputation of their hospital was lessened in the public eye.

A dull thump sounded from upstairs, catching Granite's attention and reminding him that he was no longer alone. Having Laura here would create complications. Hopefully she'd be cooperative and easy to manage.

He poured himself a drink, then went to the window. Winter wasn't his favorite time of year. The weather was unpredictable—even deadly. Sandwiched between vast prairies and the Rocky Mountains, Cheyenne was at the mercy of a variety of elements. The wind in particular could be most annoying. Throughout the year, winds often caused a great deal of misery, but when combined with snow, the town could find itself seeking shelter for days.

For tonight, though, the winds were calm, and the weather at peace. Granite walked to the fireplace and finished his drink. He would meet with some of the business leaders tomorrow and put forth his proposals for town improvements to benefit as many as possible. He knew if he could convince the others that his concepts were beneficial not only to him but also to them, they would go along with his ideas and remember Evans when it came time to vote in future elections. His popularity would also be sure to reach the ear of the president, who was charged with choosing a governor for the new Wyoming Territory. Thankfully, President Johnson had never gotten the job done, and the November election had given the office to Ulysses S. Grant. Grant was a man who was indebted to Granite. They'd met on many occasions during the war when Granite had shared information with Grant and produced supplies for the North. Of course, he'd provided them for the South as well, but Grant didn't know that.

With the money he made through underhanded means, Granite had been able to create a credible way of making money. Investing in the railroads had been a sure thing, especially after the war. The country was desperate for ways to unite once again. And of course, there was his idea for a large emporium. It was the perfect solution for moving products purchased both legally and otherwise. He'd started small at first, then increased in size—always selling at a large profit when he sold and moved to another location. Lady Luck was clearly his companion, and when he reached Cheyenne, the stage was set for the Cheyenne Ladies' Department Store—a grand and glorious emporium with multiple departments, focusing on all that any woman could ever desire in fashion, home management, and entertaining. He'd even put in a seasonal department just for Christmas decorations and gifts. That had proven quite popular.

Granite deposited his glass on the table, then headed to bed. He was quite satisfied with how he'd overcome the obstacles in his life, but now a new element had entered in.

Laura had come back into his daily life. At first he'd been rather alarmed when she'd written to say she'd completed her studies. But the more he thought of her being in Cheyenne, the more benefits he could envision. Tomorrow, he'd start to figure out what role Laura would play in his schemes.

# 2

Seeing the house's lack of Christmas decorations, Laura brought the matter to her father's attention first thing. To her delight, he had arranged for a Christmas tree to be brought in two days before the holiday. He then ordered all sorts of ornaments from his store and had them delivered as well. Laura and Mrs. Duffy had a wonderful time decorating the tree and arranging the house.

A blizzard struck the day before Christmas, burying the town in more snow. Laura had never experienced anything quite like it. On Christmas morning, the wind was still howling, and it seemed impossible to keep the house warm. Mrs. Duffy had awakened her with a cup of hot chocolate and helped her dress in a heavy quilted skirt and her warmest long-sleeved blouse and red velvet jacket. Laura even put on two pairs of woolen stockings, and still she was cold.

"When the wind blows like this, it makes all of the houses colder. Even the well-made ones," Mrs. Duffy told her. "When I left this morning, my boys were huddled up around the fireplace, and I'll bet they'll be there all day."

"I'm so sorry you have to spend Christmas here with us," Laura said as Mrs. Duffy secured her hair in a simple bun.

"It's not a problem. You're bound to need someone to help. I do get to leave just after Christmas dinner. And your father was very generous with extra pay for the day."

"I'm glad for at least that much."

Laura finished drinking her hot chocolate. She couldn't help being excited despite the cold. "I've so looked forward to this day. I haven't spent a Christmas with my father since I was a little girl. Mama died just a little less than a month before Christmas when I was twelve. We didn't celebrate that year, nor was I home to celebrate with Father all the years afterward. This is the first time we'll be together."

"How terrible for you to be alone all that time, Miss. Christmas is meant to be for family."

"I agree, but my father was never up to the challenge. I'm glad he feels he can celebrate now. I've prayed for this and waited so long. We're finally a family again."

"Well, you should get downstairs. I'm sure your father is waiting for you in the front room."

Laura hurried to the door. "I hope he's got the fire burning bright. I'm already chilled to the bone."

Thankfully, there was a large fire burning, and Father waited patiently at the mantel, no doubt keeping warm.

"Ah, there you are. Good Christmas Day to you."

"Merry Christmas, Father." Laura engulfed him in a hug. "I'm so happy I could cry. This is already the best Christmas I've had in years. Just having a home again and being with you is more than I could have asked for."

He looked at her oddly as he pulled away. "I didn't know it had been so hard for you."

"I missed you. You had to know that. I wrote it in all my cards and letters home."

He glanced down and shrugged. "I'm sorry I wasn't up to the task of having you home for the holidays."

She gave his arm a squeeze. "It's all right. Let's put it behind us. We have each other now. Come and sit. I have some gifts for you."

Laura had brought trinkets of affection to give her father. She had purchased three books she thought he'd like, a new fountain pen carved from whale bone, and decidedly masculine-scented cologne bags for his dresser drawers.

He had arranged presents for her as well, including a beautiful necklace of exquisite diamonds and sapphires. Laura argued that the gift was much too expensive, but her father told her it was in keeping with her new status and that he hoped to give her most everything she asked for. The only thing he refused her was her request to attend Christmas church services.

"It's far too cold, and besides, I don't have a church to attend." He dismissed the subject then, since Mrs. Duffy announced breakfast was served.

For the rest of the day, they quietly read in the front room. From time to time, one or the other made a comment, but it was a rather uncomfortable time for Laura. She had hoped she'd return to the loving father she remembered. Instead, she found herself wondering if she had simply invented that person in her mind. Surely not. She had good memories of him and her mother. Of course that had been a long, long time ago, but people didn't change that much. Did they?

The next day, Laura was determined to talk to him about rectifying the matter. "Father, I hope you don't mind, but I was rather hoping to talk to you about something," Laura began, midway through breakfast.

"Whatever it is, speak up." Her father had been balancing his attention between her, the food, and the newspaper.

"I was wondering why we did not attend Christmas services. I remember Mama was quite fond of us going to church together on Christmas morning. Through the years, I've found it to be such a glorious time."

His expression saddened. "I haven't been in church for years, if you want an honest answer. I'm afraid my anger at losing your mother left me unable. I haven't yet worked out a way to make peace with a God who would steal away a child's mother and a beloved wife when so many evildoers go unharmed." He picked up his coffee and met her gaze. "I'm sorry if that offends you, but I have no use for religion."

Laura tried to choose her words carefully. "I can understand your feelings. Losing Mama sent me in the opposite direction, however. And in your absence, I was most desperate for a father's love and attention."

"You always had both from me, just not face-to-face. For that, I'm deeply sorry. I wasn't a strong man back then. Your mother's death nearly brought on my own. I sent you away, Laura, because I knew I could not be a decent father to you. It wasn't for lack of love." He put the coffee down untasted.

"I had little love in my life as a child. Your mother's love was my first real experience with it. She taught me to feel and care about things and people. I had so carefully guarded myself against such things that it was an entirely new way of living for me. Then you came along, and it was easy to lose my heart to you as well."

Laura smiled. "And you were a very good father. You still are. I hated our separation, but you explained it quite well, and I held great sympathy for you. And even though I needed your attention and affection, there was a part of me that knew such a tenderness for your needs that my own seemed unimportant."

"Still, it was wrong," her father replied. "I should have been there for you. Your grief was great. It wasn't right that I should have sent you away, but please know it was never for lack of love."

She had always been certain of this and gave a nod. "You have always proven to me that your love was sincere and never-ending. I suppose that's why it was easy for me to accept God's love and to build my faith ever deeper. Mother always encouraged it, and without you to guide and encourage, I sought my heavenly Father. I hope you don't find it offensive, but my faith is a big part of who I am. I can't deny it just because you have no interest in it. I mean to attend church on Sunday and to continue being a woman of faith."

"I have no problem with that," her father replied, once again picking up his coffee. He took a long drink, then seemed to consider the contents before speaking. "Faith in God is a very personal thing. I'm sure you would agree."

"Of course."

He put the cup back on the saucer. "It's difficult for me to make peace with God. That doesn't mean that in time I won't seek to do so, but for now, I am unable to reconcile the matter. I beg your indulgence and patience, and I ask that you refrain from any attempt to rush my reconciliation."

"Of course. I have no right to impose my faith on anyone else." She felt sorry for her father. He was still deeply wounded by the death of his wife. Laura whispered a prayer for guidance. Her heart's desire was that her father would find peace once again and come to realize God's grace and mercy in the midst of his pain.

"Good," her father said, pushing back from the table. "Now finish up. As soon as you are done with breakfast, we'll make our way to the Cheyenne Ladies' Department Store. I think you'll be quite impressed. I've patterned various sections off some of the finer stores in Paris, London, and New York."

She couldn't help but smile. He seemed so excited to show her what he had created. "I'm ready. I couldn't eat another bite." Laura folded her napkin and scooted back. "Let me get my things."

The short ride through town was only slightly hampered by the snow. The blizzard winds had blown much of the snow into large drifts, and Mr. Grayson capably maneuvered the team as they made their way through the neighborhood.

Cheyenne in a cover of white seemed pristine and vast. The centralized downtown was nestled snuggly together in a crisscross of streets and contained a wide variety of businesses with everything from dressmakers and milliners to jewelry stores and an entire shop devoted to glassware. Skirting the edges of these were collections of houses and churches, expanding out to neighborhoods where even now children played in the snow. But the thing that most intrigued Laura was the noticeable lack of trees. How fascinating that the town simply rose out of the prairie, seemingly from nothing.

"We'll soon have a very fashionable city," Father declared. "Cheyenne hopes to one day be the capital of a great state. It's already an important crossroads."

"You've only just become a territory," Laura reminded. "No doubt the government will take its time in seeing it become a state. From what I've learned, Congress has the power to create states but not a set plan for how to do it. Isn't it based somewhat on population?"

"You seem to have learned a great deal at school," her father said, looking somewhat impressed.

"I did. My school was quite progressive in seeing women obtain as good an education as that offered by the various men's universities. However, they also instructed that each and every bit of knowledge we obtained would be useful in running a proper Southern household. I intend for my children, be they male or female, to value education. It's very important to be knowledgeable. Don't you think, Father?"

"I do, indeed, and it would appear my money was well spent in seeing to your education. I'm pleased that you have retained so much information."

"It might surprise you to know that I can read and write Latin and Greek, and I am fluent in French." She shrugged. "I can also speak a bit of Italian and German, as I picked those up in our travels through Europe."

He chuckled. "A well-rounded scholar to be sure."

Laura smiled. "It kept my mind occupied and saved me from being too lonely for home."

The carriage came to a stop, and rather than respond to her comment, Father exited quickly and let Mr. Grayson help Laura down.

She looked up at the wide storefront. The beautifully designed sign atop the wooden building proudly announced the department store.

"Of course, this is soon to change. This entire block is owned by me, and I am arranging for everything to be done up in brick. I have a shipment of bricks due to come in spring, and a construction crew contracted to begin building in March. This is going to be quite the place. Now, come inside and see what we have. I believe you'll be pleased."

Laura followed her father. He was obviously happy with

all that he had created, and she didn't want him to think her anything but supportive.

Inside the store, Laura noted the abundance of light. Lamps were situated throughout the floor on overhead posts and arranged so that optimal benefit could be had below. Her father had arranged a variety of departments where all manner of things could be had. Most all were of interest to women, with one section furnishing intimate apparel and another perfumes, powders, lotions, and soaps. There was a department for ready-made clothing and another for hats and shoes. It was quite impressive.

"I'm surprised that you're open on Saturday," Laura said as she took it all in.

"Just half a day. There are many women who prefer to shop today rather than during the week. I try to accommodate them, and it has paid off in a most beneficial way. Saturdays are a valuable revenue day for the store."

He pulled her along. "We have a salon in the back where our customers can sit and rest, even take tea. There are, of course, other stores that offer ready-made clothes and household supplies, but I offer everything under one roof—and of the highest quality," her father announced. "Come and meet some of my staff."

He led her to a counter where three women clad in black skirts and white blouses waited to help customers. Her father gave a quick introduction to the trio. Laura tried to memorize their names, but her father insisted on moving her on to yet another part of the store before she could speak to them.

Laura was rather relieved when one of the women she'd met approached him about a problem with one of the shipments and Father's attention was needed.

"I'll just look around the store," Laura told him. "You go ahead and see to business."

He seemed annoyed but nodded and left with the woman. Laura took a deep breath and glanced around the building. It was far more impressive than she'd imagined it to be. She was surprised by what her father had created but then chided herself for feeling that way. She really knew very little about him beyond what she could remember from childhood and his correspondence over the years.

Two women were walking down the main aisle as Laura rounded the corner. They were laughing about something and seemed to be having a wonderful time together. She smiled as they approached.

"Good morning, ladies," she said, feeling obligated to greet the customers.

"Good morning," the woman on the right replied. The other nodded and offered her hello as well.

Laura gave a nervous laugh. "This is my father's store." She wasn't sure why she made that comment. It seemed completely out of place now that the words were out of her mouth.

"How wonderful. We love shopping here." The woman on the right said. She extended her hand. "I'm Melody Decker. This is my dear friend Marybeth Vogel. You're new to Cheyenne, aren't you?"

There was an unexpected and immediate connection between the three women. Laura shook the woman's hand and nodded. "I arrived just shortly before Christmas. I'm to make my home here with my father."

"That's wonderful news," Melody said. "Do you yet have a church to attend?"

"No. I was hoping to find one." She glanced over her shoulder, uncertain what, if anything, she should say about her father's lack of attendance. She looked back at Melody and Marybeth and shrugged. "Have you one to suggest?"

"Our church is quite satisfying. We attend the Methodist church. Currently, we meet at the school on Sunday evenings. We would love for you to join us for services. We meet at seven. You and your father would be very welcome."

"I'm afraid my father would be too busy to join me." She hoped they wouldn't question her on the matter. Laura had no desire to dishonor him in any way.

"We could come by to pick you up," Marybeth offered. "My husband won't mind at all."

"Or we could. Perhaps we could take turns," Melody said, looking to Marybeth. The woman nodded.

"I would like that very much, especially given it's at night. Why are the services in the evening?"

Marybeth took on this question. "We share the school building with another church. Their services are in the morning. We have quite a few in our congregation now. We were the first church to organize in Cheyenne, but alas, we weren't the first to construct our own building. We're hoping to get started next year. It's just the matter of raising the money."

"How wonderful. Perhaps I can talk my father into donating." She heard his gruff voice barking out orders and knew he was most likely headed back to retrieve her. "We live on Seventeenth."

"I know well where your house is situated," Melody replied. "Our place is close by, next to a private school for boys that my husband and I run. One of our students lives across the street from your house."

Marybeth nodded. "It's hard not to know where everyone is situated. The town isn't that big just yet. We live on the east side as well. I'm sure we'll all get to know each other and be dear friends."

Her father joined them just then, and Laura turned to introduce them. "Father, this is Mrs. Vogel and Mrs. Decker. Ladies, this is my father, Granite Evans."

"Ladies, I'm charmed. I hope you're enjoying all that the store has to offer."

"Oh, we are," Melody replied. "It isn't our first visit here. You have a wonderful place, Mr. Evans."

"Thank you. It is my desire to afford the ladies of Cheyenne with the same services and selections as any of the larger cities. If you don't see what you need, we can always order it."

"Father, these ladies have invited me to attend the Methodist services with them on Sunday evenings. They have even offered to give me a ride with their families. Wasn't that gracious?"

"Very. I can't thank you enough for warmly welcoming my daughter to Cheyenne." He leaned forward and lowered his voice. "I will let my clerks know that you're to have five percent off anything you purchase today." He straightened and smiled. "Now, I must continue to introduce my daughter to the staff. If you'll excuse us."

"Of course," the women said in unison.

"And thank you for your generous discount," Melody added.

Laura took hold of her father's arm. She was so pleased at his kindness. "You are quite the man, Father. It's no wonder you've made good in Cheyenne. People know you for your kindness and generosity."

He patted her arm. "I find such attitude and actions to always be beneficial."

Wilson Porter sanded the table edge and ran his hand along it to make certain there were no rough places. He'd been in Cheyenne since the spring, waiting for the government to finally approve his appointment to minister on the Indian reservation. One delay after another had made it necessary to seek work, and since he was good at making furniture, Mr. Bradley of Bradley's Furniture Store had hired him on.

He didn't exactly hate the work, but it left him feeling a lack of fulfillment. He'd come west at the encouragement of his church and father, who headed up that congregation. His father was an eighth-generation man of the cloth, able to trace back his religious roots in America to a ship called the *Brethren*, which had brought his relations to the new land from Europe. His father and grandfather were quite proud of the family heritage, as was Will.

Preaching to the native peoples was something of a tradition, although his father had given that up to move his family to Salem, Ohio, where he founded their church. Despite that change, Will had felt called to continue the tradition, and once he'd graduated seminary, he had done what he could to involve himself in helping spread the Gospel to the Indians.

The War between the States had delayed him. He felt it his duty to serve and help free the slaves from the oppression of the South. During his experience on the battlefield, Will had found many opportunities to pray with his fellow soldiers and offer encouragement during times of great fear. The men started calling him Preacher, some with more affection than others. Once the war concluded, Will was able to finish seminary and complete the requirements of ordination. And through seeking to work with the native peoples, Will found himself looking ever westward.

Last spring, he had been encouraged by the Office of Indian Affairs to relocate to Cheyenne while they concluded the terms for the treaties with the area Shoshone and Bannock tribes. The newly formed Fort Hall Indian Reservation would be divided into five districts, and Wilson was sure to be appointed to one of them.

But it was nearly the new year, and there was still no word from Washington. The local Indian agent, Mr. Blevins, had tried to be encouraging, telling him it was just a matter of time, but that hadn't really helped. Especially when word came in July that Will's father had passed away suddenly. Will hadn't even had the opportunity to reach home in time for the funeral.

He could still remember the tears his mother and sister had cried when he'd left for Cheyenne. They understood his calling but wanted him to remain in Ohio. Instead, Will returned to Cheyenne and began to pray fervently for an answer as to how he could both take care of his mother and sister and answer God's call on his life. Just before the weather had turned cold, an idea had come to him: Mother and Sally could move to Cheyenne. It would put them much closer to the reservation, and perhaps in time they could even join him. With them in Cheyenne, he would have a better chance to help them. He might even find a way to be assigned to one of the other tribal reservations closest to Cheyenne.

At least, that would be his goal if he could talk them into moving west. Thankfully, his mother had money left to her from her parents. Her funds had often supported them in years when his father's earnings through the church had been lean. It had been a source of some argument as to whether it was biblical for a man of God to rely on his wife's inheritance, but in the long run, Will's father had called it God's blessing for a ministry that He had known would need extra support. Now his mother and sister could live without fear of the future. It gave Will a great sense of relief to know they were provided for since he wouldn't earn a lot of money as a missionary.

He finished his work and straightened. This table had been ordered a couple of weeks ago and was to be finished by the first of the year. Thankfully, everything was on schedule, and he could quit for the day with a clear conscience that all was well.

Will stretched and reached up to knead the muscles in his neck. He'd been invited to share supper with the Decker family this evening and had been looking forward to it all day. He enjoyed conversing with Charlie Decker, and his wife, Melody, was a very good cook. Not that his boarding-house owner, Mrs. Cooper, was a poor one. Both women were talented in their abilities. He smiled and dusted off his clothes. He was a blessed man, and if his mother and sister would come to Cheyenne, and if he could obtain a missional assignment, he'd have no complaints at all.

If.

"That table is looking good, Will," Mr. Bradley said as Will put away his tools.

"Thanks. Shouldn't have any trouble getting it stained and finished in plenty of time."

With everything taken care of, Will hurried home to the boardinghouse to clean up. He had barely stepped foot in the door, however, when Mrs. Cooper came up to him.

"You've had some news, Will. I know you'll be wanting

to see these before you head out again." She handed him two letters.

Will glanced at the envelopes. One was from his mother and the other from the Indian office. "Thanks!" He bounded up the stairs, taking them two at a time.

He hurried to his room and, once inside, ripped open his mother's letter first. A smile lined his lips. They were coming. His mother had spent most of the last few months with her sister in Mississippi, but she and Sally were finally on their way for an extended visit. They hoped to join him sometime after the new year and stay until summer. She would send another letter or telegram when she had an exact date of arrival.

Will was tempted to let out a whoop but knew it wouldn't be understood by those sharing rooms around him. Instead, he tossed the letter onto the bed and opened the one from the Indian office. He scanned the contents, a frown replacing his smile. More delays. The approval hadn't yet been given since details were still being argued regarding some of the treaty's more difficult points.

He drew a deep breath and refolded the letter. God had perfect timing for everything, and he had to trust that this was all a part of God's plan. After all, if he were to be approved for the reservation work and had to leave before his mother and sister arrived, that would put everyone at a disadvantage. This way he would be there to help Mother and Sally get settled and perhaps convince them to remain in Cheyenne permanently.

That thought brought to mind that he had no idea where they would stay. His boardinghouse was for men. Women weren't allowed. He was going to have to get right on to finding them a place. A hotel to begin with or another boardinghouse. If they agreed to stay, then maybe he could find a house where they could all live together until he had to leave. Mother could afford to purchase a place once she decided for certain, but he would need to have options for her. Tomorrow was Sunday, so Monday he'd get the table stained, and while it was drying, he'd take a little time off work and check in with the real estate office and see what he could find. He'd also ask Mrs. Cooper about places for rent or board.

A peace settled on him even as he realized time was getting away from him. Everything was going to work out right. He just knew it.

# 3

I might not be here when you return tonight," Mrs. Duffy told Laura. "I leave at nine sharp. It lets me get back to the boys to see them to bed and ready everything for the next day."

"I don't know how you do it," Laura admitted. "It can't be easy to get here at six in the morning and not get home until after nine at night."

Mrs. Duffy shrugged and pushed back an errant strand of brown hair. "My mother lives with us, and she's very helpful. The boys are too. They know the only way we can get by is if everyone does their part. Schooling is most important for them. Their father wanted them to have an education, but since classes are out for the holidays, they're busy with odd jobs around the neighborhood to add a little money to the household coffers. They're good that way."

"They sound wonderful. I didn't realize your mother lived with you. What a blessing."

The housekeeper nodded and came to do up the back of Laura's blouse. "When my husband, Tom, passed on last year, Mother came to stay with us. She had been living with my brother back in Maine. I couldn't do my job without her, that's to be sure."

"If you don't mind my asking, what happened to your husband?"

"Railroad accident. He was killed instantly."

Laura fell momentarily silent, and she wished she hadn't imposed the question. She was still trying to think of something to say when Mrs. Duffy finished with the buttons.

"There. Now you're done up."

Laura reached out to take hold of the older woman's hand. "I'm so sorry about your husband. That couldn't have been easy."

"No." Mrs. Duffy looked away. "Hardest on the boys. They were their father's pride and joy. Mine too. It's been hard for them to understand, but God has been good to us, and we'll keep trusting Him for the future."

"That's all any of us can do. When I lost my mother years ago, I was devastated and had no idea of how to get through it. One of my teachers told me to simply take one step at a time and whisper a prayer in between. For a long time, that's what I did."

Mrs. Duffy nodded. "Grief is different for everyone, but God is a stronghold that never breaks."

"Beautifully put, Mrs. Duffy." Laura's admiration for the woman doubled.

Laura turned to glance at her reflection in the dressing table mirror. She took up the matching green worsted jacket and pulled it on. It was well tailored, and as she did up the buttons, Laura turned her thoughts to the night ahead.

"I'm anxious about the church services. It's never easy to start up with a new congregation."

"Well, you look lovely, Miss," Mrs. Duffy told her, brushing off the back of the jacket. "You're certain to charm them all."

"I'll be happy if I can just get through the evening without embarrassing myself."

"Nonsense. There'll be none of that for you. You're quite the beauty, and you'll no doubt have the eye of every single man in church."

"Hardly the reaction I was aiming for." Laura sat and checked her hair one more time. It was perfect. "I don't know why I'm so nervous about this. It's just church, and I've already made friends of Mrs. Vogel and Mrs. Decker. It's not like I won't know anyone."

"I find meeting new folks to be rather daunting, but I'm sure you'll do just fine." Mrs. Duffy stepped back. I'll lay out your nightgown and robe. Would you like me to leave you a snack to eat before bed?"

"No, that won't be necessary." Laura got to her feet. "I should go downstairs. I'm sure the Vogels will be here soon. Thank you for the help. Father might not realize it, but I can do for myself. We were taught at college to be very independent and not reliant upon maids."

"I think every woman should be able to do for herself," Mrs. Duffy replied. "One can never tell when it will be required of you."

Laura smiled. She genuinely liked this no-nonsense housekeeper. Mrs. Duffy was quite knowledgeable despite having no extended education. Laura appreciated her wisdom and abilities, and she hoped to make sure the woman felt her admiration.

"I very much appreciate you, Mrs. Duffy."

"Thank you, Miss Evans."

"Call me Laura."

"And you call me Etta."

Laura stopped long enough to look the housekeeper in the eye. "I will, Etta. No matter what, I hope you know I will endeavor to be a good friend to you. Times are changing, and I believe it is possible to be friends with the people who work for you, and frankly, I need friends."

Etta picked a piece of lint off Laura's sleeve. "Well, then you have one in me."

"Thank you. Already, I feel better." Laura took up her Bible and purse and hurried downstairs. She was adjusting her hat when she heard the Vogels pull up outside.

Father was nowhere to be seen, so she pulled on her cloak and headed out to meet the Vogels. Mr. Vogel was already on the ground by the time she reached the carriage.

"Thank you so much for the ride," she said as he handed her up. "I'm quite excited to visit your little church."

"We're glad to have you. It's a very welcoming church, and I think you'll enjoy the services. Our pastor is rather new. You may have heard of Dr. Scott who started us out, but he's moved on, as has Reverend Allen. But Reverand Cather does a very nice job."

"This is our daughter, Carrie," Marybeth said. "This is Miss Evans, Carrie. Say hello."

Laura smiled at the little girl. "You are the cutest little pixie, Miss Carrie."

"I'm free."

"Free?" Laura looked to Marybeth for an explanation.

"She means three. She's almost three years old. Her birthday is coming up on the thirtieth, and she's only too aware of it. I suppose that is all my doing, but I can't help but be excited about it."

"Well, I hope you have a very happy birthday. I love birthdays."

Carrie snuggled closer to Marybeth. "You come to my birfday, please."

Laura laughed. "That would be delightful."

"We are planning a little party, and you would be very welcome. We'll have supper and then cake. Wednesday evening at six."

"I'll send word tomorrow if I can make it."

Marybeth nodded and put her arm around Carrie. Carrie patted Marybeth's abdomen. "My mama have a baby."

Edward got the carriage moving as Laura responded, "I didn't know you were expecting."

"I am. Mrs. Decker is as well. We're both due in April."

"Congratulations! How exciting."

"We're pleased to be sure. Melody is absolutely convinced we're having boys. I'm not sure why, but she feels very confident of the matter."

"Well, no matter, I'm sure you'll welcome either boy or girl and be happy for it. I wish you the very best."

"Thank you. By the way, how is your father doing?"

"Well. He's very busy," Laura answered, hesitating to explain further. She'd hardly seen him since arriving in Cheyenne and wasn't at all sure what he was up to or when they might have more time together.

"Be sure and invite him to come to the party too," Marybeth said, shifting Carrie. The child was too excited to sit still.

"I will, but as I said, he's very busy. He's had so many meetings."

"He wants to be governor, as I hear it," Edward threw in. "I think he'd probably make a good one. Folks around here admire him. He's been quite generous to the community."

Laura enjoyed hearing praise for her father. It made her proud and gave her the tiniest insight as to who he was.

It only took a couple of minutes to reach the school, and before Laura knew it, Edward was helping her down and then assisting his wife and daughter. They made such a sweet little family, and Laura already held them dear.

Inside the schoolhouse, they were immediately greeted by a man who seemed to be in charge. "I'm Reverend Cather. We're so glad you could be with us."

"I'm Laura Evans. My father is Granite Evans. You might know him."

"I do, indeed. There was a small article in the *Leader* about you coming here after finishing your education back east. You are quite welcome to join us."

"I had no idea there was an article." Laura found it strange something like that would be city news. "But thank you for the welcome."

As he turned to greet someone else, Melody Decker came to greet Laura and introduce her to the tall man at her side. "This is Charlie, my husband. Charlie, this is Granite Evans's daughter, Laura. We met her at the store the other day and plan to be good friends."

Laura gave Charlie a nod. "I'm pleased to meet you, Mr. Decker."

"Please call me Charlie. I get enough of being called Mr. Decker by my students." He grinned and took hold of his wife's arm. "I know your father quite well, Miss Evans. He heads up a businessmen's consortium to which I belong. He seems to know a lot about so much. I enjoy hearing him speak."

"I'm delighted to know he's well thought of. The Vogels were just singing his praises. It does my heart good. Oh, and please call me Laura."

"The name Granite Evans is widely respected in Cheyenne. I wouldn't be surprised to find him our new governor since we've heard that he's also well-known to President-elect Grant," Melody added.

"Goodness, wouldn't that be exciting." Laura wasn't sure what else to say. She knew her father would love nothing more. Still, it seemed prideful to boast of his plans to see that very thing put in motion.

Edward Vogel came up to them. "We'd better get to our seats. Reverend Cather is taking his place."

Laura glanced around the room as they made their way to the second row of seats. There were about fifty people gathered for worship.

She quickly found herself swept up by the congregation's joy and enthusiastic singing. By the time they had prayed and sung several hymns, she felt right at home.

The pastor preached from the book of Luke, still focusing somewhat on the Christmas story, the shepherds, in particular. Laura found it made up for having missed services on Christmas Day.

By the time the service was over and the benediction offered, she knew that she wanted to continue with this congregation. The service was simple and yet heartfelt, and the atmosphere of the worshipers was most sincere. Afterward, people came to meet her and were more than friendly.

"This is Granny Taylor," Melody told her as an older woman came to greet Laura. "Granny and her husband, Jed, are some of my dearest friends."

"It's good to meet you, Miss Evans," Granny Taylor declared. "I've heard a lot about you from Melody and, of course, from your father. He was quite excited that you were to move here to be with him."

"You know my father?" Laura asked.

"Everyone knows him," the old woman declared. "I shop at his department store, and he's always very welcoming. And lately your coming to Cheyenne was all he could talk about."

Her words warmed Laura's heart. She hadn't known that her father had made her pending arrival known to the town. The thought made her happy. She wanted so much for this reunion to be the perfect conclusion to years of isolation and loneliness. Healing had taken time, and Laura was determined not to resent the years she'd lost to grief.

Will glanced across the room to where his friends were gathered. There was a new young woman in the middle of the group. He couldn't help but wonder who she was. Charlie waved him over, and seeing that he could hardly ignore the invitation, Will joined them.

"Wilson Porter, this is Laura Evans, Granite Evans's daughter. She's newly come to live with him here in Cheyenne."

Will gazed deeply into her brown eyes and, for a moment, felt a bit overwhelmed. When she smiled, it caused his breath to catch in the back of his throat.

He cleared his throat with a bit of a cough. "Miss Evans."

"Mr. Porter," she replied. "I'm pleased to meet you."

"Will is here awaiting word from the government. He's a preacher in his own right and plans to work with the Indians," Charlie explained. "Apparently there are issues to be resolved, however. New treaties and all sorts of details. Poor Will has been waiting since early in the year to be assigned a place to minister."

"Still, that must be very exciting. I've read about the reservation system, but I've never seen one in person."

"At the rate they're taking, Will's beginning to wonder if he will see one himself," Charlie countered. "But we're happy to have him stick around Cheyenne. He's a good man."

"But we are praying for his clearance and appointment to come through soon," Melody added. "Just be patient a little longer, Will. Just as we told you last night, things will come together soon enough."

"I hope you're right." Will shrugged and looked again to Laura. "It's a pleasure to meet you, as well, Miss Evans. I've heard of your father." He chuckled. "Well, that is to say, everyone has heard of your father. He's a visionary who has done much to better the town."

"I'm glad to hear it," Laura replied. "I am rather fond of him despite our years of separation. I am very happy to be here at last."

"Do you plan to stay on?" Will asked more out of politeness than real curiosity. She was an engaging woman, and it would be easy to get caught up in socializing, but he had to keep his focus on the plans at hand.

"I do," she replied. "I don't know what the Lord has in store for me, but I do know He has brought me here, and here I will stay until He moves me on. But do tell me more about your work, Mr. Porter. Do you have a particular Indian tribe that you will work with?"

He was surprised by her interest. "I hope to work with the Shoshone. They are a peaceful and interesting people, and I've done my best to learn about them."

"What is their culture like?"

He squared his shoulders. "I don't know that I have a simple answer for that. They live off the land. They use hides for their teepees. That is to say, their houses. It's like a tent of sorts."

"And they live in these even during the cold months like we're having now?"

Will nodded. "They live quite well in them. They have figured out ways to make them warm. They usually have a fire right in the middle with venting out the top. They hunt and fish and move about as needed to get the things they need to survive. Life on the reservation will limit how much they can move about, but the government plans to supply certain foods, clothes, medicines, and such to balance the situation."

Laura seemed to consider his words. "And the Shoshone are agreeable to that arrangement?"

"As agreeable as they can be. Life has been altered for them—for all the Indians. It isn't always an easy transition, but the Shoshone have been quite amiable and peaceful. I'm encouraged to think they will readily accept the Gospel and Bible teaching."

"I hope they will. I would like to see all mankind accept God's Word."

He smiled. "As would I."

"Excuse me," Edward Vogel interrupted. "Marybeth is exhausted, and I think it's time we head home."

"Of course." Laura started to go but turned back. "Mr. Porter, I would like to hear more about your studies of the Shoshone culture. I find anthropology quite fascinating."

Will was surprised by her comment but gave her a nod. "I would be happy to tell you about them."

He watched her go. She seemed quite genuine and very personable.

"So what did you think of Miss Evans?" Charlie asked him after she had gone.

Will shrugged. "Seemed nice enough. Why do you ask?"

"I might be overstepping my bounds here, but it looked to me like you were rather taken with her."

"What? Why would you say that?" Will shook his head. "I'm not hunting for a wife, if that's what you think."

Charlie laughed. "You seem on guard to such things."

Will realized he had reacted rather strongly. "I think the long wait from the government has put me on edge. That and waiting for my mother and sister to join me here in Cheyenne. It feels as though the entire world has been slowed to a stop. I don't want anything—or anyone—to cause further delay in my moving ahead."

# 4

Thank you so much, Marybeth, for inviting me to tea,"
Laura said, accepting a cup and saucer from the expectant woman.

"I'm glad to have you join us." Marybeth poured another cup and offered this one to the old woman Laura had been introduced to yesterday as Granny Taylor. "Sometimes we sew, and sometimes we share Scripture and what God has been doing in our lives. Always, however, we have the best of times, and our friendship grows in such a precious way. When I first came here, I knew nothing about Cheyenne or the people. I've been blessed so much to add these wonderful ladies to my list of friends."

"I think we all feel that way," Faith Cooper said. Laura had met her at church but knew very little about the woman except that she ran a boardinghouse with her husband.

"I know that I feel that way," Melody Decker added. "I've known Granny Taylor the longest of all of you, but you've all become so dear and important to me. I couldn't have made it through these last months without you. Losing Da was so hard, but you were all good to be there for me and encourage me."

"The Bible says that we're to bear one another's burdens," Granny said. "I've always found that to be of vital importance. As with any burden, when more than one person helps to carry it, the load is lightened. God encourages us to do that for one another so that none of us will fall down under the heavy load."

Marybeth took her seat once everyone was served. "I know I will definitely need you all now more than ever. Edward is terrified that I'll die in childbirth as his first wife did."

Laura knew nothing about Marybeth's past and so sat quietly stirring her tea as Marybeth continued. "He's trying to give it over to God, but he can't help but worry."

"We'll keep him in our prayers, to be sure," Granny replied. "Childbearing is often a hard situation for the men involved. They cannot understand the way a woman feels about the life she carries within. She will give her life for that child."

Marybeth nodded. "I feel that way for Carrie as well. She's as much my firstborn as a child could be." She paused and looked at Laura. "I'm sorry, you don't know about my family. Carrie is actually my half sister, but her mother died after giving her life and begged me to raise her and care for her as my own. I did so, and in every way that matters, she is my firstborn."

"How lucky she is that you loved her so much," Laura replied. "My own mother died when I was young. Nothing has ever filled the void of her absence."

"How old were you when she passed?" Melody asked.

"Twelve," Laura replied.

"I was ten and Marybeth thirteen when our mothers died. Sadly, we have that in common."

"I didn't even get to grow up with my father around,"

Laura admitted. "He was heartbroken after losing Mama and sent me to boarding school."

"How awful." Marybeth bit her lower lip as if regretting her outburst.

Laura nodded. "It was hard on both of us. Father was devoted to my mother and felt he had completely failed her. We were quite poor, and the doctors wouldn't help her because we couldn't pay. Even our church was limited in their support. It's the reason my father has difficulty attending church now. He feels that God abandoned him." She paused and shook her head. "But please say nothing. I know he wouldn't like that I shared such a personal thing with others."

"Of course we'll say nothing," Granny Taylor assured. "There are a great many people who feel abandoned by God when bad things happen. Our little group here gathers to pray for a long list of people. We'll simply add him to the list. God can mend his broken heart."

"I know God has done such a work for me. I loved my mother dearly, and losing her was the hardest thing I ever had to endure. And it didn't help that Father sent me away during my mourning. But he was lost in grief. Mother was his entire world."

"How could he afford boarding school?" Mrs. Cooper asked.

"I often wondered that myself," Laura said. "I've never had a chance to ask him, but I assume he borrowed the money at first. As the years went by, he bettered himself, and he moved me to more prestigious schools. I made good friends, but still the loneliness was acute. When the summer breaks came, the other girls went home, and I was left behind to live with the headmistress or travel with one of the teachers."

"That must have been a very difficult existence for you," Granny Taylor said after a long sip of her tea.

It felt good that someone understood, and Laura nodded. "Sometimes I feared I'd never survive, but the more I missed my father, the more I turned to God. He was all that I had at times."

"I'm sure it must have felt that way." The old woman set her cup and saucer aside. "But that's often the way we grow closer to our heavenly Father. When all the world seems to have forsaken us, we seek desperately for an answer—for someone or something that will fill that void in our lives."

The other women nodded in agreement, and Laura couldn't help but smile. They all understood. They knew about the emptiness she had once felt. The emptiness she thought no one else had experienced.

"Thank you for your words, Granny Taylor." Laura nodded to each of the women. "I feel so welcomed. Thank you all."

"That's why we come together," Melody said. "We want to serve God faithfully and share His love with one another, but we also know what it is to feel alone, to need a friend. God has given us each other."

"I agree," Faith Cooper said. "No matter how old or young you are, a good friend is more valuable than riches."

"Especially here in Cheyenne," Granny added. "When we first arrived here, the town was nothing but lawlessness and greed. There were a lot of terrible people doing terrible things."

"It really was an evil town," Melody said. "We were among the first here, Laura. My father was helping lay the track for the Union Pacific. They called this an end-of-the-tracks town."

Faith put her cup down. "They called it a lot worse than that, and it deserved the monikers."

"We came a few months after everyone else," Marybeth said, rocking gently in her chair. "It was a horrible place. Edward is a deputy and worked nights then. His dear friend Fred Henderson, who owned this house, was his boss. Fred built this house for his wife and boys. He was killed by ruthless men who cared only for themselves and their greed." She shook her head. "I worried so much about Edward being the next one to die. I still must pray to keep from living in constant fear and dread. But the town is better. Your father and other men like him have had a lot to do with that."

"I'm glad Father has made a positive difference." Laura smiled at the circle of women. "It does my heart good to know he's so well loved."

"He's also very supportive of women and their right to be treated as equals, so it's made him very popular with the women here," Marybeth said, getting up to pour more tea. "He has been instrumental in pushing for women to have the right to vote."

"To vote? I would never have thought Father to be part of such a thing. Not that he isn't supportive of women." Laura felt a wave of sadness. It seemed these women knew her father better than she did.

"He's convinced a lot of men to be open to the idea," Granny said, accepting more tea from Marybeth. "I heard him speak last summer at the Independence Day celebration. He said that women had been instrumental in every good thing that ever happened to this country, from our fight for liberty to the railroad connecting this country from coast to coast. It was quite the speech, and people cheered him on for at least ten minutes."

"It's true. I was there," Faith confirmed. "I had never heard a man speak in such a way about women and their contribution to the country. He was very forthright about it, pointing out the value of women as wives and mothers. He stressed that women were the ones raising the leaders of tomorrow, be they men or women."

"I'm clearly at a disadvantage." Laura felt close to tears. "You all know him better than I do. I had only a handful of letters over the years. I feel I've missed out on so much."

"Well, you're here now," Granny replied. "That's what matters. You will catch up quickly. I've no doubt."

Laura forced a smile and nodded. "Yes. I will endeavor to do so."

Granite Evans finished looking over the inventory record, then handed the papers to his clerk. "This looks good, David. Don't forget to order those new bustles. The ladies are going to be asking for them, and we want to have them in stock."

"Yes, sir," the young man replied.

Evans liked the young man. He was industrious and kept to himself unless needed. When Granite had hired him, he knew the boy came with very little experience, but he'd proven himself over and over. Granite had put him in charge of inventory and found the hireling met the challenge with gusto. He might be the kind of man that could manage the entire store one day.

"Let me know when we get in that new order of silk flowers. I want to run an advertisement in the newspaper and have a sale. I think the ladies are going to be especially delighted to have a little beauty available to them in the dead of winter."

"Very good, Mr. Evans. I believe the flowers will be well received."

"Go on now. I have another meeting."

"Sure thing, Mr. Evans."

Granite didn't have to wait long before there was a light rap on the door. "Come on in, Gus. What do you have to report?"

The man drifted into the office like a mist. There was something about Gus Snyder that Granite found fascinating. He seemed capable of moving throughout the town almost unseen and made himself so nondescript that anyone who did manage to see him couldn't remember much about him.

Gus closed the door and took a seat in a chair opposite Evans's desk. "Got those beeves taken care of."

"Glad to hear it. I don't much care for being in the livestock business. Let's avoid any more acquisitions of four-legged merchandise."

"I agree. The men aren't cowboys. A couple of them nearly lost their lives trying to manage that bunch." There was a hint of a smile on his lips. A rare thing for Synder, to be sure.

"And you're certain no one is the wiser as to where the animals got off to?"

"No one is ever going to have a clue. When the time is right, we'll get them sold, and that will be that."

"Good. Now, what do we have on the agenda?"

For the purposes of the payroll, Gus was in charge of Granite's three warehouses. For Granite's more nefarious purposes, however, Gus was his right-hand man.

"We've been watching the stage schedule and passenger lists out of Denver. I learned from a friend that there's to be a money box sent up from Denver on the fifteenth. It's headed to the First National Bank."

"Perfect. With any luck, maybe we'll get a rich banker or

two accompanying the goods. Those men tend to be foolish enough to travel with large amounts of cash on their person as well as in their strongboxes."

"It's always possible one will accompany the money."

"Well, whoever rides the stage will hopefully be carrying plenty of cash and maybe even jewelry. We'll take it all. Can your boys be ready in time?"

"Yeah, I have to collect a few of the things we need, but it shouldn't be all that hard." He leaned back in the chair. "Oh, I got another cousin comin' to Cheyenne. He'd be trustworthy to hire on."

"Good. We can use more men like you." Granite fixed Gus with a hard look. "You know my daughter is living with me now."

"Yes, sir."

"I want it clear that no one lays a hand on her. Understand?"

"Yes, sir," Gus replied with a nod. "I'll make sure everyone knows that."

"I have plans for her, and I won't have any of those low-life hoodlums taking liberties with her. She'll be around the house and here at the shop, and I won't have anyone disrespecting her. Make sure that's understood."

"The boys will follow orders. They'll do what's expected of them."

Granite pulled out his watch. "I need to get going. I've got a meeting to attend, and then I need to get home in time for dinner. I promised Laura I'd be there." He got to his feet. "I'll trust you to take care of that other thing as well."

Gus pushed back his thick black hair and got to his feet in a slow, casual manner. "I've got everything under control. You don't have to worry about a thing."

Granite bent down to retrieve a pair of gloves from his drawer. "That's the way I like it."

When he glanced up, Gus was already gone from the room. The man was uncanny in his ability to sneak around. Granite headed for the door, where he took up his heavy outdoor coat and hat. He pulled them on as he moved through the store, then added his gloves. Several of the young women who worked for him gave him a smile. They were young and naïve, perfectly suited as salesgirls for the store. A few of them flirted with him from time to time. He found it enticing but never gave in to their charms. It wouldn't bode well with his plans for office. At least not at this point. There would come a time when he'd do as he pleased with the ladies, but for now, he had to be certain that he kept his appearance aboveboard. That's why Gus was so crucial.

Gus had shown up to work for Granite just before they moved to Cheyenne. He had proven himself to be the best of workers, yet few knew anything about him because Gus always remained in the shadows. And that was the way Granite liked it.

He thought of the meeting he was about to attend. The men there would be the wealthiest in Cheyenne. They were all of a like mind toward progressing Cheyenne forward. They all wanted to see the town become a great city. They already had a good start. The railroad made Cheyenne an important place on the map, and the tracks being laid from Denver would solidify its importance as a Western crossroads.

Not only that but it was also a gateway of sorts to the goldfields of Montana and elsewhere. With a little help, they might even be able to promote a local boom and get all the travelers moving through Cheyenne for supplies and guides.

Granite had been thinking long and hard about this. Small gold deposits had been found in the territory, so the idea of a large strike wasn't out of the question.

He wondered what Laura would think about his political ambitions. He had mentioned a bit of his interests, but he hadn't gone as far as to explain that he intended to run the entire country. Becoming governor of the territory was the first step and after that . . . the presidency. At least, that was the way Granite Evans planned it. He'd take on the position of governor and see that the territory became a state. Then with that fame behind his name, he'd move forward to endear himself to the nation.

Of course, that was probably a good ten or twenty years down the road, but Granite knew he could be a very patient man. And once he accomplished all that he planned, he could begin to expand his revenge to each and every man who had wronged him.

The thought was most satisfying.

# 5

On Tuesday, Will was still trying to locate decent housing for his mother and sister. He'd spoken to just about everyone he knew who had any connection to real estate, but nothing was available.

"How goes your search for a place, Will?" Mrs. Cooper asked as she came into the front sitting room of the boardinghouse.

"Not well," Will admitted. "Seems there are very few vacancies, and the places that are open to rent aren't at all acceptable. I don't suppose you've heard of anything, have you?"

She shook her head and moved around the room, straightening things. "No, I'm sorry. I wish I could offer you some sort of direction. But as you know, this boardinghouse is for men only, and I've already asked Mr. Cooper if he had any idea of some place they could rent. He told me you'd asked him as well."

"I did." Will put down the newspaper he'd been looking through. "I thought I had a lead on a place, but it turned out to be completely unacceptable. It was an apartment in a terrible building and hardly big enough to turn around in. My mother and sister are used to better furnishings and would never be comfortable there. I suppose I'll just have to rent them a room at the hotel and hope something opens up."

"Perhaps if your mother likes it here, she could arrange for someone to build her a house."

"I thought of that, but they wouldn't be able to start until spring thaw. Even then, an adequate place won't be built overnight." Will set aside the paper and got to his feet. "I worry that without a nice house to offer them, Mother will want to return to Mississippi."

"Would that be so bad? You said she was staying with her sister there. Seems that would be a safe place for your loved ones, especially once you've gone to the reservation."

"I know, but I want so much for them to be here with me. I've been after them to come here since my father passed away last summer. I think we'd all be better off together."

"What about your work with the Indians?" Mrs. Cooper asked. She took up the newspaper he'd abandoned and folded it under her arm.

"Maybe Mother and Sally could join me on the reservation."

"Well, I don't know that they would find that life very fitting. You've described your mother and sister as living well, and the Indian reservation certainly won't be able to offer luxury."

"No, it's not like that. We've never lived in luxury, even though there was plenty of money. My mother's people were quite well-off, and she inherited from her parents. My father often said that it was a special blessing, given his salary as a pastor was very limited. I can't put Mother in a house where there's a threat of danger. She and Sally have always been well protected. I won't expose them to anything that might compromise their safety. Even at the benefit of having them on the reservation. If life there is unsettled and at risk, I wouldn't allow them to join me."

"Just encouraging them to move to Cheyenne is threatening enough," Mrs. Cooper countered. "This isn't yet a safe part of the world to live, what with the criminal types and Indians. You know as well as I do that there's all sorts of threats to our well-being out here."

Will hadn't truly considered the dangers. He had figured to be there to watch over his mother and sister. Of course, he knew in time he'd be moved to his position on the reservation, but he would be close enough to help them from time to time.

"When do they arrive?" Mrs. Cooper asked.

"Friday the fifteenth. Mother's telegram said they would take the overnight stage out of Denver on Thursday."

"Well, hopefully the weather will hold and there won't be any problems with the Indians. Mr. Cooper said the Sioux were still up in arms over the treaties that forbid them to cross the south bank of the Platte River. He's afraid it will cause them to declare all-out war."

"I doubt that it will come to that. After all, we have the army here at Fort Russell and at Fort Laramie as well."

"Fort Laramie is over one hundred miles away. It would take days for the soldiers posted there to get here."

"Even so, Fort Russell provides a strong army presence that will deter the Indians from attacking, and they're just a few miles away. Not only that, but I believe most of the Indians in this area are peaceful. They may not be fully content with the reservation system and treaties, but they've proven to be less hostile than other tribes."

"I hope you're right. It's still a frightful thing to imagine them attacking Cheyenne. We aren't that big, and there's absolutely no place for us to seek safety if they burn down the town, given the fort is a good three miles away."

Will wasn't sure what to say. He knew there were plenty of folks who felt just as Mrs. Cooper did. But he had grown up surrounded by people who held positive opinions of the native peoples. It only seemed reasonable to think the best of the local tribes.

"We will continue to pray that God puts peace in their hearts and in the hearts of the white men in charge. I believe we can all learn to get along."

Mrs. Cooper looked skeptical. "I hope you're right, Will. I truly hope you're right."

Two weeks later, Will was relieved to find that Friday dawned clear and bright. In fact, for the middle of January, it was quite mild. He ate his breakfast at the boardinghouse and then made his way to the stage office to wait for the weary passengers to arrive.

The Denver stage was an overnight route where the passengers had to sleep on board. They usually left Denver at eight in the morning and arrived in Cheyenne around seven the next morning. There were stops along the way for meals and to change out the horses, but no overnight accommodations. Will didn't like the idea of his mother and sister having to ride with strangers and sleep on the stage, but it seemed there was nothing else to be done if they were to get to Cheyenne.

"Sorry, but the stage is running late," the stationmaster, Jim Haggarty, told Will. "We had a telegram. Apparently, there was some sort of trouble with one of the axles, and it slowed down their progress. It was repaired, and they're supposed to be back up and moving at full speed."

"Guess I'll go check on their room at the hotel and then come back." He gave a sigh and headed back out into the chilly morning air. He checked his watch. It was nearly seven thirty.

At the Rollins Hotel, the clerk assured him that the room was ready and waiting. Furthermore, he added, it was the very best he had to offer with a separate bedroom and two beds instead of one. The suite was quite expensive, but Will knew it would be worth the extra money. His mother and sister would no doubt be surprised at the luxury of it, especially after Will had reported all that he had endured in the early days of his own arrival in Cheyenne.

He left the hotel and checked his watch again. It was only seven forty-five. He let out a heavy breath and walked slowly back to the stage office, where he took a seat outside. He figured when the cold became unbearable, he'd head in and warm himself by the stove. An hour later, he did just that.

"Still no word?" Will asked the stationmaster.

"None. I telegraphed the last stop before Cheyenne. They told me the stage should have arrived by now. I've sent my boy to fetch the sheriff. Guess they could have had more trouble with that axle, but it's not likely."

"Why send for the sheriff?"

"When there's trouble, he's been the one to go and find them."

"Does this kind of thing happen often?"

Jim shrugged. "From time to time."

Will frowned. Sending for the sheriff caused a feeling of uneasiness. Maybe he should just rent a horse himself and head out to the south. The road was well marked, and it shouldn't be that difficult to locate the stage. He hated the thought of them stranded along the road waiting for someone to bring help.

The sheriff arrived just then, along with a couple of deputies. He gave Will a nod, then went to the stationmaster. "What's the trouble, Jim?"

"Stage should have been in some time ago. They had axle difficulties, but the repairs were made. Should have come straight on in."

"Where'd they stop last?"

"The twenty-mile marker. They were fine then. I telegraphed the Carr Station and was told they should have reached us by now."

The sheriff nodded. "We'll head out. The axle job was probably rushed and fell apart on them."

"Could be," Jim replied.

"I could rent a horse and ride along," Will offered. "My mother and sister are on that stage."

The sheriff shook his head. "No, stay put. It's probably nothing, but if there is trouble, I'd just as soon not have to look out for you." With that he moved out, pulling the door shut rather hard behind him.

Will felt the uneasiness return. What kind of trouble might the sheriff be anticipating? He looked at Jim Haggarty, who was busy winding his watch. When Jim glanced up, his worried expression did nothing to make Will feel any better. Twenty miles away might as well have been twenty thousand if there had been trouble.

It was nearly eleven when Edward Vogel came to check in with Jim. They spoke in hushed tones for several minutes before Edward came to speak to Will. "You doing all right?"

Will was warming up near the stove. "I'm worried about my mother and sister. They're on that stage. At least they telegrammed the day before yesterday to say they would be."

"It's always frustrating when the stage is late. I heard they had trouble with the axle. That can definitely be a problem. If they broke down again, it would take a while to get help. There's not much out there between us and the last stop. I wouldn't fret too much."

Will stretched out his hands. The stove's warmth seemed to be fading. "I doubt they'd fare well in the cold." He frowned. If they were stuck out on the front range, it was all his fault. He was the one who'd pushed them to come right away, despite the fact that it was winter.

Will shoved his hands deep into his coat pockets. "I know I should just give it over to prayer. That's what all my training tells me to do, not to mention my heartfelt beliefs. But it's hard not to worry when it involves someone you love."

Edward nodded. "I guess I know that well enough. Look, I'm gonna ride out and see if I can lend the sheriff a hand. I'm sure we'll be back soon. You should probably go grab some lunch and relax."

The two men parted company, and Will made his way into Ford's Restaurant. He didn't feel much like eating, but it was better than standing around with nothing to do. The place was packed, even though they charged a dollar for a meal. At this point, Will figured it was worth the money. The restaurant was close to the stage office, and if he could get a front window seat, he'd be able to see if the stage arrived or the sheriff returned.

He found a table where three men were just leaving. He pushed their dishes aside and took a place where he could watch the street. It seemed that the entire world went on as usual. He wondered how many folks even knew about the stage's delay.

"What'll ya have?" a rather harried woman asked.

Will glanced up and met her questioning gaze. "I guess the special."

She nodded, then gathered up the dirty dishes. "Want coffee?"

"Yes." Will eased back in his chair. "Please."

She returned with a cup of coffee. Will thanked the woman and focused on the drink. He tried not to imagine his mother and sister sitting in the freezing cold. Surely the stage was prepared for problems like that. He knew they carried lap blankets in the winter, and given there were probably quite a few travelers, the shared body heat would do a great deal to keep them warm.

He thought of what he'd do when they finally made it to Cheyenne. First thing, he'd get them installed at the hotel and let them rest. They'd be exhausted after a night on the road. Later, he had plans to take his mother and sister to Jake Landry's restaurant for supper. The place had once been a dance hall and saloon in the front half of the building with a restaurant in the back. As things settled down in the town, Will learned that Landry decided to refine his place, and now they only served meals. He knew the meals there were a little pricey, but they were also of the best quality. Jake had brought in a chef from New York City who was well received and highly regarded. Anyone who was anyone in Cheyenne knew that to eat at Landry's was a gastric delight.

The waitress arrived with a large bowl of beef stew and a plate holding two biscuits. Will picked at the food while watching the street. When an hour had passed, he paid for his food and made his way back to the stage office. By now they must have had word on the progress.

"We haven't heard a thing," the stationmaster told him. "But we ought to know before too long. They couldn't have been that far out." The man seemed to regret his comment and gave Will a smile. "I wouldn't worry, mister," he added. "Things like this happen all the time. Could be a storm blew up and they had to wait it out. Winds sometimes come down off the mountains and cause all sorts of havoc."

Will tried not to worry, but when more time passed, and there was still no word, he couldn't help but begin to fear the worst. He paced the small stage office hoping to hear something, but no news came in. Even Jim stopped trying to offer reasons for why they hadn't arrived.

Finally, a commotion grew in the streets outside the office. Will grabbed his hat and followed the stationmaster outside. The stage team was being led by two riders with a half dozen other mounted men bringing up the rear. They were all carrying their rifles as if worried about an attack. There was no one in the driver's seat of the faded red stage, making it look rather ominous. When the men came to a stop in front of the office, Will could see that one of the riders was Edward Vogel.

As Edward dismounted, Will went to him. "What happened? Driver get hurt?"

"Driver's dead," Edward replied. He tied off his horse. "Will, there's no easy way to say this." He turned to face him. "They're all dead."

"What do you mean? Who's dead?"

"The folks on the stage. They were attacked by Indians. Driver and his guard probably got hit first. Then the folks inside the stage were attacked. The Indians killed everyone, scalped the men. They took what they figured to be of value and left the rest. Surprisingly enough, they didn't take the horses. I suppose they could have been frightened off when we came along."

Will struggled to form words. His thoughts were muddled in the confusion of what he was being told. "My . . . my mother? Sister?"

"There are two women in the stage, along with all the men." Edward put his hand on Will's shoulder. "You'll have to identify them. Their personal items were taken, purses and jewelry and such. One woman is older—probably the mother of the other. The younger woman has hair about the same color as yours."

Will met Edward's gaze. Identify them? The truth was beginning to dawn on him. How could they be dead? They had only just sent a telegram the night before.

"I . . . uh . . ." He looked to where the men were unloading the bodies from the stage and lining them up on the boardwalk.

"The undertaker is on his way to collect them all," Edward said. "It's best to just get the identification done with and not dwell on it too long. I'll be with you."

The deputies quickly laid out the driver and guard, along with five other men on the boardwalk. Their faces were smeared with blood, and the tops of their heads had been sliced off to take their hair. Will thought he might lose his lunch and looked away to draw a deep breath.

He steadied himself and looked back at the bodies. The women had been wrapped in blankets and were very reverently brought to lie a little way apart from the others. They were small, and their feet stuck out from the blankets. Will didn't recognize their shoes. Maybe it wasn't his family.

Edward drew Will over to where the covered bodies waited. "I'll lower the blanket from their heads. Just nod if it's them."

Will couldn't make sense of anything going on. He stood frozen, unable to even move. He hadn't had time to process any of this. It was surely all a mistake. They couldn't be dead. It was just a mistake. It had to be.

A woman screamed and threw herself down beside one of the men. Several other people began to cry and wail. It all seemed like a bad nightmare. Will couldn't breathe.

"Will." Edward called his name, but it seemed like it came from a deep well.

"I'm . . . ready." Will forced the words. He'd never be ready for this.

Without further warning, Edward pulled down the blanket from the first body, and Will found himself gazing at the woman beneath. She looked as if she were just sleeping. Her face was relaxed and peaceful. There was no sign of any injury.

Will met Edward's eyes and gave the smallest hint of a nod. It was his mother.

Edward replaced the blanket and moved on to the smaller body. He pulled the blanket back, and the pale white face of Will's sister appeared. Will stared at her for a long, silent moment, then nodded again.

The blanket was replaced, and Edward came to Will's side. "I'm so sorry, Will."

"I don't understand why this happened. They wouldn't have been a threat. They wouldn't have tried to fight back."

"There's no way of knowing. Come on." Edward took hold of his arm. "Come back into the station and sit down."

Will shook his head. "No. No. I can't stay here. I have to

think. Please . . . have them taken . . . to the undertaker. I'll . . . I'll go there . . . later." He turned to walk away.

"Will, just wait a minute and I'll come with you," Edward called.

He heard the words and the insistent tone, but Will couldn't make sense of what his friend was saying. He'd seen death during the war. It had come in all sorts of ways. Pain-filled battlefield wounds, bodies racked with disease and infection. He'd even witnessed one older man who'd simply gone to sleep, never to awaken again. But none of those deaths had been so personal.

His mother and sister were dead. Killed by Indians.

It made no sense.

He moved without even realizing where he was going. He felt nothing but a cold-spreading numbness and heard nothing but the rush of blood in his ears as his heart seemed to pound out of control.

By the time he glanced up and saw the horse and carriage bearing down on him, Will was beyond caring. He heard someone scream—shouting for him to watch out as the team plowed into him. He felt his head hit the ground. The dull thud snuffed out the light and robbed him of all conscious thought.

Death had come for him as well.

# 6

Laura fought to control the horse and back away from the unconscious man in the street. Where had he even come from?

She glanced around as people started to gather. She quickly set the brake and jumped down from the carriage to see about calming the animal. By now she could see that the man was Wilson Porter from church.

"Hush now," she said, taking hold of the horse's harness. She gently stroked the animal's neck and continued to speak in a low, soothing tone as several men picked up Will.

He was lifeless in their arms, leaving Laura terrified that she had killed the man.

"Is he . . . is he . . . ?" She couldn't bring herself to ask the question.

"He's alive. We'll carry him over to the hospital."

"We saw the whole thing, Deputy," someone said behind Laura. "The fella just walked out into the street without paying any attention at all. It was like he was in a stupor of some sort."

"He just learned that his mother and sister were killed."

Laura turned at this news and found Edward Vogel. He gave her a sympathetic glance. "I saw the whole thing too, Laura. I know you weren't at fault."

"I want to go to the hospital." She climbed back up into the carriage. "Would you come with me?"

Edward nodded and climbed up after her. He released the brake, and with a light snap of the lines, he put the bay gelding into action.

"You said his mother and sister were killed," Laura forced herself to say. "What happened?"

"The stage was attacked about ten miles south of here. Indians killed everyone. Will's mother and sister were among the passengers. He just identified their bodies."

"How terrible. Oh, this is truly awful. I couldn't understand how he just walked out into the street without looking. Now it makes sense. Oh, the poor man."

"Indeed. I doubt he even knew what hit him."

The hospital was only a block away, and it took no time at all for Edward to bring the buggy to a halt. He set the brake and jumped down. Laura followed before he could offer his hand.

They made their way into the hospital. The men who'd brought Will were putting him onto a gurney while two nurses and a doctor were doing what they could to assess the situation.

"Who is he?" the doctor asked.

Edward spoke up. "His name is Wilson Porter. Most folks call him Will."

The doctor glanced up. "What happened, Deputy?"

"He walked out into oncoming traffic. Horse knocked him to the ground, then came down pretty hard on him. I tried to stop him but couldn't reach him in time."

"He just walked out in front of me without even trying to stop," Laura added. "I pulled back to halt the horse, but it was too late."

The doctor nodded as he examined Will's abdomen. "I fear he's bleeding internally. I will need to operate." The nurses grabbed hold of the gurney along with the doctor and moved down the hall at a rapid pace.

Edward and Laura stood watching, along with the men who'd brought Will to the hospital. It would seem there was nothing more they could do.

Laura felt horrible for having any part in Will's accident. He had just had the worst possible news and then this. She wanted only to offer whatever help she could. She turned to Edward.

"I'm going to get my father. I'm sure he'll want Will to have the best possible care."

Edward nodded. "He's going to need it for sure. He looked pretty bad."

She knew he was right but didn't want to admit it. "We should definitely pray. I'll stop by your house and let Marybeth know what's happened. She can get the others praying as well."

"That's a good idea. Tell her I'm back in town and doing just fine. She'll fret over me otherwise."

Laura nodded and hurried back outside. She had barely taken her seat in the buggy when tears came to her eyes. This was such a tragedy. She'd heard Will mention at church how much he was looking forward to his mother and sister coming to Cheyenne. And now they were dead, and he was injured.

"And it's my fault that he's hurt." She sniffed back tears and put the horse in motion.

After making a quick stop at the Vogel house, Laura hurried to locate her father at the store. She had nearly reached his office when she heard what sounded like something being thrown against the wall. She peered into her father's office and saw him shaking his fist at what looked to be a very frightened young man.

"You've been warned about this before, and if it happens again"—her father's voice lowered—"I'll kill you. Do you understand me?"

The man nodded. His eyes were wide in fear. "I didn't . . . I mean I won't, Mr. Evans. I'm sorry. I just started to—"

"Shut up. I have no desire to hear your excuses." Her father moved back to his desk. "Get out of here, and get back to work. You know what's required of you, and if you fail me this time . . . well, you know what the consequences will be."

Her father glanced toward the door as he motioned for the man to leave. He caught sight of Laura, and he looked even angrier than he'd been a few moments ago. Laura bit her lower lip, afraid of what her father might say or do. She didn't know this man. He was a complete stranger to her.

The younger man hurried through the open doorway, nearly colliding with Laura. He offered a quick apology, then rushed past her without another word. The look in his eyes was one she would never forget. He was scared . . . and so was she. Whatever had prompted her father's outburst, it wasn't a pleasant situation.

"Laura, come in here," her father called.

She stepped into the office with slow, precise steps. Keeping her distance, she grabbed the back of the chair that faced her father's desk. It was comforting to have something between them.

"I'm sorry you had to witness that. Sometimes I must be

firm with my employees. I just caught that clerk stealing from me. I've caught him before, but nothing has seemed to dissuade him."

"Why, uh, why don't you fire him?"

Father surprised her by laughing. "Yes, I should. But I made a promise to his mother. You see, she's a widow, and they have no money. I gave her son a job and have kept him on despite his thievery."

"But you said . . ." She swallowed the lump in her throat. "You said you'd kill him."

"I was angry," he said with a shrug. "I've tried so hard with that young man, and nothing seems to work. I wanted to put the fear of God into him. It was all I could figure to threaten with. He doesn't care if he loses his job. He doesn't care if his mother suffers. I figured maybe his life would matter to him."

Laura felt her fears ease. "I've never seen you like that before."

"Of course not," her father said, smiling in a reassuring way. "You've never given me any cause to act in such a manner, and you never will. I'm sorry you had to witness that. Sorry, too, that I lost my temper. Sometimes . . ." He shook his head, and his expression changed to one of sadness. "I just see such potential in that boy. He's had a hard life, but he must put aside his childish ways and be a man now. His mother needs him."

Her father's compassion overwhelmed her, and Laura couldn't help but go to his side. She leaned down and hugged him, no longer afraid of the angry stranger she'd seen earlier.

"You are an amazing man, Father." Just then, she remembered the reason she'd come in the first place. She straightened. "I need you. Something has happened."

"What is it?" He looked at her with grave concern.

"A friend from church, Will Porter, is hurt and at the hospital. He walked right out in front of me, and the horse knocked him down and stomped on him. I tried to warn him and reined back on the lines, but it was too late."

Her father got to his feet. "You say he's in the hospital?"

She nodded. "People saw the accident and said it wasn't my fault, but I still want to help him however we can. He just learned that his mother and sister were killed on the stage from Denver."

He took hold of her shoulders. "They were killed?"

Laura nodded again. "Edward Vogel—he's a deputy who also attends church with me—he said the stage was attacked by Indians. Everyone was killed, including Will's mother and sister. He was in shock. He was so very close to his family, and now they're gone."

"They were killed!" His raised voice caused her to fall back a couple of steps.

"Yes, everyone on the stage. Will had just heard, and so he wasn't clearheaded as he walked out onto the street."

The scowl on her father's face did nothing to offer her comfort. But Laura knew that he was probably as upset as the rest of the town to know that Indians had attacked so close to Cheyenne.

"I want to do whatever we can to help him, Father. Will is a good man. A preacher. He has been waiting for the government to assign him work on one of the reservations. He wants to minister to the Shoshone."

"I would imagine that will change now." Her father's voice was calmer.

Laura hadn't really thought about it. "I don't know, but I know he's badly hurt. The doctor was going to operate. I was hoping you'd come with me to wait for word."

Her father went to where his coat was hanging. "Of course I'll come. We'll do whatever it takes to help this young man. He probably doesn't have much money. I'll see to it that he has the best doctors and care money can buy."

Laura hugged her father as he pulled on his wool coat. "Thank you, Father. I was hoping you might say as much. I feel terrible for my part in this, even if it wasn't truly my fault."

Her father patted her back. "There, there. You wouldn't harm a fly. I'm sorry this happened to you, but we'll make it right."

They returned to the hospital after Father explained to one of the clerks what was happening. No one had any news on Will's condition, except to say he was still in surgery. Laura wasn't surprised to find Melody and Marybeth sitting in the waiting area. They rose and embraced her the moment Laura stepped into the room.

"Are you all right?" Melody asked Laura.

"I'm fine. Nothing happened to me at all. Except perhaps the shock of it all. Poor Will. He's had to endure so much today."

Melody frowned. "Marybeth told me about the death of his sister and mother. It must have been awful for him."

"He wasn't even able to see where he was going. It was as if he was in a fog of sorts," Laura replied. "I went and got Father, knowing he'd figure out what was to be done. He said we'll see to it that Will has the best of care. Father is such a good man."

"He is," Melody agreed. "He's helped a great many people in Cheyenne."

Just then, the doctor came to speak with them. He looked quite worried, and Laura felt her stomach tighten. Was Will going to die? Had he died already?

"He had internal bleeding, but we managed to stop it. His left foot and lower leg are broken, as well as some of his ribs. Oh, and he has a cracked skull and concussion."

"Oh, poor Will." Laura couldn't imagine how long the recovery period would be.

"I'll personally be responsible for the cost of his medical needs," Laura's father declared, "and I'll pay for a nurse to sit with him around the clock."

"I wish I had a nurse to spare," the doctor replied. "With the railroad's decision to press westward instead of stopping for the winter, we've had so many injuries to care for and a very limited staff. We've advertised back east for more nurses and orderlies, but so far, few have answered the call."

"I could take care of him," Laura offered. "I've had some nurse's training. In college, we had classes that taught us basic home healthcare and midwifery, as well as injury treatment. I learned how to care for broken bones and lacerations."

"Are you sure you want to take on the responsibility?" her father asked. "It sounds as though Mr. Porter's troubles are multifaceted."

"They are indeed, but if you feel up to the job, we could certainly use the help." The doctor's expression was hopeful.

"I know I can manage. Will is known to me from church, but we aren't intimately associated. I can be objective in his treatment. Besides, Father, it was my horse who rendered him in this condition."

The doctor continued to encourage the idea. "You could come to the hospital every day, and we'll show you what's to be done for him. Once he's home, you'll need to watch over him in case of infection and keep him from overdoing things. There will be some issues of care that would be better suited to a man, however."

"We could get Mr. Grayson to help with those things, couldn't we, Father? Or Curtis?"

"I suppose we could." Her father considered the matter for a few moments. "Yes. Yes, I believe we can make this work."

"Wonderful," the doctor replied. "Miss . . ."

"Evans. Laura Evans."

"Well, Miss Evans, if you wish to be here first thing in the morning, I will have the nurse train you in his care. It will benefit Mr. Porter greatly to have you at his side. There's no telling if he'll make it through, but his chances will be better with you than without."

"I'll be here. I know that I can do the job, and when he's ready to leave the hospital, we could bring him to our house, couldn't we, Father?"

Granite Evans appeared taken off guard, but he nodded. "Yes, I suppose we could. We can prepare a room for him downstairs."

"Mr. Evans, it's wonderful what you're willing to do for this young man." The doctor extended his hand. "I've heard wonderful things about you, but it's my first time to encounter you in such a life-and-death situation. You are quite the man."

Laura's father smiled and shook the doctor's hand. "I thank you for such high praise, but honestly, I believe it's my duty to do what I can for the citizens of this town and territory. And since this young man is a friend of my daughter's, it makes it seem even more important."

"Well, just the same, you have my highest regard." The doctor looked to Laura. "And you do as well, Miss Evans. Few people are as concerned and caring, especially when the situation isn't their fault."

"He needs help, not an assignment of blame. I want to do whatever I can. He deserves that much."

That evening, Laura thought about Will and her promise to care for him long into the night. Lying safe and warm in her own bed, the thought of him near death was overwhelming, and she prayed constantly for his healing.

She wasn't completely sure why she felt so compelled to take a stand and do what she could for this man who was nearly a stranger. Even though the accident wasn't really her fault, Laura couldn't help but feel it was her responsibility to assist Will in whatever way she could. He had lost everything and now faced his own mortality as well. When he woke up, he would remember that loss and feel alone. Laura didn't want that for him. She wanted him to know that someone cared.

She gazed upward. "Lord, help me to do whatever it is that You are calling me to do. I feel so compelled to help Will that it surely must be You who has put this upon my heart. Please show me how I might offer him encouragement and hope. Amen."

# 7

After a week in the hospital, Will was more than ready to leave. The doctor, however, made it clear that he couldn't leave without being under constant care. Laura Evans had volunteered for the job, and while Will appreciated that someone—anyone—cared about his well-being when it felt as though God and the entire world had turned against him, he didn't want her attention.

For reasons beyond his understanding, she was a constant reminder of his losses. He supposed it was because she was a caring young woman like his sister and mother had been. Perhaps it was her firm belief in God and her assurance that He had not deserted Will. That alone prompted memories of his mother. And right now, he didn't want to think of her or his sister. Not when he could still see their faces after Edward raised the blankets for him to identify their bodies.

They were dead.

Dead because they were making their way to him. Dead because he had nagged them to join him immediately and not wait until spring to come to Cheyenne. Dead because the very people he wanted to help had risen up in anger and indiscriminately killed a stagecoach full of people.

Will pounded his fist into the hospital bed at his side. The action caused him more pain than he'd expected. He moaned, forgetting that Laura was sitting quietly next to the end of the bed.

"Are you all right? Do you need more medication for the pain?"

She was quickly at his side, gazing down at him with those beautiful brown eyes. He shook that thought from his mind. She was beautiful, but he had no desire to consider her appearance.

"I'm fine." He couldn't keep the anger from his voice.

"You don't sound fine. You sound like someone who is in a lot of pain. It has been several hours since you had any laudanum."

"I don't want any medicine. It clouds my mind, and right now I need to be able to think clearly."

"Why?" She gave him a serious look. "You have no reason to do anything but recover. There is nothing at all that needs your attention. Mrs. Cooper said she is watching over your room and things, and Mr. Bradley said he'll be happy to take you back on at the furniture store when you are fully well. So you see, you can just rest."

"I don't want to just rest. I'm tired of just resting. I lie here and think of all that's happened, and it haunts me. I can't help but think of my mother and sister. I couldn't attend their funeral—I didn't get to attend my father's funeral either—and I can't even get out of bed to observe where they buried them."

"That will come in time. My father arranged and paid for everything. They were laid to rest in a lovely part of the cemetery. You'll be able to pay your respects when your body is completely mended. I don't mean to sound callous, but there is nothing you can do for them. They are with God, and their time of trouble and sorrow is done." She gave him a sympathetic smile. "Yours has just begun. The heartfelt sadness will go on for some time, so it's best to just let your body heal."

"You think you have all the answers, don't you?" He didn't mean to be harsh with her, but on the other hand, he just wanted her to go—to leave him as everyone else had.

"I suppose you think if you offend me enough," she began, "that I'll desert you. That then you'll truly be without friend or hope and able to wallow in self-pity." She smiled again. "I'm afraid you're stuck with me. I'm not easily offended, and even when you say something that strikes a nerve, I remind myself of all that you're going through. You have every right to be heartbroken."

"I'm not heartbroken. I'm angry. Angry that God would allow this to happen. Angry that He obviously doesn't care about me—didn't care about my mother and sister. They were faithful to God all these years, and He abandoned them."

"I hardly think so. The Bible makes it quite clear that God is faithful and is with us to the end. And even then, to be absent from the body is to be present with Him. Your mother and sister loved God, and He loved them. They were never alone, never abandoned."

"You can't know what they felt," Will snapped back.

Laura gave a slow nod. "That's true. I don't know what they felt, but neither do you. Will, you can't sit here and torment yourself with thoughts of what they might have felt or thought. They are safely in God's care now. They aren't suffering, but you are. Why not talk to God about it? Give it all over to Him."

"I have nothing to give Him but questions. I want answers." Will knew he was out of line, but he didn't care.

"So ask Him your questions, Will." Her soft, gentle voice was almost a balm to his wounded soul. Almost.

"A person can't question God. We're mere mortals. We have no right to question God."

"As I recall, people throughout the Bible questioned God. Even Jesus. It cannot be a sin to question Him if Jesus did it." Laura touched his hand, then gave him a gentle pat. "You've lost a lot, and you're grieving. God knows your heart. You aren't seeking to belittle Him. You aren't posing a question to taunt Him. Ask your questions, Will. You might get answers. But even if you don't, perhaps God will give you comfort."

Laura hoped her words were consoling rather than troubling. She knew that Will was lost in his sadness and fighting a battle within himself regarding his faith. He had been ready to leave the comforts of the world he knew and to minister to the Indians. Now the Indians were responsible for him losing the last of his family. How could he not have questions and confusion over whether he wanted to continue with his plans?

After their earlier discussion about questioning God, Laura had left Will alone for a few hours to sleep. She hoped he might spend at least a little of that time in prayer, posing the questions that haunted his soul.

She had prayed before returning to his room to read her Bible while he slept. Prayed for him as she had no other. A teacher had once told Laura that prayer was an intimate and loving gift that one could give at any moment to any person. *"You don't have to know them well or even know their needs, but by praying for them and asking God to help them, you have done the very best that you could ever do."*

The teacher gave the example of being just a regular citizen but having the ability to go into the office of the president of the United States and put forth your requests. Not only would the president receive you, but he would honestly listen to you and regard your requests with great consideration. As a Christian, a person had the ability to go before the King of kings and make their petitions known. And not only would God receive you, but He would honestly listen and answer.

Sometimes the answer wasn't what a person might want to hear. Laura remembered that perhaps even more than the rest of what her teacher had said. Laura had prayed for her mother to recover from her sickness, but God had said no. As her mother's condition deteriorated, Laura remembered a sense of confusion. Even her mother was baffled as to why God wouldn't heal her body. She had trusted in Him and asked for healing, but His answer had been no. At least for healing on earth.

When her mother died, Laura had asked God why it had to be that way and never felt that God had offered an explanation. She was sure Will felt the same way. It touched her deeply that he should be so alone. She wanted to make certain he knew that she was there for him.

She glanced up from where she sat reading her Bible and found Will watching her. She smiled.

"Did you rest well?"

"I suppose."

"Would you like to sit up for a while?"

He shook his head. "Not yet."

"That's fine." Laura put her Bible aside. "I can remember mornings at boarding school when I'd awaken before it was time to get up. I loved just lying there with my eyes closed, listening to the sounds around me, wondering about what the day might hold."

"You spent an awful lot of time at boarding schools."

"Yes, I did. My father was grief-stricken after the death of my mother, as was I. He was unable to face his grief and knew he wouldn't be a good father, so he did what he felt he had to do and sent me away."

"Did that make you angry?"

Laura shook her head. "It deepened my sadness. It was like losing them both. Mother through death and Father through sorrow. I wanted to stay with him, but I felt confident that if this was what he needed to heal, I had to be willing to give it. It was my sacrifice. One that only I could give."

"You were just a child. Why should you have to give anything?"

She shrugged. "I don't know. I suppose what came to me was that I was being called to give up what was most important to me to benefit my father. I loved him with all my heart and wanted only good for him. Did it hurt to lose him? Of course. But I saw that as my personal challenge—a way of picking up my own cross to follow God."

Will shook his head. "I think it's cruel."

"I'm sure others thought so as well. I saw it as a gift that only I could give." Laura stood and walked to Will's bedside. "Just as I see my time here with you as a gift that only I can give."

"Why do you even care?"

She considered the question for a moment. "To be perfectly honest, I can't really say. I mean, I was taught to care for all who were in need. And then, of course, there is the fact that my horse was the one who ran you down."

"But it was my fault for not paying attention to where I was going." His voice softened. "I don't blame you in any way."

"Yes, I realize that, but it doesn't absolve me from my Christian duty to help a brother in the Lord."

"But I don't want to be anyone's obligation." The anger returned to his voice.

"I see mankind as a Christian's obligation. I believe you do, as well, when you aren't wallowing in self-pity."

"What?" He narrowed his eyes. "You think I'm wallowing in self-pity?"

Laura shrugged. "You have genuine grief to deal with, but there is also an element of you feeling sorry for yourself."

"And why shouldn't I? I've just lost the remaining members of my family. Am I not entitled to feel sorry for myself?"

"Does it help? Will it make the situation better for you?"

He opened his mouth to reply, then closed it again. He stared at her as if trying to figure her out. Laura moved closer to the bed.

"Will, I'm not trying to belittle you, nor say you haven't a right to grieve. Sometimes, however, grief turns to something else. Something very destructive. I know because I experienced it myself. You have a mix of feelings right now, and that is perfectly normal, but don't let yourself go into that dark place where you shut out everyone else. God has not abandoned you, nor will He. I won't either. I pledge that to you here and now. You do not need to walk this road alone."

"I don't even know you. You owe me nothing."

"As a Christian sister, I owe you much. I am charged to help you bear your burden."

Will met her gaze. Laura had never seen such sorrow emanate from anyone. "No one can help me bear this."

"Well, how's the patient today?" the doctor asked as he bounded into the room.

Laura turned and greeted the doctor. "Good afternoon, Doctor. Will has just awakened from a nap. His incision was cleaned and redressed this morning and is healing nicely. He's still having headaches, but the head wound seems better."

The doctor helped Will to sit up and removed the bandages on his head. "This looks very good," he said as he inspected the wound. "You will probably have headaches off and on for the next few months. Maybe even the occasional dizzy spell. I'm going to remove the stitches before I send you from the hospital, but you'll still need to be mindful of the injury. Try to rest often, even after you're up on your feet."

"When do you plan to release him?"

"He's still able to come to your home, is that correct?" the doctor asked.

"Yes. Father had the housekeeper prepare a room for him on the first floor. It was originally a small library and sitting room. Now it has a bed and the other things Will might need. I'll be able to care for him there, and if there's something I can't do for him, we have a young man who will help."

"Good. Then I see no reason to keep him here another day. Can you arrange someone to drive him to your place today?"

"Yes, of course. We have a driver and a landau. I believe we can transport him with minimal difficulty."

"He won't be able to walk. I don't want him even attempting it. It would probably be better to arrange a buckboard and stretcher. I can provide the latter." The doctor was already checking the incision on Will's abdomen. "He needs to heal from the surgery and the head wound. The leg and foot breaks are nothing compared to those two things. I want Will to remain in bed for at least one more week before attempting to sit in a chair. I'll come and see him every couple of days, but if something goes wrong, I want you to send for me sooner."

"Of course." But Laura felt confident she wouldn't need the doctor. Will was doing quite well, and with the household staff willing to lend a hand, Laura knew they could handle his every need.

"How does that suit you, Will?" the doctor asked.

"I'll be very glad to get out of this place."

The doctor chuckled. "Haven't we treated you well? We fed you and gave you a pretty girl to oversee your recovery. What possible complaint can you have?"

Will frowned. "It just feels as though death is all around me."

"Well, I suppose I can't fault you on that. We have had our share of folks dying. There was another bad accident this morning, and I'm afraid we'll probably lose at least two of those men." He looked to Laura. "I'm glad you and your father agreed to care for Mr. Porter. It will free up this bed for another. I will say this, Miss Evans, if you desire to become a nurse, we will happily receive you and continue your training. You're quite good and have such a kind heart."

Laura hadn't considered becoming a nurse, but the idea did give her pause. "I'll keep that in mind, Doctor."

"Miss Evans, if you would go ahead and arrange transportation to your house, I believe we can have Mr. Porter ready within the hour. You might want to bring him a robe and a nightshirt. There's no sense in trying to put him in clothes."

"I'll arrange it right away." She looked at Will. "Have you those things at the Coopers' boardinghouse?"

"Yes. Mrs. Cooper can get them for you."

"Are there other things you'd like her to pack as well? Your Bible? Other books?"

He gave a long sigh. "Tell her to pack whatever she thinks I'll need."

Laura went to where she had put her coat and hat. She hurriedly donned them and turned back to give Will a smile. "I think you'll like staying with us. Our cook is very good, and she will enjoy coming up with new ways to encourage your appetite."

Will said nothing, but Laura didn't let that discourage her. She was excited to move him to the house. She felt there it would be possible to take his mind off his injuries and death and help him to focus on living again.

Two hours later, she had him tucked into bed with a fire going in the hearth and a supper tray on his lap.

"I think you're going to like Mrs. Murphy's roast beef. It was one of the first things I had when I came here, and it was so tender. I don't know how she does it, but I intend to learn. I believe I should learn all that I can. One never knows where God will lead."

She came to his bedside and put her hand to his forehead. "Good, no fever. Let's keep it that way."

"How can you tell by merely feeling my head?"

Laura shrugged. "It was part of my training. There's a certain heat that the body puts out when it has a fever. It doesn't feel like anything else. A warm day gives the body one type of heat, but a fever is completely different. I was told that with practice, you can actually learn to tell the varying degrees of fever just by touch. Our teacher proved it when a couple of my classmates fell ill. I have to admit I was very surprised."

"What kind of school was it that taught such things?"

"Mary Sharp College in Tennessee. I attended there until the war broke out, and then Father arranged for me to go to Europe with one of my teachers. After the war, I returned and continued my education. They were very good about teaching women some of the same things men learned, but they also focused the work to teach us to run a household and be a good wife and mother. I learned a great deal."

"Such as feeling a forehead for fever?"

She laughed. "I actually get a better accounting from the neck, but I didn't want to be too forward with you. Along with that, I learned Greek, Latin, and French. Oh, and some math and classical literature, as well as government. I had quite the well-rounded education, I assure you."

"I can tell you're very intelligent."

"Why, Mr. Porter, I think that might be the nicest thing you've ever said to me."

She was surprised when his face reddened a bit. She turned away to take up another blanket. It wasn't her intention to embarrass him.

"I enjoyed school. I suppose learning was something I was good at, and so it made me feel accomplished."

"And what are your intentions for that education? Will you become a nurse as the doctor suggested?"

"Hmm, I don't know. I've been trained to believe that God's will for every woman is to be a wife and mother."

"And do you believe that it's God's will for you?"

Laura met his questioning gaze and shrugged. "At one time I had hoped for such a thing, but . . . I don't know." She turned away as she felt her own cheeks heat up. "Now you'd best eat, and I'll go fetch your dessert."

She left the room and headed for the kitchen, pausing a moment to lean against the back stairs wall. A painful memory caused her great discomfort. Talking about marriage and being a mother had made her feel . . . vulnerable. It wasn't Will's fault. He couldn't know what had happened to her before.

Laura straightened and drew a deep breath. Even so, it was silly to get the vapors over his question. Who could say at this point what God's will was for her life?

# 8

On Sunday evening, Laura joined her friends at church. They sang several hymns, then the pastor spoke on the parable of the lost sheep. Laura had heard the words of Luke fifteen many times in her short life, but tonight they touched her in a special way as she thought of Will.

The pastor read the text. "'What man of you, having an hundred sheep, if he lose one of them, doth not leave the ninety and nine in the wilderness, and go after that which is lost, until he find it? And when he hath found it, he layeth it on his shoulders, rejoicing. And when he cometh home, he calleth together his friends and neighbours, saying unto them, Rejoice with me; for I have found my sheep which was lost. I say unto you, that likewise joy shall be in heaven over one sinner that repenteth, more than over ninety and nine just persons, which need no repentance.'"

The pastor closed his Bible and looked out on the congregation. "There are many ways to be lost. One can be lost to God because he has refused Him obedience. One can be lost because the trials of life have sent him on the wrong road. One can be lost in sorrows, and one can be lost in pleasures. But in the account of our text, we can be assured that no matter the cause, this loss creates a separation from the Shepherd. From God Himself.

"Now, there are those who are lost who have never come into the fold. They are not a part of the flock and yield themselves to no shepherd. But our story today speaks of those who belong to the Shepherd. This is a shepherd who has one hundred sheep, and one of them goes astray. One of them leaves the safety of the shepherd and wanders off, making his own way. For whatever reason, he leaves the flock. But the shepherd loves him and cares for him just as he does the other ninety-nine. And he goes in search of him until he finds him.

"And when he finds him, the shepherd calls to his friends and tells them about his success, and there is great rejoicing. For God so loves the world that each and every person in His flock is precious to Him. He will seek you and come to bring you home."

Laura loved this parable. The thought of God coming after her, searching for her when she chose to walk away, had always encouraged her to stay close to Him, where she was safe and protected from all attacks.

Thoughts of Will again came to mind. Will had grown up among people who had a strong faith in God. He had chosen to be a minister, and not just any minister but one who would give up the comfort of all he knew to go to a new and different place. That thought truly touched something deep in Laura's heart. The sacrifice that was necessary for such a thing was tremendous.

Will had to know that he was risking his very life. Just because the government assigned him a place to minister didn't mean that the native people would accept him. Someone could easily take offense and put an end to Will's life.

And had his mother and sister lived, it would have required complete separation from the people he loved. He'd already endured many months in Cheyenne without them nearby. He'd lost his own father and was unable to get back in time for the funeral. There had been no opportunity to say good-bye. Just as there hadn't been with his mother and sister. It grieved Laura to imagine his pain in that sense of void. She had always been glad that she'd been at her mother's bedside for those final days. Laura and her mother had been able to talk about everything—to share their love. Mother also spoke of her hopes and dreams for Laura. It had been a precious time. One that Will hadn't had a chance to have. Not with his father, nor his mother and sister.

"Little flock, precious lambs of God, you are loved with an everlasting love. God will not give up on you. He will seek you until He finds you. He will pursue you because you belong to Him. The ways of this world might lay you low. Sin might darken your vision and lead you into places where you should not stray, but God is mighty and loving. If you don't already know Him, I encourage you to pray and repent of your sin and ask that He take charge of your life. It's a very simple act. Romans ten, verses nine and ten declare, 'That if thou shalt confess with thy mouth the Lord Jesus, and shalt believe in thine heart that God hath raised him from the dead, thou shalt be saved. For with the heart man believeth unto righteousness; and with the mouth confession is made unto salvation.'"

He stepped toward the congregation. "And if you have already made that confession and belong to Him, but you've strayed away like the little lamb, come back to the Shepherd. Return to where you belong and repent before you face overwhelming consequences that might take you even further from the love of the Father."

Before Laura knew it, the service was over, and the congregation was standing for the benediction. Once the final "amen" was said, the people broke into groups to talk to one another about the coming week. Laura found herself immediately caught up with Granny Taylor and Marybeth Vogel. Melody and Mrs. Cooper soon joined them.

"How's the patient?" Granny asked. "I want to come see him one of these afternoons."

"I want to do that as well," Mrs. Cooper added.

"I think we'd all like to pay a visit," Melody said.

"Why don't we gather at my house on Wednesday for our sewing circle? It's well past time for me to host." Laura had already planned to ask them to come, and now seemed the perfect moment for the invitation. "I've been worried about Will. He's lost in sorrow and blames himself for the death of his mother and sister. He's quite angry at God, although perhaps I shouldn't say as much. I don't mean to gossip about him. I'm just worried." She glanced at each woman's sympathetic face. "I think it would do him good to have you ladies come and visit."

"Poor lad," Granny said. "I can only imagine that his guilt overwhelms him. He told me how he had been after his mother since summer to come here to Cheyenne. I'm sure he feels that had he done otherwise, they would both be safe and alive."

Laura nodded. "That's it exactly, Granny. He says it's all his fault. Well, his and God's. I've tried to reassure him that he's not to blame and that God hasn't abandoned him, but he won't hear it from my lips. Perhaps from yours."

Granny shook her head. "He won't receive it until the pain lessens a bit and he's able to think rationally. Right now, he's in the throes of grief, and that can make a person believe outrageous things."

"It's never easy to deal with death," Marybeth assured. "And often there is regret and the sense that so much was left unsaid. I can still remember the day my father died. He went off to work driving his freight wagon as he did every day. We had flapjacks and maple syrup for breakfast. My father always preferred eggs and sausage, but I hadn't had a chance to go shopping, and we didn't have but a couple of eggs. He made light of it, but after he died, I remember being so sad that he hadn't been able to have his favorite breakfast that morning. I found myself wondering if I'd even told him that I loved him when he left the house. I started second-guessing myself on all sorts of things."

"That's why I always make sure I tell Jed how much I love him before he leaves for work each day," Granny said, glancing over at the man with whom she'd shared most of her life. "I know that no matter what happens through the day, he knows that he's loved."

Marybeth nodded. "I remember you saying that, so I make sure Carrie and Edward know how I feel before we part company."

Laura could well imagine that Will was full of regret for not having been able to say good-bye. "I'm glad you can come. I know Will can use cheering up. I'll furnish lunch, so plan to stay a few hours."

"Sounds perfect," Melody replied. "I'll see you on Wednesday."

When Laura returned from church, she was surprised to find that her father had gone out for the evening. She knew he was quite independent and used to doing as he pleased, but the fact that he'd told no one where he was going bothered Laura a great deal. She would never be so thoughtless as to leave him wondering about her whereabouts.

She hung up her coat and set aside her hat and gloves before heading down the hall to check on Will. She found him struggling to sit up and chided him for not ringing the bell for help.

"You aren't going to do yourself any favors by trying to do everything without help. You could cause more harm than good." She came and helped him to sit. Once he was more upright, Laura grabbed a couple of pillows and put them behind Will.

"Have you had supper yet?"

"Yes. I ate an hour ago. That new girl came and took the tray away."

His reference to the new maid her father had hired made Laura smile. "Rosey's quite good at her job, don't you think?"

"Yes, I suppose. She lays a good fire."

Laura straightened the covers around Will. "She's very young. Just nineteen, but I've watched her work, and she pays close attention to detail. I think she'll be very helpful."

She pulled up the rocking chair and sat without seeking Will's approval. "Church was quite crowded tonight. I am hopeful that they'll soon have enough money to begin to build their own building. The pastor spoke on the parable of the lost sheep in Luke fifteen. Are you familiar with that story?"

"Of course." Will's tone was biting.

Laura paid it no attention. "I was deeply touched by the fact that if I stray, God will seek me out. He will leave the ninety-nine and come to urge me home."

"If He cares so much, why does He allow us to stray in the first place?"

"Hmmm, that's a good question. After all, He is God and can do whatever He wants since He's all powerful. You've had seminary training. What did your teachers say about this?"

Will met her gaze momentarily, then looked away. "That God gives us free will. That we are allowed to choose obedience or disobedience for a time."

She nodded and began to rock. "I suppose God doesn't wish us to feel forced into a relationship with Him. He wants us to come willingly and to abide in Him once we've made that choice. I can't imagine trying to walk away from God."

"Even when the worst happens in your life, and you feel abandoned by Him?" Will continued to stare at the wall.

"What are the alternatives? Where would I go? I can abandon my faith because things don't work out the way I think they should, or I can abide and trust that even though things haven't gone the way I wanted, God is still faithful. Still loving. Still God."

Will fixed her with a hard look. "And you believe that?"

"I do. And whether you want to admit it or not, so do you. It's the fact that you do believe that is causing you such anger."

"You don't even know me. Don't judge me."

Laura smiled. "I know we haven't been around each other for long, but I feel as though I do know you. There's something about you that just seems very familiar." She held up her hand when he opened his mouth. "I know that sounds silly, but it's true. When we first met, I could tell you were a man who was completely devoted to God. You still are, but you are hurt and angry. The questions you have seem to have no answers, and the loss you've experienced is devastating. But you still believe."

"You have no right to say that. You *don't* know me."

"I'd like to know you better. I'd like to be your friend."

"I don't want a friend."

Laura could see the frustration in his expression. Her words had struck a chord. "I understand. You fear the loss that could come. And it always comes in one form or another."

"I don't want to talk about it."

Laura ignored him. "In many ways, life is but a series of losses and disappointments—of counting on God for one result and getting another. My mother was strong in her faith and had trusted God since she was a child. But when she realized He wasn't going to heal her in a manner that would allow her to remain on earth, she was deeply disappointed. I was as well. She had always taught me that God heard and answered our prayers. Each and every one of them.

"I was distraught that He wouldn't save my mother. Nothing hurt more than telling her good-bye." The memory pierced Laura's heart, and for a moment, it was as if it had happened yesterday. She could still see the despair on her mother's face when she told Laura that she wasn't going to get better.

"But Mama didn't want me to give up trusting God. I would imagine your mother wouldn't want you to do that either." She looked at him and smiled. "What mother would? I know my mother longed to stay. She wanted to be there for me and for my father, but she was also racked with pain. She wanted the release that only God could give her. How could I deny her that?"

"You were a child. You needed her."

Laura nodded as she looked deep into his brown eyes. There was something about this man that drew her in . . . made her feel as if they'd known each other for years rather than weeks.

"I did. I needed my father but lost him as well. At least for a time. I can tell you from my experience that I learned to guard my heart. And the time that I didn't . . . well, it taught me a lesson I'll not soon forget. So I can understand how you feel, and I'm so very sorry. Just know that I care . . . that I'm a friend who understands the pain of loss."

She got to her feet. "Can I get you anything else before I head up to bed?"

He studied her for a long moment, then shook his head. "I don't need anything." He tried to lie flat in the bed. A moan escaped his lips.

Laura was immediately at his side. "Well, for now you may not need a friend, but you do need a nurse, and you're stuck with me." She helped him to a better position, then straightened to put out the lamp.

"Miss Evans . . . Laura," Will said, his voice much softer. "I'm sorry. I know I'm difficult. Thank you for your help."

She gave him a hint of a smile. "You're welcome, Will."

# 9

Will was relieved to sit in the leather wingback chair rather than be propped up in the bed. Curtis had helped him to get into the chair and put his leg and foot up on the ottoman. It took another pillow under his leg to make things comfortable, but Will found it improved his spirits.

He leaned his head back and closed his eyes as he considered what his future might hold. His plans to work with the Indians used to be so clear, but now he didn't know what he wanted to do. The Indians were responsible for killing his mother and sister. How could he possibly go and work alongside them after what had happened? What if he even ended up assigned to the very men who killed his family? His anger at the thought of anyone attacking innocent stagecoach passengers was enough to make him desire revenge rather than sharing the Gospel.

For days now, Will had tried to pray about the matter, but he couldn't move beyond the anger he felt toward God. Why bother to pray? He had prayed for his mother and Sally, and it did them no good.

*I don't understand any of this. None of it makes sense. Why were those people allowed to die? They didn't do anything wrong.*

Will had heard that there was a strongbox aboard the stage. That, along with other possessions from the passengers, had been taken. The driver and his guard had both been armed with rifles as well as revolvers. Those were gone, and they were dead. There had been a fine saddle on top with the luggage. That was missing, and the luggage had all been riffled through. The contents left behind had been strewn on the snowy roadside.

Will could picture it all, including the way the people had been left to die. Edward had given him the details as best he could when Will insisted that he needed to know. Will had been certain it would help ease his mind to understand the way things had happened, but it didn't.

The Indians—most figured they were Sioux, from the arrows left behind—had come charging at the stagecoach. The driver and guard had been killed first, causing the horses to go out of control. The passengers who had weapons returned fire. Apparently they weren't very good shots, however, because while there had been a bit of blood found in the snow, Edward said there were no additional bodies, and so the sheriff figured the blood had been left by one of the victims when they were tossed out of the stage and searched.

Whether Edward lied about the situation regarding Will's mother and sister, Will didn't know, but the deputy said they'd been treated in a most humane fashion. Each had been shot once in the heart with guns. Where the men had been scalped, the women had been untouched and left in their seats in the stagecoach. They had been searched and their purses taken, as well as their jewelry. Mother's wedding ring and her grandmother's emerald ring, which she always wore, were missing. As was Sally's necklace and the pearl ring their parents had given her on her eighteenth birthday.

The necklace had been a gift from Will on Sally's last birthday. She had been so enthralled with the inscribed gold locket that she pledged to never take it off. Each time Will had seen her after that, the necklace had been prominently displayed around her neck. He'd shared all this information with Edward and promised to write to his aunt Willa in Mississippi to see if the two were carrying anything else of value. He'd still not managed to work up the courage to write that letter.

How could he tell his aunt that her beloved younger sister was dead? That her niece had been slain at her side by savages? That his insistence they come to Cheyenne had put them in the wrong place at the wrong time, and it resulted in their death?

His head pounded, and he pressed his hands on either side to ease the pressure. What was he to do? How could he ever make any of this right?

Perhaps he should send word to Mr. Blevins and tell him that he'd changed his mind regarding the reservation work. He didn't see how he could move forward, but at the same time, he didn't know how he could walk away. This was something he'd wanted since he was a boy and heard his grandfather's and father's stories about working with the native peoples. His mother's and sister's deaths weren't the result of all Indians, just a handful of malcontents who had plotted and carried out the attack.

There were good Indians and bad, just as there were good and bad white men. Will could hardly blame all tribes and their numbers for the actions of a few. But at the moment, he felt an overwhelming hatred for everyone. The Indians for the attack. The stage driver and his helper for not having been wiser or more alert. The men in the coach who weren't good shots, and frankly anyone else who had even the most remote role in what had taken place.

He even wanted to hate Laura for her part in running him down, but he couldn't bring himself to that. He didn't know why he wanted to hate her, except that her presence reminded him of what he'd lost. She offered the kind of tenderness and gentle healing that his mother would have given. In fact, Laura reminded him a great deal of his mother. He nearly smiled at the thought of how Laura refused to be put off by him. His mother would have been the same way. She would have ignored his whining and growling, and followed it up with a stern reminder that there were folks elsewhere who had it worse than he did. But this time, Will wasn't sure that was true.

A light knock sounded on the door, and Laura swept into the room. She had her dark auburn hair carefully pinned in place and had donned a dark navy skirt and matching jacket. Her white blouse was trimmed with ruffled lace down the front, and she'd pinned a cameo at the base of her throat.

"Good morning, Will," she said, moving to the window to open the drapes. "You simply must see the day. It's so bright and beautiful. There isn't a cloud in the sky."

"I have a headache."

She stopped midstep. "I hadn't thought of that. I'm sorry. I'll leave the drapes closed." She moved to the fireplace and stirred up the burning wood before adding a log. Once there was a roaring blaze, she stepped back and turned once again to face him. "I hope you are staying warm enough."

"It's been fine. Mrs. Duffy checks on it every hour."

"She's a wonderful lady. So capable," Laura replied, coming to where he sat. "Are you ready to return to bed? I can call for Curtis."

"Maybe in a little while. I'm trying to push myself to endure a little more each day."

"My friends from church are coming here in a few minutes. They're all ladies that you know, and they want to pop in to say hello and let you know that they're praying for you. After that, I'll serve lunch. We can set you up at the table with us if you really want to push yourself."

"No, I wouldn't be good company. I'd just as soon eat here alone."

"Very well." She felt his forehead. "I'm so glad you've no fever. The doctor was quite worried about infection, but I would say we no longer have to worry about that. You're healing nicely from the surgery. I know you're still having headaches and the light still bothers you. Is there anything else that is causing you trouble? What about the nausea?"

"It comes and goes. Mostly it's not a problem. I'm fine." He thought again of his mother. She would be appalled at how badly he had been treating Laura.

"And what of the ribs and incision? Has the pain lessened there?"

"I still feel all bruised up inside but not as swollen. Of course, it hurts when I move because of the broken ribs."

"Yes, it will take some time before those mend, but I think you're making good progress." Laura moved toward the door. "If you have need of anything, just ring the bell. I will be very close at hand."

"Wait!" He hadn't meant to call out in such a panicked tone and hurried to continue. "I want to apologize for the way I've been acting." He paused and thought carefully about what he wanted to say.

"I'm not at all myself, and while that's still no excuse for rudeness . . . well, I have no other explanation. I do appreciate what you've done for me. I know I would have been stuck in that hospital with minimal care had you not taken up my cause."

Laura smiled, and his breath caught. Maybe it was just the broken ribs, but whatever it was, Will was momentarily unable to breathe. He gave a cough and straightened.

She frowned and moved to his side. "I really do think we should get you back to bed. You can get up again this afternoon after you have lunch and take a nap. I'll make sure of it. But for now, you should rest. When the ladies come, I'll see to it that they don't visit you for too long."

She went to the remade bed and pulled down the covers. "I'll go get Curtis to help."

Will said nothing. He wasn't sure what he could say. How could he possibly tell her that his feelings for her were a jumble of anger, gratitude . . . and perhaps a fleeting bit of enticement? That he found her quite beautiful and a great conversationalist, but he also saw her as a bitter reminder of his loss.

"I think those doilies you're crocheting are absolutely beautiful," Laura said, inspecting Granny Taylor's work. "Please set some aside for me the day of the fundraiser. I'll pay double what anyone else is offering."

"I can hardly pass up an offer like that," Granny said, chuckling. "The church will appreciate that."

"The church fundraisers are always so beneficial and fun," Melody said, continuing work on a piece of embroidery. "I'm glad you can be a part of it, Laura. Your own work is quite lovely."

Laura looked down at the baby blanket she was knitting. "I love handiwork. I find it gives me time to reflect and pray when I'm doing it alone. I think of each piece and who I plan to gift it to, and then I pray for them."

"I do the same," Granny admitted. "I knit a lot of shawls. In fact, at the sale you'll find I have several to donate. I pray for the person who will buy them and wear them. I want God to bless them and help them on their daily path. It blesses me to think of how He will work in their lives."

Marybeth returned just then from visiting Will. "Poor Will. He really is dealing with a great many things. I feel so sorry for him."

"I think we all do," Faith Cooper said as she put aside her crochet work to take a sip of her tea. "He was such a hardworking and enthusiastic young man prior to losing his mother and sister, and of course . . . the accident."

"I didn't know him as well as you ladies did," Laura began, "but I can sense that he was far more outgoing and excited by the prospects of what was yet to come."

"Oh, he was. He was so excited about getting his assignment on the Indian reservation. He came out last spring with such enthusiasm and love for those people." Faith lingered over her tea. "I remember him sitting and talking to me and my husband for over an hour one evening after supper. He spoke of some of the cultural things he'd learned about the Shoshone and of how he thought he could help them to see how much God loved them. He said everyone longs for love and a sense of purpose. I thought that was insightful for one so young."

"He's not all that young," Granny countered. "He's thirty years old. By that age, my Jed already had a wife and children and a ranch to work. He was older than his years because of all we'd had to face. I have a feeling that beyond the war, this situation is the first time Will's had to dig deep to get the living water he needs to survive."

"What an interesting way of putting it, Granny." Laura loved the old lady's way of looking at life and speaking her mind.

"Well, it suits the moment. Will's grown up in the Christian faith. And his faith may never have been tried like it is right now. The war was terrible, and no doubt it grew him up a great deal and tested his spirit. I won't be sayin' that it didn't. But now he's dealing with life in a very personal way. He's lost his family, and now the one thing that gave him purpose and goals is questionable to him. His faith has been shaken."

"I hadn't really thought of his faith being shaken," Melody said, rubbing her expanding abdomen. "The baby is sure kicking up a storm today."

"You've got what, about two and half months left?" Faith asked.

"Something like that. Early to mid-April as best as the doctor can figure."

Marybeth nodded. "I can hardly wait, and poor Edward won't sleep well until I safely deliver this child. I wish he weren't so worried, but having lost his first wife in childbirth, he can't help it."

"We'll keep praying for him. Just as we'll keep praying for Will. Our fellas need our constant prayers. They have a lot of strength in spirit and body, but they need that extra bolstering in order to make good." Granny put her crocheting aside and got to her feet. "Time for me to stretch a bit."

"Would you like more tea?" Laura got up and placed her knitting on the chair.

"I think that would be nice," Granny said. "After that, I think we should gather round and pray. I have a feeling that we should pray long and hard for each of our fellas today. Seems like testing times are upon them all."

Laura waved good-bye as the ladies headed off on foot to their various homes. She had thoroughly enjoyed their time working and praying together. It was refreshing in a way that she had never known. Back in school, there had been times of silent prayer, but they weren't encouraged to pray out loud. There was something quite intimate and deeply encouraging about praying with friends.

A noise sounded nearby, and Laura turned to see what it was. To her surprise, a little gray-and-white-striped kitten dashed across the snowy yard and came to brush up against her skirt.

"Where did you come from, little one?" she asked and leaned down to pick up the cold animal.

Drawing him close, Laura was rewarded with loud purring as the kitten snuggled up against her.

"You are such a little thing." Laura glanced around the neighborhood, wondering who had lost their pet. "Well, I'll take you inside and let you warm up. Then I'll talk to Curtis about finding out where you belong."

The kitten mewed again, and Laura couldn't help but laugh. "How can anyone ever be sad around a kitten?" She thought immediately of Will. Oh, wouldn't it be fun to share this with him?

She made her way into the house and down the hall to his room. "Will?" She called softly from the door just in case he was sleeping.

"Come in," he answered.

Hiding the kitten under her shawl, she pushed open the door and stepped inside. "I've come to show you something." She closed the door behind her, then made her way to his bed.

"Look what I found." She unwrapped the shawl and placed the kitten on the bed beside him. "I think he got lost. I'm going to have Curtis check with the neighbors and see if they are missing their pet."

Will stared at the animal for a moment, then surprised Laura by running his index finger down the back of the baby. "He's pretty young to be out on his own."

"I thought so too." She moved to the door. "Will you please watch him while I go speak to Curtis?" She didn't wait for an answer but hurried to the kitchen, where she hoped she'd find the young man. The cook had mentioned earlier that she was going to put him to work rearranging the pantry.

"Mrs. Murphy, is Curtis here?"

The stocky woman looked up from where she was rolling pie dough. "He's in the pantry."

"Thank you. I need him for a little errand, but he can finish for you first," Laura said as she moved toward the pantry.

She found Curtis on a ladder placing several jars of pre- serves on a high shelf. "Curtis, when you're finished here, I wonder if you would do me a favor."

"Sure, Miss Evans. What is it?" He climbed down and stopped directly in front of her. "I'm almost done."

"I found a kitten. He's with Will right now. Stop by and see him for yourself so you can describe him, but then I want you to go around the neighborhood and see if any- one has lost him. He's so little—too little to be out in the snow."

"Sure thing. I'll go in a few minutes and see what I can find out."

"Thank you, Curtis." She glanced around the pantry, but having never seen it before, she couldn't really say if the young man had done a good job or not. However, she knew his work was generally quite thorough. Surely praise was in order.

"This looks very nice, Curtis. You've done a good job."

"Thanks, Miss Evans. I've always been able to organize things. Your pa said he might hire me on down at the store."

"Well, if you are gifted with organization, I can't think of a better place to work." She left him with that. Back in the kitchen, Laura grabbed a saucer. "I wonder if I could have a bit of milk?"

Mrs. Murphy looked at her oddly but fetched the milk and poured a little into the saucer. Laura smiled. "I found a kitten, and I believe he's hungry."

"And cold if he's been outside long."

"Exactly. Will is warming him up right now."

Laura made her way back to Will's room and found him quite entertained as he allowed the kitten to crawl around his face and neck.

"Looks like you two have made friends already. I've brought a little milk for him."

"The way he's been mewing, I'd say he's starved."

Laura brought the milk to the bed and carefully placed it beside Will on top of the quilt. The kitten hurried to the saucer and began to lap at the offering.

"See there, you were right." Laura gave the animal a little stroke as he continued to lap up the milk. "I asked Curtis to find his owner. Hopefully we can reunite them soon."

But by late afternoon, they were no closer to finding the

animal's home. Laura thought it fine and made plans to keep the baby, but Will seemed less enthusiastic.

"You'll just get attached and something will happen to him," Will said, shaking his head in disapproval.

"And I suppose I should never get attached to anyone or thing because something might happen to them?" Laura asked before realizing how it might affect Will.

"It'll save you a lot of hurt if you did things that way."

"It'd keep me from a lot of love and happiness too." She met his gaze. The kitten was sleeping next to him, curled up against Will's neck on the pillow.

"Is that why you haven't married?" she asked Will, deciding to make it personal.

"I learned during the war to guard my heart. It served me well. And of course, given all that's happened of late, I should have done a better job. What about you?"

"I suppose I should have learned that after losing my mother and, to a degree, my father, but I didn't. I had a hard lesson when I was seventeen. My college in Tennessee decided to temporarily close in 1863 because the war was on our front steps. I accompanied one of my teachers, Mrs. Nelson, to Europe to escape the horrors of war. That was my father's desire anyway.

"Mrs. Nelson was a childless widow, but she had a sister in Paris, so we went to stay with her for the duration of the war. She had a son who was a little older than me. His name was Andrew Mansard. We saw each other day in and day out. He was attending college, and since I was being schooled by Mrs. Nelson, we often studied together. I found him to be quite entertaining and enjoyed learning about his experiences in life.

"As you remember, the war went on until 1865, so my time with him was extensive. He was often my escort to various parties and outings. I couldn't help myself. I fell in love. It was my first experience of losing my heart. Andrew was quite suave and devilishly handsome. He had made conquests all over the city. I didn't know it at the time, however, and fell rather hard. I thought he felt the same way, since he declared it to be so with his romantic speeches and promises."

"I had friends who were like that," Will said, shaking his head. The kitten stirred but didn't wake.

Laura could still remember how much it hurt when she realized she'd been duped by Andrew and his well-crafted words.

"When we heard the war was over, I was so excited. I knew I'd finally be able to go home again, and I wanted my father to meet Andrew and approve him as a husband. Andrew had talked on and on about how we would be married once the war was over, and I took him at his word."

"But he didn't mean it, did he?" Will asked.

"No. No, he did not. One morning at breakfast, Mrs. Nelson announced we would soon book passage back to America. I made the mistake of asking Andrew if he would accompany us or come soon after. He acted surprised and said I had misunderstood him. That my little girl infatuation had caused me to imagine all sorts of promises when none had been made."

Laura shrugged and eased back into the rocking chair. "I was such a foolish child. I had no suspicion of him being anything less than truthful in his feelings. I didn't have a mother to warn me about such things, and Mrs. Nelson obviously didn't want to create a problem with her nephew."

"Figures. Never mind that it hurt you. What happened?" Will's voice was soft and full of sympathetic tones.

"Nothing. That was the problem. I found Andrew and

asked him about all the promises he'd made. All the words of love. He laughed and told me that this was just the way of things in Paris. That he was merely enticing me and teaching me to enjoy romance. I told him that given the outcome, it wasn't worth the pain. He thought me quite silly and childish. And perhaps I was. But I grew up that day."

Will nodded. "I can understand that."

Laura shrugged again. "What of you? Have you ever been in love?"

"No. And given the pain of losing the people I loved, I don't plan to love again, especially not in the fashion you're talking about."

"I suppose some would call you very wise." She got to her feet and headed for the door. "I'm going to let you get some rest before supper. Sleep well."

After Laura had gone, sadness washed over Will. He could see in his mind's eye the innocent and loving young woman she'd been. Her first experience of romantic love was all a game. How that must have crushed her spirit.

She had been soured on love. They both had, but Will found it especially troubling where she was concerned. Laura Evans was a beautiful and intelligent young woman. She was kind and generous as well. She deserved to be loved and cared for by someone other than her father, who hadn't been man enough to set aside his own selfish needs for that of his grief-stricken child.

Will had no trouble imagining Laura as a wife and mother. Her family would be blessed to have her, and there would be an abundance of love and joy. Laura was the kind of person who could draw love quite naturally from others.

If she would allow it.

He frowned and closed his eyes. But she wouldn't. She'd been hurt, cut deep. She had trusted and given her heart and found it was all a farce. She was much too logical to allow it to happen again. Anger at Andrew coursed through Will's thoughts. He was older. He knew better. He had toyed with her affections as if they were nothing more than a childhood game.

Cruel.

Very simply the man was cruel, and Will hated that Laura had ever had to endure him.

# 10

H e's just the sweetest kitten, Father. I knew you'd want me to shelter him from the cold," Laura told her father the next morning over breakfast. "I asked Curtis to check around the neighborhood, but no one seems to know anything about him. I've put him in with Will. I think it will do much to improve his spirits."

"Well, I can't say that I approve of having a wild animal in the house." Father frowned as he helped himself to a platter of bacon.

"He's hardly a wild animal. It's just a little kitten. Barely even weaned from his mother." Laura slathered butter on her toast, then reached for some jam. "I think he's darling, and if he doesn't belong to anyone, I'd like to keep him."

Her father said nothing and concentrated instead on adding sugar to his coffee. Laura wasn't sure why he was opposed to the kitten, but she felt confident she could win him over.

"When you're away for long hours, a kitten will help me not to feel so alone."

Her father glanced up. "Well, there are other solutions, you know. I've been thinking long and hard about it, in fact."

"What are you talking about?"

"A husband. It's high time you married. You are, after all, nearly twenty-three. By most standards, folks would say you're pushing toward being an old maid."

"And that bothers you?"

He gave a half smile. "It should bother you, my dear. No woman wants to be forgotten in situations of matrimony."

"Such things aren't all that important to me. I fell in love once, and it was a brutal and sorrowful situation."

"When did you have opportunities to fall in love?"

"You seem surprised." She dabbed the napkin to her lips. "Just because I went to schools for girls doesn't mean I was never exposed to the company of young men."

"I suppose I never thought much about it. Still, being exposed and having time to form a relationship and fall in love are two different things." His brows furrowed together. "I can't say that this news sits well with me."

"Don't let it upset you, Father. The young man was the nephew of a teacher. The one you arranged to take me to Europe. Remember, I was there for nearly two years. That's a long time to be around a dashing and ambitious young man."

"I'm appalled to imagine you having an intimate relationship. I never anticipated you would be put in such a dangerous situation."

She shook her head. "I was carefully supervised for the most part. And Andrew did not take liberties, if that's what worries you. We spent a lot of time together, that much is true, but he was mostly full of words. He professed his love, but he did so to many young women." Laura hated to even bring up the subject again but was determined for her father to understand.

"I learned that the heart can be easily deceived if the parties are either deceptive or naïve. I was the latter and will not make that mistake again."

Her father lowered his coffee midway to his mouth. "Why didn't I hear about this when it happened?"

Laura picked up her own cup. "Why would I bother you with such a thing? What was to be done about it?"

"If he played you false or took advantage of you, then he deserves to be called to account. Even punished."

She chuckled and sipped from the china cup. She could well imagine the debonair Andrew facing her imposing father. There might have been a bit of satisfaction in it when she was younger and nursing her wounds, but now it just seemed humorous.

Putting her cup aside, she shook her head. "It's of no consequence now. I just want you to understand why I have no interest in pursuing courtship."

"Still, it's important for your future. Perhaps even for mine. Making a good connection would see our families supporting each other in crucial matters."

"Such as you being appointed governor?" She raised her brow and eyed him carefully. "Surely you wouldn't trade my happiness for the governorship?"

Her father said nothing for a moment. Finally, he shook his head. "Of course not. However, I know a bit more about life than you do. Women are happier with a mate. Men are too, but they often don't realize it. The team of husband and wife can face the future with a strength that comes from no other place."

"I believe that strength comes from God," Laura said, picking up her fork once again. "A man and woman who serve God first and then each other are, in my opinion, unbeatable.

When times of hardship come, they will seek their heavenly Father first."

"While those things sound encouraging and hopeful, I can tell you from experience that it doesn't always work that way. Your mother and I had a great deal of faith in God. We sought Him when your mother fell ill, and He ignored our pleas. God doesn't always answer prayers."

"Oh, but He does, Father. He just doesn't always say yes. As hard as that is to accept, God often says no and directs us to a better way."

"And how could there have been a better way at the price of your mother's life?" Father all but growled the question. It was clear he was thoroughly upset by the conversation, and Laura hated that their discussion had turned so dark.

"Father, I'm sorry. I never meant for us to argue. I trust that you are wiser than I am when it comes to affairs of the heart. If it's your desire for me to meet some young men, then I will." She gave him a reassuring smile and saw the tension ease in his expression.

"I have no desire to fight either. I will keep in mind your thoughts and feelings. Perhaps we could have a gathering—a party. You could mingle among the guests and get to know some of the men who reside in Cheyenne. I would choose only such men as I know to be honorable and of marriageable age. You could see if any of them appealed."

"That would be acceptable to me, Father." Laura would rather walk barefoot on hot coals, but to keep her father from being upset, she was happy to agree.

"It seems you've made several good friends already," Father continued. "I'm glad you have managed to do that."

"Yes, they're all women from the church, and their husbands are quite active in Cheyenne. One used to be a banker, but now he owns and runs a boys' school. Charlie Decker is his name. I believe he's a member of one of your business groups. Then there's Edward Vogel. He's a deputy with the city's police department. He works for the city marshal. Mr. Cooper is retired but keeps himself involved with town politics. You probably know him."

"Cooper? Yes, I believe I do. Owns a boardinghouse, if I'm not mistaken. I know Decker as well. The man is quite intelligent—has a good mind for figuring out details."

"That doesn't surprise me. Their wives are quite knowledgeable too." Laura held each with great affection. "And there's Granny Taylor's husband, Jed. He works for the railroad but used to own his own ranch in Texas. Granny is always giving sound and sage advice. I really like her."

"It's good that they're such decent sorts. There are plenty in this town who aren't. A lot of ruffians remained after the train moved west. I intend to see this town cleaned up. Now that we've passed laws against gambling and prostitution, we should see some real changes. And we will, of course, continue to pursue law and order."

"I'm sure Cheyenne is a much better place for your attention. I know that you have interests in being appointed governor, but I don't really understand why. What has driven you down that road?"

Her father finished eating and pushed back from the table. "The power and ability to carve a way in history so as to actively effect change."

Laura hadn't known what she expected him to say, but it wasn't that. "You desire power to make changes? What kind of changes?"

"There's a whole variety of things I would change. A lot of it, however, has more to do with the people I would eliminate from their positions of power. People who have flawed ideas and plans for this town and territory. I'd get rid of all the Indians, eliminate the reservations and the people on them."

Her mouth dropped as her eyes widened. "Father, you would have them killed?"

He looked at her oddly. "No, of course not. I would have them removed. I am of a mind that we allocate one area in this country or perhaps Canada and send all native people there. There's not that many of them left, and having all these separate reservations in our great country is ridiculous. Let them all be thrown together in one place where they can be controlled. As you know, they can be very violent."

"But they're of different tribes. They speak different languages and have different cultural stories. Throwing them together won't work."

Her father rose from the table and tossed his napkin down. "Nonsense. America is the very symbol of that. We are a conglomerate of nations. Irish, Germans, Swedes, as well as Mexicans and Asians. We have come together and live and work as a collective group. It shouldn't be that difficult for the Indians to do the same. It would take an adjustment, but it would work in time, I assure you. Now, I must get to the store." He came around the table and leaned down to kiss her cheek.

"It's so good to have you with me," he said. "Don't worry yourself over political affairs. I've the head for such work, and you must trust that I know what I'm doing. With your suitors as well. I'm quite anxious to put you on the path toward matrimony."

After her father left, Laura wanted to kick herself. Why had she encouraged him to bring suitors? She had no intention of choosing a husband. Her only desire was to know her father better, and it seemed to her that breakfast had given her quite a bit of insight into his heart. The problem was, she wasn't entirely sure she cared for what she saw there. Power and marrying for social connections were hardly things that she valued. It made her uncomfortable to know they were what her father desired. After all, they would do nothing to draw them together as a family. The thin line of connection they had would only be made weaker by adding a third party. Laura sighed and put her napkin on the table. Maybe if she said nothing, Father would forget all about it. She could only hope.

A week later, Will had to admit he wasn't anywhere near as strong as he'd hoped to be. The doctor told him he'd lost a lot of blood, and they'd been forced to remove his spleen to prevent him bleeding to death. Will had asked but been denied the right to get up and walk on crutches. The doctor told him it was still too dangerous, and his broken ribs would never have the strength to hold him. But as much as this had soured Will's attitude and spirit, a visit from Mr. Blevins only served to make it worse.

"I had come to bring you good news. The government is ready to move ahead and assign additional workers for the various reservations. I went to the boardinghouse this morning, hoping to give you the good word," Mr. Blevins began. "However, Mrs. Cooper told me you had been in a terrible accident and were staying here for constant nursing care." The older man lowered his wire-rimmed glasses to the edge of his nose so that he could peer over them at Will.

"Yes, I was injured on the fifteenth of January when a horse trampled me. I suffered broken bones and a ruptured

TRACIE PETERSON

spleen. I also took a hard hit to my head," Will replied. "The doctor tells me I'm lucky to be alive."

"Yes, well, while it's good that you lived through your ordeal, it hardly helps me." Mr. Blevins tsked. "No, sir, it doesn't help at all."

The little man rose from his seat. "You'll no doubt be weeks, maybe months, at recuperating from your injuries. I can hardly set aside a position for that long."

"It seems to me if you've waited this long, a few more weeks isn't going to be the end of the world." Will's frustration brought out a sarcastic tone. How could the man only consider his own circumstances? Will had nearly died.

"Well, there's also the other thing," Mr. Blevins said, eyeing Will with a serious expression. "I understand your mother and sister were on the stage that was attacked by the Sioux."

"Yes, they were killed."

"And you're still of a mind to go and work with those who were responsible?"

"I never intended to work with the Sioux. I've studied and learned about the Shoshone. We talked at length about my heading west to their reservation with the Bannock."

"They're still Indians. Are you sure you can handle working with people who might have been responsible for killing your kin?" Blevins straightened to his full height, which couldn't have been more than five feet. "It's something to think about. Maybe you'd be happier starting a little church right here in Cheyenne and avoiding contact with the Indians."

Will had to admit, only to himself, that the same thoughts had occurred to him. His emotions were still torn when it came to the idea of working with the natives. He had wrestled with his lifelong plans over and over. After all, mental

123

arguments and contemplation were about all he was good for. Well, that and spiritual battles. He had even given thought to giving up on preaching altogether. He felt abandoned by God, and his heart didn't seem to be able to move on past that point.

At his silence, Blevins gave a nod and moved toward the door. "I will check back in with you in a week and see what the doctor says about your recovery. I can wait that long to decide."

Will met his grim expression and nodded. "Very well. Thank you."

But his heart wasn't full of thanks at all. He wanted nothing more than to get up and give the man a shake. In fact, Will would have liked to give most everyone around him a good hard shake. No one seemed to understand how difficult it was to be laid up—to not even be able to attend your own family's funeral. Forced to rely on everyone else for the simplest of needs.

Will heard the wind pick up outside. The staff had been talking about the possibility of a blizzard, and wind usually came before a storm.

"I see your visitor is gone," Mrs. Duffy said, coming into the room unannounced. Rosey followed behind her, along with Curtis. Both carried armloads of wood. "The weather's gone bad on us, and we're stocking up on dry firewood in each of the rooms. I'll be sure to check frequently to see that you're staying warm enough."

"Is Laura home?"

"She hasn't returned just yet. She went out to meet with her sewing circle friends," Mrs. Duffy replied. "I expect her most anytime. The ladies are usually good to keep track of the weather."

Will nodded. "Curtis, would you help me back to bed? I'm feeling a bit done in."

"No problem, sir," the boy replied after depositing the firewood. Mrs. Duffy motioned to Rosey, and the young woman hurried to pull down the covers.

Will found the kitten had burrowed under the covers up by the pillow. He stretched and opened his eyes as Will joined him in the bed, but otherwise had no interest in moving. Will almost laughed as the cat closed his eyes.

"He has no more energy than I do."

"Probably knows it's going to storm," Mrs. Duffy said, coming to tuck Will in. "Animals seem to know. I'm thinking this storm may be a bad one, and all the animals will hole up wherever they can to avoid the cold. This little fella's lucky Miss Laura found him. Otherwise, I hate to think what might have happened to him."

Will thought for the briefest of moments that the same might be said of him. Laura was determined to care for him, but since she had been the one to run him down, Will thought it rather . . . well . . . expected. He knew, however, that it really wasn't. He was the one who'd paid no attention to where he was walking. Laura had gone above and beyond to ensure he had good care. He really needed to be more grateful.

The staff exited the room, but in a moment, Mrs. Duffy was back, and on her heel was Charlie Decker.

"Mr. Decker has come calling. Are you up to a visitor?"

Will nodded and motioned him in. "A blizzard is about to start as I hear it. You should be home, Charlie."

The man doffed his hat. "I brought Laura home in our carriage since the snow had already started. I thought I might as well stop in and say hello," Charlie said as he stepped up to the bed. "I promise I won't stay long."

"What about school?"

"Oh, I dismissed the students early. The weather was just too threatening. The wind came up, and the sky is heavy with snow. I told the boys to go straight home, and I pray they did as they were told for once." Charlie took a seat in the ladder-back chair by the bed.

Will didn't feel much like visiting. "You need to get back before the storm moves in and you're unable to find your way home."

Charlie smiled and ignored the suggestion. "I told Melody I was going to visit with you for just a moment or two. I wanted to see how you were doing. I heard Blevins was back in town."

"He is, and he's already been here," Will admitted, realizing he had no choice but to talk. "The news is that the government is finally settled and ready to take on preachers for the reservations, but I'm not ready to take on a job."

"You'll heal up soon enough. Can't they wait?"

"I guess not."

Charlie's eyes narrowed just a bit. "Will, do you even want them to wait?"

Will knew his friend meant well, and frankly, he did need to talk it out with someone. He just hadn't expected to have to do it at that very moment.

"Truthfully, Charlie, I don't know if I do. Indians just killed my family. How can I go to them and show the kind of love and encouragement that God expects? I don't even have a good relationship with God right now. I feel so abandoned and angry."

Charlie chuckled. "Sounds like you have a lot to work on. Maybe we could start with a little prayer."

The wind gusted hard against the house, and Will shook

his head. "We don't have the kind of time needed to pray through this issue. You need to get home, Charlie. Melody needs you there."

He saw the battle waging in Charlie's eyes, but finally his friend got back to his feet. "I'll go for now, but I promise to return, and I'll be praying about your troubles while we're apart. I think you'd do well to do the same, even if you are put out with the Almighty."

Will nodded. "I'll do what I can, Charlie. But I make no promises. I'm not sure God wants to hear from me anymore."

# 11

L aura finished pulling on her gloves before heading downstairs to bid her father good-bye. She was heading out to church despite the deep snow left from the storm. Her father had plans to be gone for the evening as well, so he could hardly complain or forbid her to leave the house based on the weather.

"Father," she said, coming into his study, "the Vogels will be here shortly, and I'll be going to church. Do you know what time you plan to be home tonight?"

He glanced up from his desk and shook his head. "Hard to say. Sometimes these meetings go long."

"Seems a shame to have to have them on the Sabbath." She pulled on her wool bonnet and began to secure the ties. "I think there must be those who would prefer to do business on other days."

"It's really none of your concern, Laura." He gave her a look that suggested she had crossed a line, but then he smiled. He could so easily change his manner. "My, don't you look pretty."

Laura came around his desk to offer a kiss on his cheek.

"Thank you, Father. And as for my concerns, I just worry that you're overextending yourself. You never seem to rest, and I fear you'll fall ill."

"Don't worry about me. I assure you I am healthy and capable. You haven't had the experience of being in my presence long enough to realize that this is a normal manner for me."

And whose fault was that? She wanted to ask but didn't.

"Well, the weather doesn't help." She didn't want to make too much of the snow for fear he might suggest she stay home. "The cold causes all sorts of illness."

"If I thought that to be true, I'd forbid you to traipse off to church. Now stop your fretting."

Laura headed toward the door. "I'm sorry. You must remember that I love you and want only the best for you."

Her father gave her a wave. "I want the same for you. By the way, what say we host a party on Washington's birthday? I still want to get you properly introduced to my friends, especially my single friends."

"The twenty-second of February?" Laura considered the fact that she likely wouldn't get out of this no matter what she said. "I think that would be a good time. Spirits will be high in celebration, and as good Southerners we can hardly host a party on Lincoln's birthday." She smiled.

"I've never yet celebrated that man's birthday and never will. Now go on with you. I'll make the arrangements, and you make sure you have a pretty dress to wear. You know I have a fine collection of ready-made gowns at the store. You should come and pick something out."

"I have a great many clothes already. I'm sure I'll have something appropriate."

Just then, someone gave a light rap on the door and

opened it before her father could speak. The man was tall and lanky. He was dressed in a dark brown duster and dark trousers. A black broad-brimmed hat was worn low over his face. There was an air of danger about him, and Laura immediately disliked him.

"Laura, this is one of my men. I need to speak to him," her father said. "You and I can finish up later."

"Yes, Father. We can talk in the morning." She wanted nothing more than to get out of the room. She knew it was probably silly, but the man made her most uncomfortable.

"Yes, yes. Go on with you now."

She stepped into the hall and pulled the door partway closed. She would have closed it all the way, but strangely enough she heard her father mention the kitten.

"Remember I told you about that blasted kitten? Laura kept it, and I want it gone. While she's at church tonight, take it out and drown it."

Laura put her hand to her throat. Was he serious? She knew her father hadn't been all that welcoming of the kitten, but since it stayed in Will's room, she hadn't thought it to be a real problem.

"Do you really want me to kill it?" the man asked.

"I hate that thing. I don't care what you do with it. I just want it gone. I'll tell her it ran off."

"If that's the way you want it."

Laura heard her father confirm his desires before going off onto something else he wanted the man to oversee. She hurried down the hall to the kitchen. There she found one of the cook's market baskets and grabbed it and a couple of dish towels. She'd take the kitten with her to church and find another home for it. She wasn't about to leave it here to be killed. And no doubt if that was her father's order, the man would carry it out. She knew her father well enough to know that his hirelings would heed his orders or risk being fired.

Laura nearly ran into Mrs. Duffy as she was coming out of Will's room. "I'm so sorry. I'm in a bit of a hurry. Would you mind watching for the Vogels? I need to tend to something, and they should be arriving most anytime now."

"Of course, Laura." The woman headed for the entryway. "I'll get your heavy wool coat ready as well."

"Thank you." Laura pushed back the door to Will's room and immediately spied the kitten on the bed. She closed the door behind her, then hurried to place the basket on the bed.

"Something has come up. I can't take time to talk about it, but I'm taking the kitten to church with me. I'm hoping someone else can give him a home." She took the kitten in hand and drew it to her face. She kissed his little head as he mewed.

"But why? I thought you enjoyed him."

Laura met Will's gaze. "My father doesn't want him around. He . . . he told his man to take it out while I was at church. He told him to kill it."

"He what?" Will glanced at the closed door. "But why?"

"I don't know, and I can't take time to try and figure it out right now. The Vogels will be here any minute to take me to church. All I know is I can't risk that horrible man finding him and carrying out his orders."

"Of course not." Will looked again at the door. "How will you explain his absence?"

"I don't know. I suppose, if need be, I'll tell the truth. That I found a home for him." She tucked him into the basket and closed the lid. "Hopefully I can get him out to the wagon without anyone questioning me."

"I'm sorry it's come to this."

Laura nodded. "Me too. I know you've come to care for him."

"It's not me I'm sorry for," Will replied.

For a moment, Laura just looked at him. His expression was one of sympathy, but it was Will's eyes that caught her attention most. He seemed to look through to her soul. As if he really understood her feelings in this matter.

There was a knock at Will's door, and Etta Duffy looked in. "They're here, Miss Laura."

"I'm coming." Laura grabbed the basket and hurried to where the housekeeper stood holding her coat. She handed the older woman the basket and took the dark green coat from her. Slipping into the warmth, Laura found it did little to help the cold that permeated her heart. How could her father be so ruthless and cruel? Surely, he didn't really mean for the man to kill the kitten. It was too much to accept, much less try to sort out in a rush.

Climbing into the carriage, Laura held the basket tightly as the kitten mewed from within. Carrie was asleep on Marybeth's lap, and Laura was grateful she only needed to explain to adults.

"I have a kitten in this basket," she said. "It's a complicated story, but I need to find it a home and didn't feel that I could leave him at the house."

"We were just saying that we could use a cat," Marybeth replied. "In fact, a kitten is even better. Carrie would love a pet."

"It'd be better to have a full-grown cat," Edward chimed in. "The idea is for it to kill mice. This cold weather has really driven them inside."

"He'll be a good mouser in time," Marybeth said. "Why don't you swing us back by the house, and we can leave the basket there? We have plenty of time."

Edward said nothing but turned the horse toward their place. Laura felt a huge sense of relief. "Thank you. I would hate it if something happened to him. He's so little and sweet."

"A three-year-old, a kitten, and soon a new baby," Marybeth said, shifting Carrie in her arms. "Sounds perfect."

"Sounds like more than we bargained for," Edward muttered.

"Our entire marriage has been more than either of us bargained for," she said, laughing. He chuckled as well.

Their levity gave immediate relief to Laura's spirits. She still found it hard to stomach her father's orders, but at least the kitten would be safe. She could figure out the rest of the matter in time.

Exactly a month after Will's accident, he received the doctor's approval to try to use the crutches Laura had found for him. His ribs and left side were still plenty sore, but he had been bed bound for too long and getting up on his feet was what he most wanted now.

"You seem to handle yourself very well," Laura said as she swept into his room. She was gowned in a forest-green silk that had been trimmed in black cording and lace. The long sleeves were full to the elbow and then fitted to the wrist. It was done up in the new postwar style that eliminated the full belled skirts and had instead a bustled back. She looked quite lovely, and her dark red hair complemented the color of the gown.

"I . . . uh . . ." He tried to move his thoughts away from how beautiful she looked this evening. "I'm doing my best."

"I'm here to encourage you to join us for dinner. Father

said he'd like to know you better, and I know it's been weeks since you sat at a table."

"I'd like that too. The doctor said it won't hurt for me to have my foot down. The swelling should be gone." Will straightened. "I'm hardly dressed for a formal dinner, however."

"Well, I can help you with that. You need only to don your coat and you'll be proper enough." She went to the wardrobe and opened it. She took out a suit coat that Mrs. Cooper had brought for him along with some of his other things when he'd first taken up residency at the Evans house.

She helped Will into his jacket, and that was when he noticed the scent of her perfume. It was new.

"What's the new scent you're wearing?"

She looked surprised and gave a light laugh. "I hardly expected you to notice such a thing. It's a new floral perfume from my father's store. Do you like it?"

"I do. It suits you better than the other."

Laura studied him for a moment, then smiled. "You never cease to amaze me, Wilson Porter. Now, come along. Father is waiting."

He followed her slowly, making certain to manage the crutches without mistake. The last thing he wanted was to reinjure his foot and leg. Once they entered the dining room, Rosey was there to help Laura get him settled at the table.

"Look who has decided to join us, Father."

"Mr. Porter. It's good to see you up and around." Granite Evans gave him a nod.

"Thank you, sir. Your generosity has been a blessing to me, but I'm certain to be headed home soon. At least as soon as the doctor tells me I can manage the stairs."

"I'm not sure how you would even attempt that with a

broken leg." Laura took her seat and placed her napkin on her lap.

"I suppose a little finessing will be needed, but I'll figure it out," Will assured them.

Dinner was served, and to Will's delight it was one of Mrs. Murphy's delicious beef Wellingtons. Apparently, this was a favorite of Mr. Evans, as they had it at least once a week. When everyone was served, Will noticed that Mr. Evans picked up his fork and knife to dig right in while Laura bowed her head for an apparent silent prayer.

Still feeling rather distanced from the Almighty, Will picked up his napkin and arranged it on his lap until Laura had finished. When she glanced over at him, she smiled.

"I'm so glad you felt up to joining us this evening. It will no doubt give Father some better and more lively conversation."

"Your conversation has always been enjoyable, Laura." Her father cut into his beef. "However, it is good to see Mr. Porter doing so well."

"It's all due in thanks to you two. Had you not taken me in, I would probably have fared far worse in lingering in the hospital. I thank you both."

"You're quite welcome. It's only right to help out our fellow man," Laura's father said.

"Especially when I was the one responsible for having run him down," Laura added.

"No, the fault was all mine."

"Still, I felt obligated, and I'm glad I did. It's been nice to get to know you better. The Vogels and Deckers as well as others have spoken so highly of you."

"I understand you're a preacher and your plan is to go to the reservation to save the souls of the Indians," Granite Evans commented.

"I don't know that it's my ambition to do that any longer. After all, it was Indians who killed my mother and sister."

Granite picked up a goblet of wine. "I suppose that would cause a fella to reconsider his heart on the matter. I personally don't believe the Indian has a soul to save. As far as history shows me, they've failed to contribute anything of quality to our society."

"But, Father, they are people. Of course they have a soul. You can't be one of those who believes them to be nothing more than animals."

Her father shrugged. "I've seen no proof to suggest otherwise. They have been vicious killers all along the rail line. Ask some of the others. It seems in this town anyway everyone knows someone who has suffered at the hands of the Indians. Why, prior to the war, we were always reading in the newspaper about some skirmish or attack in the West."

"You have to admit they have been provoked on many occasions. Fired upon at first glance, rather than waiting to see if they were friend or foe." Will was surprised to find himself defending the Indians and began eating to hide it.

"Will makes a good point, Father. All of this land was once theirs. Their homelands have been ripped away and their needs compromised. They were reliant upon hunting and fishing, and a lot of that has been taken from them."

"Bah! They owned nothing. They don't believe in land ownership. They think it all belongs to the Great Spirit or some such thing. They believe it their right to move freely and take their people from one place to another."

"So as not to completely use up the resources of an area," Will offered without thinking.

"Exactly. I've read about the Indians, Father. They are very mindful of the land's ability to produce for them, be it from the animals on it or the plants that grow. I believe, given the fact that they've been around here for who knows how long, they know well enough how to maintain the grounds and animals for their benefit."

Her father looked at her oddly. "You sometimes surprise me with your comments, Laura. I would never have expected such talk from you. I suppose that women's college taught you this."

"No, my own reading and discussion with others did. You'll find that I'm quite well read, Father. I read newspapers and books of every kind. I also read Godey's for all the knowledge and wisdom a woman might need in dressing in the fashions of the day, learning a new embroidery pattern, and reading short stories and poetry. I like a wide variety of reading, and the more topics, the better."

"Well, it's not exactly fitting for a proper lady to be reading details about Indian living," her father countered. "Some of their activities can be quite scandalous. Not to bring up bad memories for Mr. Porter, but the Sioux did scalp those men from the stagecoach."

"They did indeed," Will replied and looked to Laura. "I think it is admirable that you take an interest in the Indians. Personally, my family has a long history with them, and we've found most tribes to be amiable when we offered kindness and friendship."

"Before I came here, I read all I could about Cheyenne and the territory. It's all very fascinating to me. I believe the better educated a person is, the more solutions they will have to the problems they face."

"And what problems are you facing?" her father asked. "I do my best to protect and shield you from having problems."

Laura laughed. "And you do such a good job, Father. Now,

tell me, what is this I hear about giving women the right to vote? Is that truly something the Cheyenne founding fathers are supporting?"

"Indeed. The word across the territory is that we don't have enough voting males to establish statehood. Congress won't even consider us for statehood until we reach a higher number of voters. It's been suggested that if we allow women the right to vote, we would have our numbers."

"I wonder if Congress will see it the same way."

"I have my doubts," her father admitted. "But it is worth the try."

"So you are supportive of women voting?" Will asked.

Granite Evans shrugged. "I don't see how it could hurt. They'll vote the way their husbands tell them to. It's really no different than every man having two votes."

"And what of single women like me?" Laura asked.

Her father shrugged again. "You'll do what I tell you to do."

Laura thought to remark but refrained. Sometimes her father's attitude disappointed her, but she was determined not to love him any less. No doubt he had his reasons for the things he said and did. She obviously needed to know him better to understand his comments. Even if she couldn't agree with them.

# 12

H ow are the boys doing?" Granite asked, looking around the small shack of a home.

Gus Synder poured a cup of coffee, then handed the mug to his boss. "Doin' good enough. You keep them in money, and they're happy as pigs in mud."

Granite took a sip of the bitter brew and nodded. "You know, I pay you enough. You could live better than this."

"Yeah, but that would raise suspicions. After all, I'm just your warehouse overseer. Living better would cause folks to wonder how I got the money to live that way. Besides, I've lived like this all my life. It suits me well enough." He poured another mug of coffee, then sat down at the table where Granite was sitting.

"So everybody's keeping their mouth shut?"

"Yeah, they know better than to talk. It'd be the last thing they ever did. Harvey keeps them in line."

Granite knew Harvey Breckenridge was one of Gus's cousins, and the family was loyal to each other. In fact, Granite had never seen the likes. Gus employed two of his cousins, and the men would die for him. Granite had no idea what had instilled that kind of loyalty but knew that, besides being related, the men had gone through the war together.

The war had done strange things to men. He'd seen it on both sides, and it fascinated him. The very idea of a man giving his life for another was so very foreign. Granite himself had never been loyal to anyone but Laura's mother. She was the reason he pursued wealth and power. Her memory was the driving force behind everything he did. Well, that and his own self-satisfaction and greed.

"Harvey say anything about the last job?"

"He outlined it for me. They waited in that hilly area just to the south. Hid in some of the rocks. It was simple enough to jump out at the last minute and take the stage down. Driver and his man didn't know they were under attack until it was too late. Problem came with that new man, Abe Johnson. We had to let him go."

"He started the killing?"

"Yeah. Thought he was back at Gettysburg. Totally lost his sense of where he was and what was going on. He was the one who scalped those men. The other fellas were collecting the valuables like you wanted, but Abe acted like an animal."

Granite lifted the coffee Gus had poured for him when he first arrived. "But he won't be a problem anymore?"

Gus shook his head. "No. He's been dealt with."

"What about the money? Anyone getting greedy?"

"Those boys have been with us too long for that kind of nonsense. Like I said, they know if they dared to cause trouble they'd be quickly dealt with—like with Abe. They've also seen it happen before when we had fellas less inclined toward loyalty. Now that most of them have been with us for a time, they know how things go."

"Good. Our system is working well. They know what's expected and do what they're told, or they die. It's that simple. And no one but you needs to know I'm holding the reins. Keeping my identity a secret is to everyone's benefit."

"Yes, sir." Gus drank the rest of his coffee and got up to get another cup. "What did you have in mind for us to do next?"

"We're laying low for a time. The army is still out there trying to locate the Indians who robbed the stage and killed the passengers." Granite finished off his coffee, then continued. "And that money box was full. It'll hold the boys for quite a while and help me build my new house."

"What about that fella you've got in your house?" Gus asked, holding up the pot toward Granite. "More?"

Granite shook his head. Gus made the worst coffee in the territory, and he had no desire to suffer through another mug. "Don't you worry about the man in my house. It's done wonders to keep Laura busy. She's been the dutiful nurse, and the preacher is lost in his mourning. I guess I am a little sorry for him. It wasn't in my plan that there would be women on the stage. Seems we seldom get women traveling this time of year, and the fact that they happened to be his mother and sister is a tragedy, to be sure."

"If Abe hadn't lost his mind when the older woman pulled a derringer out of her bag, they might still be alive."

"A derringer, eh?" Granite had to admire Mrs. Porter's gumption. "Well, it's done, and the haul was excellent. The law believes it was the work of Indians, just as they will on the next job we pull."

"And when will that be?" Gus asked, reclaiming his seat.

"Those soldiers and lawmen are gonna be searching until spring. By then, the Indians will be getting itchy to get off the reservations, and the army will have their hands full. The lawmen will be busy with new settlers coming in, and I've already gotten word that there will be at least ten different new herds of cattle coming our way. A group down in Texas is planning to unite and push up here to resettle. Not to mention sheep. There's a herd of a couple hundred that are being relocated here from Colorado Territory. The owner came and finalized his purchase of land last week. Ought to be interesting. I never did see a time a sheep man and cattle rancher could get along. With all that going on, you'll get your chance for a new adventure.

"In the meanwhile, talk to that other cousin of yours and lay in more of the Indian wares. That always serves us well."

"Harvey will handle it. As long as you supply him with rifles and ammo to trade, the Sioux will give him whatever he asks for."

"You've got quite the interesting family, Gus."

The man shrugged. "We know how to deal with the law and those who get too out of hand."

Granite got to his feet. "Thanks for all you do. There's gonna be some extra cash coming your way. Oh, and thanks for taking care of that kitten."

"I didn't." The man looked at Granite with a blank expression. "Never did find the thing."

"Hmm, well, it's gone. I suppose that's good enough. Since Laura's said nothing about it, maybe she found it another home. I made it clear I didn't like animals in the house. Could be she cared enough to do something about it. Wouldn't that be something? An unselfish act from an Evans."

"Your daughter seems to be a good sort."

Granite gave a slight smile. "She does, doesn't she? She never gets into my business and seems content to just sew with her lady friends, nurse Mr. Porter, and go to church. She's the kind of good sort that would make a quality wife, and I intend to find her a husband as soon as possible. If I can connect her to one of the more powerful and wealthy men of our town, we might be able to create a force that people will have to deal with. And eventually that force might put me behind the governor's desk."

"As I hear it, you may be put there by the president. Rumor has it you're in the top running with one other fella."

Granite nodded. "But I've never relied on rumors, nor trusted them. It's hard to tell who's putting out the information. Washington is a long way off, and a lot can get misinterpreted along the way. I hope they're right, but I'll rely solely on myself to make it happen."

Will heard the front door open and wondered if Laura had returned. He found himself almost hoping she had so that they could visit. Lately, her company had become more and more appealing, although he continually forced away thoughts of how perfectly suited they were. Will had often thought of the kind of woman he'd one day marry, and Laura met his requirements and then some. She cared deeply about the people around her and took responsibility for things whether they were hers to deal with or not. Just taking care of him was an example of that. Making sure the kitten had a home was another. She was also respectful of her father even when he said things that were harsh and uncalled for. The man always apologized after his outbursts, especially if he caught sight of Laura's pained expression, but there was something of a mystery about him that Will didn't quite understand.

Just then, the very man looked into Will's temporary room. "Am I disturbing you?"

"No, sir. This is your house, after all." Will did his best to sound welcoming.

"How's the recovery coming along?"

"Good, I believe. The doctor seems to think it too soon for me to master stairs, and Mrs. Cooper is still unable to offer me a ground floor room. Otherwise, I would be thanking you for your very kind help and letting you have your room back."

Granite Evans surprised him by laughing heartily. "You haven't been any trouble at all, and this is just an extra room. If all houseguests were as quiet and easily dealt with as you've been, I'd have them all the time."

"Still, I know you're a very busy man and having a stranger around all the time can't be easy."

"Honestly, son, if you were a problem, you wouldn't be here." Granite stepped in closer. "But seriously, how are you feeling? You seem rather . . . dark of mood."

Will didn't know how the man knew what he was feeling. He'd been around so seldom that unless someone else had told him, Will wasn't sure how he'd deduced this.

"I guess I am." Will hated admitting his feelings to anyone, much less a stranger, but he did owe this man his life in some ways.

"The loss of my mother and sister is quite overwhelming to me, and it's made even worse knowing that I was the reason they were in a position of danger." Will looked away, trying to steady his emotions.

"And being laid up hasn't helped my mood at all," he added, glancing back at the older man with a shrug. "Although the care has been exceptional."

"Yes, indeed. Laura is a remarkable young woman," Evans replied. "I can say that with pride, even though I've had little to do with it."

"You sent her away right after the death of her mother, as I understand it."

Mr. Evans frowned. "It was for the best of us both. I was a very wounded man after losing my beloved wife. Perhaps that's why I recognize the darkness in you."

His conclusion made perfect sense and caused Will to relax a bit. "Yes, that's how I feel in losing my mother and sister. A part of me wants to fight with everyone I encounter. Another part wants only to pour out my heart and yet another to hide from the world."

Evans nodded. "Exactly. I didn't have it in me to comfort Laura. She was just a child and had been very close to her mother. I knew she needed someone to care for her, to listen to her." He looked away, and Will thought his expression bore a great deal of regret. "I knew it couldn't be me. I failed her miserably. I missed out on so much of her life, but what was I to do? I couldn't expose her to my rage."

"On the other hand, you might have found solace in her presence."

"I might have. But she was so young and needy, and I just couldn't take the chance that my anger would rise against her one day."

"I can understand your concern. It would seem the people who played a part in raising her did a good job. She's devoted to God, intelligent, beautiful, and as kind and gentle as any woman I've ever met."

"She is." Granite glanced out the window for a long moment, then turned back to Will. "But enough about Laura. What about you? What plans have you now that things have changed?"

Will shook his head. "What do you mean exactly?"

"Now that Indians have killed your mother and sister. What have you decided?"

"I gave it a lot of consideration. I'm not going." The answer surprised Will. Had he really come to that conclusion? Could he just turn away from a lifetime of planning to follow in his father's footsteps?

"I should clarify. I know that there are good Indians as well as bad, just as there are good and bad amongst every race of people. But right now . . ." He fell silent. Why was it so hard to sort through his feelings?

"What were you doing while awaiting your assignment to go?" Evans asked.

Will glanced up. "I was making furniture over at Bradley's."

"Are you any good at it?"

"Mr. Bradley was pleased and told me I was a blessing. People often sought me out for special projects, so I guess I'm good enough." Will shifted in the chair. His side ached. He hoped Curtis would come soon to help him to bed.

"Well, if you ever want a job with me, I know I could find something for you. I've asked around, and you have a sterling reputation. Preachers usually do, but given your age and lack of wife, I suppose I did wonder. But everyone I talk to tells me that you are uncompromised and reputable. You have even earned high praise from Judge Kuykendall."

Will remembered the man and his request for a blanket box for his wife. He had wanted it carved with intricate scrolling to match another piece of furniture. Will had gone to his house and studied the piece to get it just right. It had taken an impressive number of hours to complete, but when he was done, it looked as though the pieces had always been together.

"The judge is kind to offer praise. I merely created a piece of furniture to his design."

"Well, even so, the fact that you were able to please him speaks volumes to me." Evans turned toward the door. "I am always happy to find a place in my company for men of quality. It seems to me that you'd be wasted out on a reservation."

"It's hard to just give up on the idea, even with what happened. I come from a long line of preachers who worked with various tribes of Indians. It's something I figured I was called to do . . . to follow in their footsteps." But the idea of working for Granite did linger in his thoughts. If Will was to truly believe all things happened for a reason, then maybe Granite Evans was a part of his future. Maybe he'd been so fixed on what he believed was his destiny that he missed seeing that God actually had another plan for him.

"Maybe you have another calling now," Granite said as if reading Will's mind. "Ever think of that? I don't walk with the Almighty in the same manner that you and Laura do. I'll give it to you that there is a God, but I am not at all convinced that He cares about us."

His words caused feelings of defense to rise in Will. "But how could He give such attention to the details of His creation and then play no part in our daily lives? It seems to me that He must care, even love us dearly."

"But he allowed your mother and sister to be cruelly killed. He stood by as death stole away the mother of a young child and a beloved wife—my wife. How does that support a case for His love?"

Yesterday, Will would have considered himself the wrong person to ask. He would have been far more inclined to think as Evans did. But there was something about hearing the words aloud from someone else.

"The world holds a great many flaws. Sickness, death, evil. We endure as best we can. We see throughout the Bible examples of those things and God's dealings with His children."

"He allowed His own son to die a hideous death on a cross," Evans interjected. "How is that love?"

"It was love for us. It made a bridge for us to the Divine. Jesus came to deliver us from the evil of this world. By accepting Him as Savior and repenting of our sins, we can come into the presence of the Father. We are forgiven and accepted as children."

"But to what purpose, Mr. Porter? God doesn't keep us from experiencing the evils of this world. We still know sickness, death. We aren't set free from those things."

"No, but we are set free from eternal damnation, from a hopeless end that will separate us eternally from God."

"It sounds like your loss has not shaken your faith, as I presumed. I suppose that's a good thing given your desire to preach. However, I cannot make my peace with a Creator who stands idle while His creation suffers."

"Nor could I, but I don't believe God is idle. I believe He grieves over us as a father would his child. If Laura were hurt, you would grieve. If she were threatened by some evil that she willingly allowed in her life, would you not fight for her and intercede in whatever way possible?"

"Of course I would. I would eliminate whatever that evil was, proving my point. If I were God and knew of what evils were to come, I would never stand by and allow it to touch Laura. If I, an earthly father, flawed as I am would do that, how much more should we be able to expect it from God?"

"But we have no idea of the ways He guards us and keeps evil from our door. We live in a very flawed world. A world full of sin and death that came at mankind's choice. God does not impose His will upon us, Mr. Evans. But I am convinced that He loves us, beckons us, and delights in us when we turn away from sin and return to Him."

Will could feel his anger toward God ease a bit. Maybe he just needed to hear the words aloud—to hear what his own father had told him many times when Will was a boy.

"Evil men will always do evil things, and yes, there will be times when we suffer the effects, even as God's beloved children. However, I still believe in His love and goodness."

Granite Evans shrugged. His face was void of expression. "To each his own, Mr. Porter. I'll bid you goodnight. Please know that you are welcome here as long as you need a place to stay." He started to go, then turned back. "And that is my grace. Not God's."

# 13

There had been some great celebrations in Cheyenne for Lincoln's birthday, but the real celebratory plans were slated for the birthday of George Washington. At the Evans house, a grand party of outrageous proportions was being planned. It had already been decided that most of the larger pieces of furniture would be stored in tents behind the house to leave plenty of space for musicians and food tables inside.

Will had heard from Mrs. Duffy about Granite Evans's plans for some of the town's wealthier bachelors to meet his daughter. Having been able to join them at the dinner table for the evening meals, Will was surprised to hear Mr. Evans talk openly about the reason behind the party. Evans spoke as if Laura were a commodity to be auctioned and was confident that she would be able to pick a husband by the end of the evening. Will was appalled and even commented that he thought the idea ridiculous. He had suggested that a deep abiding love needed time to develop, but Granite Evans just waved him off.

"I'm not talking about deep abiding love. That will come

in time," he had said. "No, what I'm talking about is the most advantageous union that might bring benefit to both families. Laura can tell immediately if she will get along with someone. She's a brilliant woman of deep feeling. I'm confident of this."

Will could still hear Laura's tactful reply, explaining she had plans to not hurry into marriage. She had been quite surprised at her father's confidence that she'd know by the end of the night who she'd want to marry. Will had been glad to see her take a stand, but her father was insistent and even verged on being angry at times. He reminded her that a lot of planning had gone into this party—and into his career—and he hoped he could count on her to be helpful rather than harmful.

"You look a million miles away," Laura said, joining Will in the foyer. "Are you all right?"

"I am." Will balanced on his crutches. "I'll be so glad when the doctor removes this cast. He said it should just be another couple of weeks."

"I know. I'm excited for you to be able to walk around unimpeded, but I'll be sorry to lose my houseguest. Are you ready for our walk?"

He pulled his felt hat low as she opened the front door. "I am. But as for your sorrow over losing your patient, I'm sure you have better things to do than take care of me."

"Like pick out a husband?"

Will maneuvered the crutches as he stepped from the house. "No. Not that."

Laura pulled on her gloves. "Shall we walk around the block? The snow is nearly all gone. I don't think you'll have any problems." She closed the door and turned to face Will.

He thought she looked quite lovely in her plum-colored

full-length coat, white scarf, and plum-and-white wool bonnet. She was pretty as a picture.

"Are you all right, Will? You look . . . well, I can't really say, but your silence concerns me."

"I'm fine. I was just thinking that I've not seen this coat and bonnet before."

"No, it's new. Father insisted I have it. It just arrived with the store inventory. It is quite warm, and giving it to me seemed to please him so much." She gave a shrug. "I didn't really need it, but I couldn't deny him. He insisted on a new gown for the party as well."

"The coat and bonnet suit you, even with auburn hair."

"I never really worry about such things. I once had a house mother at one of the boarding schools who refused to allow me to wear any shade of red or pink. She said redheads had no business in such colors. It was most annoying and never sat well with me at all. When I moved to another school, the first thing I did was buy a red hair sash."

Will couldn't help smiling. Her cheerful demeanor was like good medicine. "I'm glad you don't worry about such things."

She chuckled. "Oh, by the way, did you ever get a letter off to your aunt?"

"I did. It was probably the hardest letter I ever had to write."

"I'm sure it was."

They began to walk toward the street in silence. Will concentrated on the path to make sure he didn't hit any hidden patches of ice, but all the while, he wanted to watch Laura.

"The party plans are coming together in good order," Laura continued. "Mrs. Murphy has all sorts of delicacies planned. She makes the most delicious pastries."

"You forget I've been eating her food for a month now. I'm quite aware that she's gifted," Will admitted.

"Well, I hope you'll enjoy yourself at the party. I know it hasn't been that long since . . ." She let the words trail off.

"I have to say that your positive outlook and kindness have helped me a great deal. Then there's the encouraging visits from the pastor and my friends. Those have also helped. I'm sorry I've been so depleted of hope. I'm still wrestling with all that's happened. Just when I think I have some sort of understanding, something comes to discourage me and causes confusion over the entire matter.

"The other day I was speaking to your father about salvation and the priceless gift God gave us in His Son. The words came easily, and I felt confident, but later that night, I awoke from a nightmare and was saturated in doubt and despair. I've never had a crisis of faith like this before, and I honestly don't know what to do."

"Have you talked to the pastor or even to one of your Christian friends?" she asked, her voice soft and not in the least condemning.

"I'm talking to you."

Laura smiled. "I meant have you talked to one of the men you call a close friend?"

"Some, but not as I suppose I should. Look, I know the answers. I can quote the Bible from front to back. I can tell you about times of doubt in the lives of many biblical patriarchs. I can tell you the words Jesus had for those in despair. I know what I ought to know, but I can't seem to . . . take it into the deepest part of me . . . past the hurt and anger. I need to talk it through with someone."

They turned the corner and came back in view of the

house. Laura pointed. "There are Edward and Charlie. Ask and it shall be given."

"What do you mean?" Will looked at her oddly and then back down the street to where his two best friends were waiting.

"God knew what you needed and has sent your friends to help."

"You were helping me just fine."

She smiled again. "I'm hardly qualified for this one, Will. I can pray and will do so, but I have no insight for this situation. You see, when God allowed everything to be taken from me, I clung to Him all the more. The thought of putting Him from me—of blaming Him or of turning away—never entered my mind. My faith was all that got me through. Knowing that God was there and would never leave me was everything I longed for because everyone else had gone. You aren't in a place where you want to receive that kind of reassurance." She stopped as they reached the house and turned toward him.

"But from the stories I've heard them tell, I'm almost certain that either Edward or Charlie knows exactly how you feel. Talk to them. And when you get it figured out, I'd love to hear all about it. I am confident that you won't walk away from God. I think you know that as well."

Will couldn't help but nod. Laura reached out and touched his arm with her gloved hand. "You are an amazing man. You've served God all your life and never doubted Him, never considered your life without Him at the helm. You aren't truly doing that now either, but I know you're hurting and need some help. I also know that this is a test of your faith. Sometimes God allows those moments so that our faith might grow. How else will we make it stronger for the more difficult times in life?"

She squeezed his arm through the heavy coat he wore, but to Will it felt like a branding iron. It was as if she knew exactly what his heart had been telling him for days, while his mind acted in protest like a small child. Even so, there was no condemnation.

Laura moved away without another word. Will heard her speak in a soft, welcoming manner to Edward and Charlie, and he moved forward to join them.

"I'll have Mrs. Murphy put on some coffee and bring out refreshments. If you need anything at all, just have Will ring for it." She went into the house while Will worked his way forward on the crutches.

"Laura seemed to think you were hoping we'd stop by," Edward said.

"I guess I was." Will shook his head. "Sometimes I think she knows me better than I know myself."

"Uh-oh," Charlie said, laughing. "Sounds like maybe you two have been together too much."

"I'm not sure that's possible," Will replied, staring at the closed front door.

After an hour of talking to Edward and Charlie, Will knew that God had sent them to help him through the mire.

Will spoke of his mother and sister as he considered all that they'd discussed. "I know I will mourn their death for a long time to come, just as I am still mourning my father's passing."

"Of course you will," Edward said, setting aside Will's Bible. "I still mourn the loss of my loved ones. I still wonder what it might have been like had my boy lived. There are all sorts of things that come to mind from time to time."

"We all still carry the scars of battle. Those friends who stood side by side with us will remain in our memories, both the good and the bad," Charlie offered. "Death is a constant companion in life, but we must keep our eyes on Jesus. He's overcome death, and we can overcome it as well—through Him."

Will rubbed his left knee. "I know you're right."

"But don't think either of us is saying you don't have a right to grieve," Edward added. "I needed a long time to move beyond losing Janey and the boy. You may need a long time to deal with your family's passing. We're here to help, and I know Marybeth and Melody feel the same way. Laura obviously cares a great deal too. You have people who want to walk this path with you. You don't have to walk it alone. God hasn't abandoned you, and neither have we."

Tears formed in Will's eyes. It was as if all the pain surfaced at once. A sob broke from deep within, and he buried his face in his hands. He hadn't yet allowed the tears of grief. Not even for his father. Back then, he had tried to be strong for his mother and sister and hadn't allowed himself to face the sadness of loss.

As he wept, he heard Edward begin to pray. The whispers were barely audible, but Will knew that was what he was doing. When he stopped, Charlie picked it up and continued. They went back and forth like that for some time, and all the while Will wept.

Laura heard her father's raised voice at the back of the house and went to investigate. He was shaking his fist at Curtis. When he saw her, his expression softened, and he looked embarrassed. He dismissed Curtis and tried to address her as if nothing had been amiss, but Laura wasn't about to allow it to pass unnoticed.

"What in the world happened to make you so angry at Curtis?"

"It's none of your concern."

"I think it is. I live here too, and I feel that I am constantly coming upon you in one rage or another. Not only that but . . ." She stopped, wondering if she dared go on.

*I can't leave things unsaid. They must be resolved, or it will harden my heart against him.*

"I overheard you tell your man to drown my kitten." She stared at him, waiting to see if he would deny it.

"That was a terrible thing, and I am sorry," her father admitted. "But you must understand . . . since you returned . . ." He sighed, walked into the kitchen, and took a chair at the empty table where the cook took her meals.

Watching him bury his face in his hands, Laura was surprised by his reaction. For several long moments he said nothing, prompting Laura to take the chair opposite him.

"You have to understand." He looked up to meet her gaze. "I've been so afraid that something might happen to you. Afraid that you wouldn't make it here, and then when you arrived, well, I was afraid something might hurt you or that you wouldn't like me. When you announced that you'd brought a wild animal into the house, I'm afraid I didn't handle it well. I feared diseases and the harm that might come. I didn't want to see you hurt. I still don't."

"But a kitten wasn't going to harm me."

Her father shook his head. "It could have. We've had cases of rabies around here. People have died. I couldn't bear the thought that you could be infected."

Laura hadn't considered that, and seeing her father's

obvious distress, her anger faded. "It's just that you've been so different from what I expected. You've yelled and threatened many people while I've been here, and . . . well, that's not the father I remember from when I was little."

"We've both changed, Laura. You must allow for that, but I suppose my anger has been a bit out of control. I just wanted things to be perfect for you. I wanted you to be safe and happy. I feel like such a failure as a father."

Laura could see there were tears in his eyes. "I'm so sorry you feel that way. I don't think that at all. You've been a wonderful father."

"I deserted you. I left you alone when you needed me most. I failed to do what I promised your mother I would do."

Laura reached out and took hold of his hand. "You did what you thought was best for us both. You are a good father and a kindhearted man. You didn't fail me at all. I've grown stronger because of all you did. I might have fallen apart or become a weak and desperate woman. Instead, I learned to put my faith in God and hold fast to my beliefs. I remained convinced that we would one day be rejoined, and that our love for each other would see us through the sorrow of losing Mother. And it has."

"You're an impressive young woman full of kindness and love. Your ability to forgive is humbling. I pray you forgive me for whatever flaws I have. I want to do right by you, and I'm sorry that I grieved you with the kitten. We didn't kill it."

Laura nodded. "I know. I gave him to the Vogel family. I couldn't allow him to be killed."

"I'm so sorry. Please understand, what I did was out of my fear of harm coming to you."

"I do understand, Father, and I don't hold it against you. I just wish that next time you will talk to me and explain why you feel as you do. I want to understand and grow closer to you, but I can't do that if I feel I cannot trust you."

He squeezed her hand. "You can trust me, Laura. Everything I do—everything I've done—has been for you."

⁓

"Do you need anything before we leave?" Edward asked Will.

"No, not a thing. I'm exhausted and plan to go straight to bed. But thank you both for helping me. I know God sent you to break through my iron heart. I have a long way to go, but at least I don't feel that terrible separation from God any longer."

"I'm glad to hear it. By the way, Charlie and I came today for an entirely different reason. We were wondering if you could make us a couple of baby cradles."

"Cradles?" Will repeated. "That's easy enough. I'm not sure where I'd work on them. I could talk to Mr. Bradley."

"No need. I have a woodworking shop behind my house. I'm sure you will find everything you need. Just come over when you're up and around."

"I would like to do that," Will admitted. "It sounds like a perfect arrangement. I could work at Bradley's during the day and then come over there in the evening."

"What about your work with the Indians?" Charlie asked.

Will shook his head. "I had decided that I wasn't cut out for it, but now I feel it's such a part of who I am that I can't refuse. Still, I'm not sure that it will ever happen. Mr. Blevins said he had to move forward, and he couldn't wait for me to mend. I wasn't sure if he meant emotionally or physically, but either way I knew I wasn't going to get a job offer."

"I'm sorry about that, Will," Edward said. "I guess we have a lot to pray about."

"Yeah," Charlie said, smiling, "just because Mr. Blevins has given up on you doesn't mean God has."

"I know He hasn't given up on me," Will said with a sigh. "I'm just not sure what it is He wants me to do now. Granite Evans offered me a job, so that's another possibility. I don't know what I'd do for him, but at least I'm not without options. Hopefully, the Lord will make things clearer than they are now."

# 14

Frigid temperatures settled over Cheyenne on George Washington's birthday, but it didn't deter the gathering of the socially elite at Granite Evans's fine house. Laura had dressed carefully for the occasion, donning a pale-yellow silk gown. The bodice was somewhat lower than she cared for, but with a little lace strategically positioned, Laura felt presentable.

When the party first started, she stood at her father's side and greeted each new arrival, commenting on how pleased she was to make yet another acquaintance in Cheyenne. She marveled over the ladies' fashions and gave brief conversation to the gentlemen as her father declared their position or interest in the city.

Names like Whitehead, Kuykendall, Sloan, and Baker were given. Laura tried to memorize each person, but after the first ten or so found it impossible. Her father commented that most of the city council was there, along with the mayor. It was important to him that they attended. Everyone who had even a remote possibility of seeing him put into the governor's seat was significant.

Ulysses S. Grant had won the presidential election the previous fall and would take office in just a couple of weeks. Andrew Johnson had been unable to appoint a territorial governor for Wyoming, and everyone now knew it would fall into the hands of Grant. The man was a Northerner, and it was anticipated that he would appoint someone who shared his political beliefs. Still, Laura had heard someone say that her father had friends who were of a Northern persuasion— friends who had contacted Grant as soon as he won the election to suggest Granite Evans as a perfect choice for the job of governor.

Her father acknowledged that it probably wouldn't happen the first time around, but with any luck, he could prove himself in the next few years. It was even possible that Grant's appointment would hate Wyoming Territory and give up his position. If that happened, Granite Evans intended to be available and well-known to the president.

"You look absolutely beautiful."

Laura had been so lost in thought that she hadn't seen Will approach on his crutches. She smiled and gave a nod at the dark navy suit he wore. "As do you."

"Mrs. Duffy helped me with the trousers. She opened the seam, and once they were on, sewed it shut again. She said she'd help me tonight and cut it open once more."

"She's full of ideas." Laura pointed to the lace at her neckline. "She helped me to be a little more modest tonight."

Will motioned his head toward the alcove in the front room where a small string quartet was playing. "It's wonderful that your father was able to find musicians of such quality."

"I find Father usually gets what he wants. He arranged for them to come from Omaha on the train. Not that there weren't musicians already in Cheyenne, but he wanted to be able to boast about these men who once played in Canada for the governor-general."

Will smiled. "Sounds like something to boast about."

"Are you able to enjoy yourself at all?" she asked. "I know it must be hard to get around on crutches in a room full of people."

He lost the smile and gazed out across the room. "It is difficult, but you and your father have been so gracious to me. It seemed only right that I honor you both. I hadn't expected an invitation to the party, but to refuse would have been akin to snubbing those who rescued me."

Laura shook her head. "I never would have seen it that way. I told Father it wasn't right to expect you to attend, but I am glad you did. I feel that I have at least one friend here. Father wasn't interested in inviting my other friends. He said this was to be a party of Cheyenne's cream of society."

"Well, that clearly leaves me out. But I'm glad to be that one person you can call friend."

His reply stirred something within Laura's heart. It seemed honest and perhaps even heartfelt. She hoped it was.

"You're also the only single man in attendance who isn't looking at me as if I'm a slab of beef to be purchased." She shrugged and gave a laugh. "I'm hopeful that most here are men who prefer chicken or lamb and bypass me quickly."

Will chuckled and shook his head. "Haven't you heard? This is beef country. More cattle are being brought in every day."

"Well, then maybe there will be so many prized animals that they'll soon forget about me."

"I doubt any are as charming, witty, smart, or beautiful as you. It would be impossible to forget you."

Laura was touched by his words as they seemed to come with a deeper sentiment than mere teasing. Every day Will seemed to do or say something that endeared him all the more to her. What would she do when he was gone?

"I suppose I must continue to circulate and play hostess to our guests." She smiled and gave a sigh. "Pray for me."

Will nodded. "I can finally say with confidence that I will."

Granite Evans was delighted by the number of prominent citizens attending his party, especially given the fact that the weather was cold and snow seemed impending. His only frustrations were the small size of the house and lack of a great room for dancing. The new house would have a third-floor ballroom to rival any home in Cheyenne. But little good that did him now.

Still, the people of Cheyenne knew he was an important figure. His department store was so successful that he was considering adding another floor next year. He had three warehouses full of goods to fill every inch of the new addition. It would be a wonder unlike anything west of the Mississippi. Then, of course, Granite had his investments, and they were doing quite well. It wouldn't be long before he could forgo the stage and wagon robberies along the routes into Cheyenne. Underhanded dealings and thieving had gotten him to this place of success, but he certainly didn't mean to continue with it forever. If his illicit activities were ever found out, he'd be taken off the president's list of men to consider for the position of governor—or worse.

He made the rounds from one gathering of guests to another, pausing here and there to listen to the gossip and comments with keen attention to anything political. Second to that were the comments given about Laura. He hadn't come right out and said he was seeking a husband for her, but given that many on the list were widowers or single men, no one could have failed to realize his intention.

Throughout the evening, he also watched Laura as she moved among their guests. She was all graciousness and ease. She seemed to have a natural affinity for entertaining and small talk. Nothing seemed to cause her discomfort or distress. Such confidence was uncommon with most of the women Granite had known, with exception to the wife he'd lost.

Laura's mother had been equally self-assured. She hadn't had grand parties to host, but with the small responsibilities she faced, Meredith Evans had managed her duties with great skill. She had been the most beautiful and exceptional woman Granite had ever known. And now her daughter took that role.

"I wonder if I might have a word with you about your daughter." The young man who approached him was one of Granite's top prospects for Laura.

"Of course, Mr. Aldersgate. What did you have in mind?"

Will tested his walk while the doctor observed. Except for feeling a little off-balance now that the weight of the cast had been removed, he had no pain and felt just fine.

"There's nothing wrong with me," Will said, giving an abrupt turn to prove his point. "I do still have the occasional headache, but you said that would pass in time. I believe I'm back in good order for the most part."

The doctor closed his bag. "I agree. Perhaps you'll be able to dance a jig at the St. Patrick's Day celebration. I do hope, however, you'll avoid the streets from now on, or at least the wagons and teams on them."

"I can assure you I will be more observant. I've waited too long to enjoy this freedom. I won't be eager to put myself back in the position of invalid very soon—if ever."

"I'm glad it worked out well," the doctor replied. "Now, if you'll excuse me. I must be on my way. I have a surgery to tend to at the hospital."

They shook hands, and Will walked the doctor to the door. Outside, it was as if spring had come to Cheyenne and the world was made new. After a week of rain, the sun shone down from endless blue skies above, and there was a warmth to the air that was deceiving. A person could easily get caught up in the momentary turn of the weather and forget that it was barely the first week of March. There was always the possibility of late snow.

"A glorious day," the doctor said, raising his free hand to the sky. "Hard to believe we could see an icy rain or snow before nightfall, but that's the way of things in Cheyenne this time of year."

"I was just thinking that very thing," Will agreed. "Good luck with your surgery, and thank you again. I'll be by tomorrow to pay my bill."

"No need. It's already been covered by Mr. Evans. He insisted, so if you have a problem with it, take it up with him."

The doctor waved and moved off toward the street. The hospital wasn't all that far away, so he'd come on foot and would return the same way. Laura had offered to take him back by carriage, but the doctor assured her he enjoyed the walk.

"I see you're on your foot, bare though it might be," Laura said, coming up behind Will.

"Oh!" He looked down. He hadn't even realized or thought about the inappropriateness of parading around his host's house without shoes. "I'm sorry for my thoughtlessness."

Laura giggled. "It's really not a problem." She followed him as he made his way back to his room.

He went to the trunk where he kept his clothes. He rummaged around, looking for a matching sock. "I've been so used to only needing one sock and shoe, I'm not even sure where the other shoe has gotten off to."

"It's over here by the door. And the mate to the sock you're wearing should be right there on top of your clothes."

Will slowed down and realized he'd knocked it aside in his hurry to locate it. He pulled it from the trunk just as Laura returned with his shoe. He sat on the edge of the bed. "It's going to feel so good to walk about once again."

"I suppose this means you'll be leaving us." Laura handed him the shoe. She looked rather sad. "I will miss being able to just come here and talk to you about things."

"Speaking of which, the doctor told me that your father paid my bill to him." Will placed the shoe on the floor beside him.

"Yes. We discussed it, and Father felt that since I helped to cause the accident, he would cover the charges. Given the situation, I feel it's only right."

"As I've stated on many occasions, it was my own distraction that caused the accident. You could hardly know that I was going to step out into traffic."

"Well, it's done now, and you're on the mend. I'm so grateful it wasn't worse than it was. So what will you do next?" she asked.

"For now, I'd like to hear what was accomplished in regard to proper suitors for your hand."

Laura went to the chair she'd so often occupied when visiting with Will during the early days of his injuries and sat down. She was dressed quite simply in a high-necked white blouse and navy skirt. Her hair had been plaited down the back and tied with a dark ribbon. She looked so much younger that way, and Will had a hard time believing she was nearly twenty-three.

"There was plenty of interest, unfortunately. Many people believe my father will one day be governor, and they're impressed with the power he might wield. Marrying his daughter would be a feather in their cap."

"I suppose so." Will hurried to pull on his sock. Once this was done, he grabbed his shoe. "And what of you? Did any man there catch your attention?"

Laura shook her head. "Not really. I would just as soon have spent my evening talking to you."

Will didn't tell her that he would have preferred things that way as well. He hadn't stayed long in the company of the partygoers. After about an hour of explaining who he was, Will grabbed a plate of refreshments and hid himself away in his library oasis.

"Did you father make arrangements for you to see any of them?"

Laura sighed. "He decided he would have them over individually for dinner. It would be us three, and we'd talk about the expectations each young man might have toward the future. Thankfully, Father is too busy to start this until after the first of May. He's hoping President Grant will decide on who is to be governor by then. He's doing all he can to keep his name and good works ever on the president's mind. However, the other person at the top of the list is a good friend of Grant's—or so the newspapers proclaimed."

"John Campell is the man in question, and I know him personally. We lived next door to his family in Salem, Ohio. He's a good man and would definitely make a great governor."

"Well, until the matter is settled, Father will be focused on the appointment. I'm hopeful he'll get the position and then not have any time to worry about anything other than the territory."

"I doubt a father can just forget about his daughter, even if he does have an entire territory to worry about."

She leaned back in dejection. "I honestly wish Father would just give up on the idea. I had my heart broken once, and I don't care to risk that again. If God wants me to marry someone, then He'll have to make that very clear to me. Reveal the truth in such a manner that I cannot doubt it is from Him."

"I'm sure He can do that," Will said, uncertain what else he could say. He got to his feet and walked around the bed and back. "I seem to be fit as a fiddle. The doctor cautioned me when I first stood and said I might want a cane, but I feel just fine."

"What of the ribs. Do they hurt you anymore?"

"Not a lick. I am completely recovered."

She gave a slow nod. "I believe most all of your things are ready for you to pack up. Etta said she finished with your laundry earlier today."

"That's wonderful." Will went to the trunk. "There's really very little left to worry about. Most of my clothes are in here, and everything else belongs to you and your father. Speaking of your father, is he here?"

"No, I believe he's at the store. Why?"

Will shrugged. "I wanted to say good-bye. I'm not sure when I'll see him again. I'll probably go right back to work for Mr. Bradley, and I promised Edward and Charlie that I would make cradles for their babies. I'm supposed to go over to the Vogels' in the evenings. They have a woodshop behind the house."

"I suppose you shall be very busy," Laura said.

Her tone left Will convinced she was unhappy. No doubt she was worried about what was to come from her father's plans. He turned toward her. "Try not to be overly worried about your father's plans. It isn't the Middle Ages, and a woman still has to agree to be married. No decent pastor would allow for a union between a man and woman who didn't both want it."

"I suppose you're right. It's just that I'd rather Father not bother with it at all. I'd like to have more time to focus on getting to know him. Or spend time talking to you. I mean . . . well . . . I know you may or may not have plans to remain in Cheyenne, but I feel that we've become good friends. I enjoy hearing your thoughts on a variety of topics."

"And I enjoy hearing yours as well," Will replied. "In fact, I doubt there's anyone I enjoy talking to as much as I do . . . you."

Laura straightened. "That's about the nicest thing anyone has ever said to me. Thank you, Will. Do you suppose you might stop by from time to time? Or do you think it would be all right if I came by the house to see how you're doing? Faith Cooper is a good friend, and I know she would welcome me, but I don't want to if . . . you would be offended or think me too forward."

She wanted to come by. She wanted him to return to see her. Will found this information delightful. He hadn't been able to figure out how they might stay in touch except for church.

"I believe that would be perfectly fine. I am not at all offended at the idea." He grinned. "Good friends should keep in touch."

She got to her feet. "Exactly. That is precisely what I think."

Laura continued to think about all that Will had said as the days went by. She wondered how long she should wait before going to see him. She didn't want to seem too eager or pushy. She had rather hoped that he would stop by to see her first. But it had been over a week, and Will Porter had not graced her doorstep.

She'd seen him at church, but there had been a lot of other people who wanted to talk to him, so she had held back and kept to sharing news with Marybeth and Melody. Both were nearing their final weeks of pregnancy and were quite excited about the babies to come, so the conversation was mostly about that. A subject Laura found interesting, but not overly helpful. After all, who knew if she'd ever have children of her own.

With Will gone from the house, Laura found her days were empty. She still read her Bible and spent time praying. And of course, once a week she gathered with her friends to sew, but it wasn't the same. Will had been around all the time. If she was feeling frustrated or upset about something, she could discuss it with him. If it was evening and her father was out playing politics, she and Will could share supper together and talk about the events of the day. Sometimes they had read each other articles from the newspaper. It was almost as if they were an old married couple.

That comparison caused all sorts of concerning thoughts

to race through Laura's head. Had she grown too attached to Will? He was easy to care about, and she had to admit he was constantly on her mind. She told herself that was only because she'd nearly killed him and owed it to him to take care of his every need. But now . . . it was frightening her to find other ideas surfacing.

Was she falling in love with Will? And if so, whatever was there to be done about it? He wasn't interested in taking a wife. He'd made that abundantly clear. And if he managed to get himself back on track with his goals and ambitions of preaching to the Indians, a wife would only complicate the matter. Mr. Blevins had given up on him as an agent of the government. How much worse would it make things if Will convinced Blevins to give him another chance, and then he had to go back to the man and explain that he'd taken a wife?

She tried to push all such thoughts aside and busy herself with reading or sewing. Once she'd even attempted baking. Mrs. Murphy nearly had a fit of apoplexy when she discovered that Laura had come into her kitchen the night before and made numerous batches of cookies. Laura had done her best to clean up the mess and leave things as they had been, but apparently there were enough misplaced items that Mrs. Murphy demanded it not happen again.

How could the absence of one man make a house seem so big and time pass so slowly?

# 15

March tenth was Laura's twenty-third birthday. All day long she'd waited for her father to say something about it, but so far he'd barely even acknowledged her presence. He was obviously busy with his business matters. He was so preoccupied that at breakfast he had spooned salt into his coffee instead of sugar. Shortly after that he'd thrown down his newspaper in exasperation and locked himself in his office. An hour later, he left the house without a word to Laura.

Now as evening approached, Laura wondered whether to say something, but when her father came home, he stormed off into his office once again. If he planned to celebrate, she would need time to get ready. She decided to chance it and followed him. She waited until he was seated behind his desk to pose her question.

"I wonder . . . well, that is . . . do we have plans for this evening?"

He looked at her blankly for a moment, then glanced down at the calendar on his desk. "You think I've forgotten your birthday, don't you?"

He smiled. "But I haven't. It's just been an extremely trying day with business issues and problems that have kept me going from one thing to another. Still, I know my daughter's birthday, and we are going to celebrate. I have a gift for you and figured to take you out to dinner this evening. As a matter of fact, that's why I'm home early. Run upstairs and change your clothes, and we'll make our way to Belham's."

"You always remember." She kissed his cheek. "Thank you for making me feel special."

She hurried upstairs and found Etta. Together they managed to get her changed and ready to go in record time. When Laura once again reached her father's office, she found him speaking in hushed tones to Curtis. The young man nodded enthusiastically, then pulled back in a surprised manner when Laura entered the room.

"I'll get right to it, sir," he said and dashed from the room, barely giving Laura a nod.

"He certainly seems in a hurry," Laura said, pulling on her gloves.

"I promised him a bonus if he does what I asked in half the normal time. I have several businessmen who are waiting to hear from me on something; Curtis will deliver my decision."

He pushed his papers aside and reached for the top drawer. "Now for your gift. I'm quite excited to see what you think. I had this specially made for you."

He drew a little box from his desk and handed it to Laura. She opened it and found a gold heart-shaped locket inside.

"Oh, Father, it's lovely."

"Open it up."

She set the box aside and took the locket into her gloved hand. She thought for a moment that she might have to remove her glove but finally managed to get the clasp to open.

Inside she read the engraved words, *Jesus is the way, the truth, the life.*

"Oh, Father. I love it. It's wonderful." How unexpected that with her father's negative feelings toward God, he had gone to the trouble of engraving Scripture. It touched her that he had put aside his resentment to honor her faith.

Laura came around the desk and kissed the top of her father's head. "I will cherish it always."

Her father stood and took the necklace from her. "Shall I secure it for you?"

She turned around. "Yes, please."

The day had turned out so much better than she'd expected. If only Will had come to visit her, it might have been perfect. But it had been ten days since she'd seen him, and Laura was starting to think that perhaps he didn't share her eagerness to continue their friendship.

By the evening of March sixteenth, Laura was done waiting for Will to act. Earlier in the day she had decided she would pay him a call and instructed Mrs. Murphy to make Will's favorite gingersnaps. The older woman had been happy to comply when she learned they were for Will. She even cut them in the shape of shamrocks to celebrate St. Patrick's Day.

Laura was delighted at the woman's creative gesture. She loaded a basket with the treats and made her way to Faith Cooper's boardinghouse just after supper. With Father tied up in political meetings, Laura wasn't about to spend another evening home alone.

She arranged for Curtis to drive the carriage, despite it being a lovely evening for a walk. It was rather forward for a single woman to go in search of a single man, and at least with Curtis driving her, it would seem a bit more formal than if she just arrived on foot. Especially when it required visiting a boardinghouse full of men.

Laura wondered how she would explain her unannounced appearance all the same. Faith wouldn't mind, Laura felt certain of that, but Will might find it embarrassing for her to just show up to see him. She prayed that wouldn't be the case.

They reached the Cooper place, and Curtis set the brake and helped her down before reaching back up to get her basket.

"I don't know exactly how long I'll be, so please wait here." Curtis gave a nod.

Laura made her way to the house and knocked on the door. The evening was still a bit chilly, and she was glad she'd chosen one of her heavier cloaks.

Faith opened the door and smiled in greeting. She stepped back and motioned Laura inside. "Come in, come in. What brings you here?"

"I know it's the height of bad manners to show up this way, but I wanted to check on Will's recovery and bring him— well, really all of you—some of Mrs. Murphy's gingersnaps in celebration of St. Patrick's Day tomorrow." She held up the basket.

"That was so kind. Will isn't here. He's been spending most every evening at the Vogels', where he's making baby cradles. He's quite good at building furniture, you know." She took the basket Laura held out. "These will be well received. They're my husband's favorites."

"Will's too," Laura replied, not quite sure what to do. If she stayed and visited for a while, she wouldn't have time to go to the Vogels and see Will. But to show up as she had and then not stay for at least a brief time was also rude.

"Come with me, Laura," Faith commanded, and Laura did as she was told.

Faith paused at the opening to the front room. "Gentlemen, Miss Evans has brought us gingersnaps. I shall bring some for you with the evening coffee."

"Thank you, Miss," one man after another offered.

Laura smiled and gave them a nod. "You're quite welcome."

She went with Faith to the kitchen and waited for further instruction. Faith took the cookies from the basket and transferred them from Laura's plate to one of her own.

"Now you'll be able to return these things to Mrs. Murphy. I know she keeps a tight hold on her kitchen."

Laura laughed. "She does indeed. I once baked cookies without speaking to her about it first. I thought she might pop a blood vessel. She was quite firm on telling me not to do that again."

"I can well imagine." Faith took down another plate and set several of the cookies aside. "I'll keep these for Will. If I know these fellas, they'll gobble these down without concern for anyone else. My own husband will be the worst of offenders."

"Thank you. I appreciate that you would do that for him."

Faith put the cookies under a cloth, then hid them away in the cupboard. "You like him a lot, don't you?"

Laura was taken aback by the question. "Well . . . I suppose I do. We got quite close when I was taking care of him after the accident."

"He seems to esteem you as well. He often talks about you."

"Me?" That was strangely pleasing to Laura. The thought of Will talking about her to others surely suggested he kept her in his thoughts.

"Don't be so surprised. I think he cares a great deal about you, and how could he not? You probably saved his life. He might have died in the hospital without constant care. Many's the man who has passed on due to blood poisoning or some other condition that might never have been an issue had he received decent care." Faith held up her hand. "I'm sorry. That was overly critical of me toward the hospital. It's just that I know they need more staff, and that alone makes it difficult to have any confidence in them."

"It was my privilege to care for Will. He wasn't a bad patient, and once he managed to get past the truly darkest days, he was quite agreeable. Of course, Edward Vogel and Charlie Decker are mostly to thank for that. They were good to visit him and help him deal with his anger."

Faith nodded. "I'm glad he wasn't able to come back here. These fellas would have kept him quite bleak, I fear. Most don't have a faith in God, or if they do, it is nominal at best."

"I was grateful for the company. Now that Will is gone, the house seems very quiet. I'm so glad to be hosting our sewing group tomorrow. It won't seem so lonely."

"Say, I have an idea." Faith reached back into the cupboard and took down the smaller plate of cookies. She wrapped the three she'd saved for Will in the cloth that covered the plate. "Why don't you make your way over to Marybeth's house and take these to Will? It will give you the perfect excuse to see him."

Laura felt her cheeks heat and lowered her gaze. "Am I that obvious?"

"Only to me. Maybe Marybeth. The menfolk won't have a clue. They seldom do when it comes to matters like these."

Laura took the cookies. "Thank you for not making me feel bad about . . . well . . . about . . ."

"Caring for Will?" Faith laughed. "You would never receive condemnation from me for falling in love."

Was that what she was doing? Was she falling in love with Will? For so long she'd ignored that question, and once more she pushed it to the farthest reaches of her mind. She would contemplate that later. Right now, she needed to get going before she lost the evening light.

"I didn't figure to see you before tomorrow," Marybeth said, opening the door for Laura. "Come in. I was just getting ready to give Carrie a bath."

Carrie stood back away from the door, holding the kitten Laura had given them. Her attentiveness to the animal made Laura smile.

"I see you've become good friends with the kitty. And just look at how he's grown," Laura said, stepping to where Carrie stood. She knelt and gave Carrie a smile. "What do you call him?"

"Dis is Dandy," Carrie told her.

"Ah, that's a very nice name."

Marybeth chuckled as Laura stood once again. "She would consider no other suggestion. Edward commented that he was a dandy, and that was the only name Carrie wanted after that."

"I suppose when confident of a thing, one should move forward with it," Laura said with a shrug.

"I should be more understanding of that," Marybeth replied. "After all, Edward and I have been quite fixed on what to name our baby."

"And what names did you choose?"

"We're keeping it a secret for now," Marybeth said, rubbing

her hand over her abdomen. "But I never wanted any other names, especially for a boy."

Laura glanced around the room. "I don't want to be rude, but I've actually come to check on Will. Faith said he'd come here to work on something."

"Yes, he's in the woodshop out back. I'll show you. Carrie, take Dandy to your room and get ready for your bath. I'll be right there to help you."

"Yes, Mama." Carrie didn't even wait for her mother's reply but hurried down the hall. Dandy mewed with each bouncing step.

"She really is the most adorable child."

"She can be a real handful, but I think she's finally grown accustomed to this house and our new life here. The kitten helped a lot. I wish we'd thought of it sooner."

"I'm so glad you could take him. My father has an aversion to animals, especially wild ones."

"Well, Dandy is certainly not wild. He's very alert and attentive. I do believe he'll be a good mouser when he gets older. I'm hoping his instincts will take over when he's big enough since he won't have a mama to teach him."

Marybeth led Laura to the back door. "You can see the shop just down the path there."

"Oh yes, thank you. I won't be long. I'll just walk back around the house to the front when I'm finished. That way I won't disturb you giving Carrie a bath."

Marybeth gave her a quick hug. "I'll see you tomorrow."

"I'm so looking forward to it."

They parted company, and Laura made her way to the shop. She didn't know if Will was alone or not, so she kept the cookies tucked under her cloak in case she needed to give them to him in a more discreet fashion. She hadn't even considered that she didn't have cookies for Marybeth and her family.

She knocked on the door and waited a moment. Will opened it and looked at her with such an expression of surprise Laura couldn't help but laugh.

"I can tell you weren't expecting me."

"Not at all. Please come in."

Laura stepped inside and was immediately aware of the scent of cedar and pine. "It smells wonderful in here."

"I agree. I've always loved the scent of wood." He smiled. "It's good to see you. I meant to stop by before now, but I've been so busy."

"It's all right. I wanted to bring you something." She pushed back the cloak and drew out the wrapped cookies. "Mrs. Murphy baked your favorite gingersnaps, and I took some to the boardinghouse. Faith said you were most likely here, so I brought you some in case the others were eaten up before you got home."

"Most likely they will be. Those fellas have big appetites."

Laura extended the cookies. "I hope you're doing well."

Will reached for the cookies, then stopped. He stared at Laura for the longest moment, but not at her face. She glanced down, wondering what had captured his attention. The only thing she could see was the locket.

"Where did you get that?" His voice seemed almost strangled.

"My father. It was a birthday gift. He had it engraved for me. Let me show you." She set the cookies aside on the countertop.

Will stepped back and finally looked her in the eye. "You don't have to. I know what's engraved there."

"You do? Did Father tell you about it?"

Will shook his head very slowly. The color had drained from his face. Laura grew concerned. "What's wrong? Are you ill?"

He pointed at the necklace. "'Jesus is the way, the truth, the life.'"

Laura nodded. "Yes. How did you know?"

"I had . . . It was made . . . for my sister. I gave it to her for her birthday last summer."

"Your sister?"

"That's her necklace. I picked it out myself."

"It can't be." Laura shook her head and reached up to take hold of the piece. "My father said he had it made for my birthday . . . for me."

"I ought to know. I spent days figuring out which locket to get her. Then I worked with the engraver. It was difficult to fit the Scripture in the locket. We had to cut it down, yet I was determined it wouldn't lose the meaning."

Will looked as if he'd seen a ghost. He stumbled back a step, then took a seat on a high stool. "Where did your father get it? It was stolen from her during the Indian attack."

For a moment, Laura couldn't draw breath. She felt as if he had hit her hard, knocking the wind from her. Having no explanation, she backed out of the open door. "I . . . I . . . don't know." She needed space to think. Unable to look at Will any longer, she turned and hurried across the yard.

How could this be? What in the world had possessed her father to give her the necklace of a dead woman and claim it to be something he'd had made just for Laura?

She reached the carriage and didn't even wait for Curtis to help her climb up. "Get me home. Hurry."

If this locket belonged to Will's sister, how did it come into the possession of her father? Had someone wandered into his store to trade it for something? Had someone sold it to one of the local jewelers, and they in turn offered it for sale?

None of this made sense. Will had to be mistaken. He just had to be.

# 16

L aura barely slept that night. She wrestled with the idea of her birthday gift belonging to Will's sister and found sleep impossible. By morning, she knew she would have to face her father and ask him about the necklace, but when she came down to breakfast, her father was already gone for the day.

"He said he had some important business to tend to, Miss," Rosey told her after pouring her a cup of coffee.

Laura added some cream and slowly stirred. The aroma of the nutty brew did nothing to soothe her as it usually did. She took a sip and found it bitter in her mouth.

Rosey left and returned with a plate of eggs and bacon, as well as a rack of toast. Laura had no appetite, however. She could still see the strained look on Will's face from the night before. What a horrible shock. How terrible he must have felt.

How had it all happened? There had to be an answer to why her father had possession of the necklace. Throughout the night, Laura had considered so many possibilities, but always it came down to the fact that her father had lied to her. He had told her he had the necklace made for her.

Nothing about him had turned out to be as she expected. She had believed him to be a stellar individual who always told the truth and, despite not wanting a relationship with God, maintained a godly sort of presence. Although, as she sat contemplating that very thought, that didn't make sense either.

Father had never tried to pretend that he was a man of God. Even in letters, he had made it clear that he blamed God for his woes. Laura had always tried to defend God's position. She had found God to be her only comfort. To contemplate Him taking her mother in the heartless manner her father declared it to be threatened Laura's serenity.

"I really know nothing about him," she murmured, still holding the coffee cup close to her lips. She sighed and finally put the cup down.

*How could Father have come into possession of the necklace?*

"Miss, Mrs. Murphy wants to confirm that the ladies will be coming at precisely eleven," Rosey said.

Laura looked up to find the woman standing just across the table. She nodded. "Yes, eleven. We'll serve them luncheon in here upon their arrival, then retire to the front room for our sewing."

"Yes, Miss. Curtis has already set up the table and chairs."

The anticipation of seeing her friends was the only thing Laura could find any joy in. Confusion was holding her hostage, and with her father already gone, she had no way to resolve the situation. Laura briefly considered going to the store to confront him but knew that would be inappropriate. She was upset, and her questioning would only serve to upset her father as well. It would keep. Her decision was further confirmed when Rosey brought her the paper.

"I thought you'd want to see it for yourself," Rosey said. "The president didn't pick your father to be the governor."

Laura read the headline announcing John Campbell would be the first territorial governor of Wyoming. She knew her father would be livid, but it didn't matter. She still had to get answers as to how he ended up with the necklace.

In the meantime, Laura decided to share the matter with her friends. Granny Taylor always said that sharing the load made it easier to carry, and Laura felt as if the weight of the world were on her shoulders. If she told the women about the situation, they would pray with her, and Laura knew that would offer comfort and peace of mind.

By eleven, everything had been prepared, and Laura had donned a simple but fashionable gown in which to receive her friends. Marybeth and Carrie arrived first. Carrie held a little basket and showed it to Laura like a prize.

"Dis is my sewin'," she said with great pride.

"How nice," Laura replied. "I'm so glad you could join us."

"I've just started her on learning to sew a straight line. She's always wanting to do everything I'm doing, and I figured before the baby arrived, it might suit us both if I started teaching her to stitch," Marybeth said, placing her larger basket on the table by the door.

"I think you are very wise." Laura helped Carrie take off her bonnet and little cloak. The child was very polite and cooperated in every way as Laura unfastened her buttons. Just as Carrie slipped out of the wrap, she whirled around and wrapped her arms around Laura's neck.

"Tanks you."

"Good girl, Carrie. It's always good to thank someone when they help you," Marybeth said as Laura battled not to topple over.

As Carrie let her go, Laura straightened. "It's not any trouble. Here, let me assist you with yours." Laura reached over and helped Marybeth with her cloak.

"I woke up feeling particularly huge," Marybeth said, rubbing her stomach. "I think the baby is starting to drop."

Laura looked at her swollen abdomen and nodded. "It does look that way, although Granny spends more time with you and would probably be able to judge that better than I."

"I hope I'm half as wise as Granny is when I'm her age," Marybeth said, reaching to take back her basket. "There isn't anything she doesn't know. At least I've not found it yet."

"She's probably delivered her fair share of babies over the years. I learned midwifery at college, but I've only helped deliver one baby."

"That's one more than me," Marybeth replied. "I never thought of a school teaching such things."

"They wanted women to have practical educations."

Just then, a light knock at the door drew their attention. Laura quickly received her guests and found the others had come together.

"I'm so glad you're all here." Laura helped them inside. Once the coats, gloves, and hats were dealt with, she motioned them to the front room. "Everything is ready for us. Feel free to set up your place for sewing."

"Miss Laura, luncheon is served," Etta announced from the doorway.

"Well, perhaps just leave your baskets and we can set everything out after lunch." Laura hadn't expected the announcement quite so quickly, but when she glanced at the clock on the mantel, she saw they had already kept Mrs. Murphy waiting fifteen minutes.

"Tell Mrs. Murphy we will shortly be assembled in the dining room."

The ladies made their way to the table, and as had happened before, Etta offered to take Carrie with her to the kitchen where she could eat separately and the mess would be easier to clean up.

"We saw that your father didn't receive the appointment to governor," Granny said.

"I'm sure it is a disappointment to him, but I haven't had a chance to even see him this morning." Laura shrugged and gave a little shake of her head. "Let's pray."

Prayers were offered up, and Laura waited until the soup course was served before saying anything about her troubled heart. She had intended only to ask the ladies to pray for her to have wisdom in dealing with a pressing matter, but Granny wouldn't hear of such an abbreviated request.

"I knew from the minute I came through the door that something was troubling you, Laura. Why don't you just share it with us while we eat?"

"I didn't want to cause anyone discomfort. It's not a pleasant topic." Laura looked down at her soup.

"Does it have to do with the governor's position?" Granny asked.

Laura put down her spoon. "No. Something happened last night. I'm so disturbed by it that I can hardly make sense of anything."

Everyone stopped eating and looked at Laura.

She lowered her voice and leaned in. "I don't want the staff to overhear."

"Perhaps it should wait until we are assembled to sew," Granny suggested. "There's more privacy there."

"I agree," Faith said, nodding.

The other women did likewise, and Laura leaned back. "Of course you're right. We'll wait."

Luncheon was rather hurried and silent after that. The women seemed to understand the urgency of the matter, and when it was suggested that dessert be served after sewing, everyone agreed.

They adjourned to the front sitting room, after which Laura dismissed Rosey and closed the pocket door. Thankfully, Carrie was still busy eating in the kitchen. Laura joined her friends at the table, wondering how they would receive her story. No one had even bothered to retrieve their sewing.

"My birthday was on the tenth, and my father gifted me a locket."

Laura omitted the details of their dinner and went right to her visit with Will. As she concluded with the basic details, Granny held up her hand.

"The obvious question is, Have you spoken to your father?"

"No. I had hoped to approach him on the matter but had no opportunity. He wasn't here when I got home last night and was already gone this morning when I came down to breakfast."

"Then fretting over it and making supposition here won't do a bit of good. Matter of fact, I've seen far more harm come from taking up a subject and imagining all the bad possibilities without any of the actual facts. I suggest we pray for comfort and resolution, but that we don't waste our time trying to figure out what happened. When your father comes home, sit down first thing and ask him what you need to know.

"But don't do it in anger or accusation. Simply explain what you know—how Will recognized the piece. Don't make a fuss over the fact that he lied to you about having the locket made. You can discuss that later," Granny continued. "What's important is to find out where he got it."

"I agree with Granny," Melody said, rubbing her stomach.

"Well, there is one other thing I wanted to ask," Laura said, looking at each of the women. "Should I give the necklace back to Will? I feel like that would be the right thing to do, but I don't want to cause him even more pain."

"I don't think it would cause more pain," Marybeth answered. "If it belonged to my sister, I would want it back."

The others nodded, but it was Faith who spoke up. "I wondered what was going on with him. I expected him to be happy when he returned last night because I knew he'd seen you. Instead, he went straight to his room and hadn't come out by the time I left this morning. He didn't even join us for breakfast. No doubt this has been very upsetting to him."

"I'm sure it has left him overwhelmed," Laura replied. She gave a heavy sigh. "Poor Will. It seems the worst is still upon him."

"Let us pray," Granny said, bowing her head.

Will sat staring at the wall. He'd never even gone to bed. He couldn't have slept if he'd wanted to. He kept seeing Sally's necklace hanging from Laura's neck. Why did she have it? How had it come into Granite Evans's possession?

A knock sounded on his door, and he glanced at his pocket watch. It was nearly two. He got up slowly and went to see who it was.

He opened the door just a bit. "Yeah?"

"Will, it's Reverend Cather. I stopped by to see you, and Mr. Cooper said you weren't feeling well."

Will opened the door a bit more. "He's right. I'm under the weather."

"Could I come in and pray with you?"

"I don't know if that would be a good idea. I . . ." Will let the words trail off. He wasn't physically ill, at least not in a sense that would infect the man. "Come in."

He backed away from the door, and the reverend entered. Will motioned to the chair, then went to sit on the edge of his bed.

"What seems to be wrong, Will?"

"Everything. Just when I think I've managed to get my heart and mind back on the right track, something comes along to send me careening off the rails."

"How can I help?" the older man asked.

"Besides praying for me, there's nothing you can do to fix it or help me."

He had tormented himself all night, imagining the necklace being torn from his sister's throat. Had she still been alive when it was taken, or had the thief pulled it away after shooting her in the heart? Had there been blood on the tiny gold links? On the heart-shaped locket?

"I'd say prayer is the best of all we can do for one another, Will."

"I want to believe that too." He put his hands on either side of his head and squeezed. "I can't get the terrible images out of my mind. I keep thinking of how it happened."

"The death of your loved ones?" the pastor asked.

"Yes. That and . . ." He heaved another sigh. "Something happened last night, and it brought everything to the forefront once again."

"Would you like to talk about it?" the reverend asked.

Will looked at him for a long moment. "Not really, but I suppose it might help."

---

After the pastor had gone, Will felt a little better. He knew he needed to speak with Laura's father. If anyone could answer his questions, it would be that man. Only he would know how he came by the necklace.

But what if he didn't know the origins? What if the necklace had changed hands many times? What if the Indians had traded the things they stole to someone else, and then that person had brought it to Granite Evans? Or they might have sold it to another store, and Evans, needing a birthday gift for Laura, had purchased it from them.

Laura.

He thought of how frightened she'd looked when she'd run from the woodshop. Will had caused that fear. He knew he hadn't been able to mask his shock. He had been so happy to see her. He was finally to a place where she stopped reminding him of his mother's and sister's deaths, and then the necklace had ruined it all.

A part of him wished he could go to her first and offer an apology, even comfort. But frankly, Will wasn't sure he had anything to offer. He went to the window and raised the shade. It was a beautiful spring day outside, but even that couldn't cut through the darkness in his soul.

"Why, Lord? I know I keep asking that question. I've asked it since I first got here and couldn't seem to coordinate with the government. I just wanted to serve You, but nothing would come together. I've asked You why over and over these last few weeks, and You remain silent."

Will's eyes went to the billowy white clouds overhead. "Where are You, Father? You feel so far away. I thought I'd found my way back. I felt Your presence when I prayed, but right now I feel alone again.

"I don't doubt Your existence. I don't even doubt that You have a plan in all of this. I guess I just doubt . . . No, that's not even the right word. I just feel like it's all too much. You've required too much of me. Given me more than I can handle."

*Give it to Me.* It was as if an audible voice spoke in his head. Will closed his eyes and heard the words again. *Give it to Me.*

"I want to, Lord. I want to turn it all over to You. I want to trust that You will show me the way—that I won't bear any of this alone."

Will leaned against the wall. He felt so weak, so depleted of any real strength. He dropped to his knees.

"Take it, Lord. I give it to You." He thought of Jesus on the way to His death, carrying His cross through the streets of Jerusalem. Even He had needed help.

"I can't carry this alone."

Laura looked at the clock for the tenth time in as many minutes. It was nearly nine o'clock. Soon she'd have no choice but to go to bed and wait until morning to speak to her father.

But she didn't want to wait. Didn't feel that she could wait. This was far too important to let another night pass without answers. Where was Father?

She needed to see her father and hear him tell her the truth, but he was nowhere to be found. After the women had finished sewing and went home to get supper on the stove, Laura went to the store, hoping to find her father in his office. But he wasn't there, and no one seemed to know where he was or when he'd return.

Then she made her way to his men's club. There she was told in no uncertain terms that women were not allowed to bother the men once they entered the walls of their sacred club, and the doorman could not tell her if Granite Evans had taken refuge there. She gave the man a dollar, at which point he told her that her father had been there earlier but now was gone. She hoped it was the truth but couldn't be sure.

There had been no other choice but to return home and await his arrival. But what if it turned out to be another late night? What if he decided his business dealings were so important that he couldn't come home until the wee hours of the dawn?

Laura paced in front of the fireplace and looked again at the clock. She had to speak to him. She had to have answers. This was a matter of greatest importance. Will had a right to know how the necklace had gotten into Granite Evans's hands.

And Laura had a right to know why her father had lied.

# 17

At four minutes after ten, the front door opened, and Laura's father stepped inside. Laura had dozed off on the settee and jumped up with a start.

"Father, is that you?" she called.

He looked around the corner into the front room. "Good grief, Laura. What are doing up at this hour?"

"I needed to speak to you. I tried to find you earlier, but it didn't work out." She came forward, tightening the sash of her robe. "I must speak to you. It's of the utmost importance."

"All right, but I'm quite exhausted. It's been a very busy and disappointing day, and if this could just wait for morning—"

"No!" She tried to calm her voice, knowing she sounded close to hysterics. "I'm sorry. I know that you're disappointed in not receiving the appointment, but this is something else entirely. Something that isn't going to be pleasant for either of us, but it must be done."

He frowned. Laura could see that he had no idea what she

wanted to say. She stepped back. "Please sit down for just a few minutes. It won't take long."

"Very well. I must admit you have my curiosity piqued."

Laura reclaimed her seat on the settee. "I have a couple of very important questions to ask you."

"In regard to what?" Her father sat and stifled a yawn.

"My birthday gift." She waited to see if there might be some response, but when none came, she hurried to continue. "I was wearing the necklace when I stopped by to bring Will some cookies the other night, and he happened to see it. Father . . . the necklace belonged to his sister. The one who was killed in January with his mother."

Her father's face remained blank. Why didn't he say something? He didn't even try to deny it.

"I, uh, I know you said you had it made for me. I suppose you said that to make me feel special."

His eyes narrowed slightly as he fixed her with a look, but he remained silent. Laura found his behavior most disturbing. She couldn't figure out why he didn't at least acknowledge that he had lied about having it made for her.

Laura looked away, feeling a bit unnerved at his stern expression. "Will had it engraved for his sister for her birthday last summer. She must have been wearing it when the stagecoach was attacked."

She finally looked back at him. "Father, we need to know where you got it. Who did you buy it from? It's important that we know so that Will can speak to them and find out where they got it."

For several long moments, Laura wasn't at all certain her father would answer her questions. Finally, he stretched and yawned.

"I got it off a man who was just passing through. I don't

know his name or where he was headed after he left Cheyenne. He said he'd gotten it in a trade, and since he knew my store sold fancy trinkets to women, he thought maybe I would buy it from him. I felt sorry for him and wanted to help him out. I could see the piece was quality and bought it."

"So you have no idea where we could find this man and question him?"

"What is with the *we*? Seems to me this is Mr. Porter's business, not yours."

His comment irritated her. "I took care of Will, and I care about what happens to him now. He was so shocked by the appearance of the necklace. If you had seen him, you would feel equally a part of the search. You should anyway. Will's family was killed and finding the man who sold you the necklace might help us find those responsible."

Her father shook his head and shrugged. "But I don't know who the man was. He was just someone passing through. Had a horse and his gear and not much more. He offered to sell me the necklace and some other things."

"But don't you see, those other things might have also belonged to Will's mother and sister or others from the stage. We must find him." Laura knew she had started to raise her voice, and she drew a deep breath to calm herself. "You should speak to the sheriff and perhaps the commander at Fort Russell."

"I will if it helps to calm you down. Honestly, Laura, I don't know why you're so worked up about this."

His demeanor frustrated her, and Laura couldn't keep quiet. "The entire situation disturbs me. Not only because the necklace belonged to Will's sister and was obviously taken from her during the attack on the stagecoach, but because you lied to me."

She hesitated for only a moment. She hadn't planned to make a big deal about the lie, but now she felt as if she had to in order to make her father see how desperately important the matter was to her.

"You told me you'd had that necklace made for me. That you'd had it engraved with Scripture, knowing I would like it. Instead, I find out it's the property of a dead woman."

He sighed again and got to his feet. "I have been so busy with trying to get the governorship that I didn't have time to buy you a birthday present. I knew the day was coming and had fully intended to do something wonderful, but time got away from me. I am without excuse. I'm a terrible father."

Laura shook her head. "No, you aren't terrible. But I don't want you to think you have to lie to me."

"I knew it was wrong to give you the necklace. I wanted you to have something new, something all your own, but there wasn't time. The necklace was everything I knew you would love, and . . . I suppose it was exactly what I would have had made for you had I taken the time to arrange it.

"That's what makes me so terrible. I could just as easily have gone to the jewelry store and had something similar created, but I've been so wrapped up in my desires. Oh, Laura, I am sorry. It was deplorable of me. Can you forgive me?"

Her anger faded. "If you'd just admitted to me that you'd forgotten my birthday, I wouldn't have been upset."

"But you're my everything, Laura. All that I've done, I've done for you. You alone. You're my entire world. After your mother died, I kept driving myself forward, thinking of you. I had to find a way to give you a better life. I had to find a way to make enough money that you would never be denied the medicine you needed or doctor's care you deserved.

"Laura, I must admit, I did things during the war that . . .

well, let's just say that if realized, would have been considered traitorous to the North. But also to the South. I played both sides against the middle because I hated that we'd gone to war. Despite it being profitable to me, I hated that it sent you even farther from me. Tennessee was right in the middle of everything, though. I couldn't risk something happening to you by having you remain there. And I couldn't send you deeper into the South. I knew things weren't going to bode well for them in the end. They were already struggling for supplies and food. How could I leave you there to endure such things?"

Laura was touched by his words. It broke her heart to think of him having no alternative but to send her away to keep her safe. She went to her father and touched his arm.

"I've always understood, Father. Please don't grieve so. I am no worse for my experiences, and it certainly didn't diminish my love for you." She put her arms around his waist, and he wrapped her in a warm embrace.

"I just wanted good things for you, Laura. I wanted to give you all the things I could never give your mother. You will always be so precious to me."

"I know that, and you are precious to me too." Laura rested her face against his chest. "I'm so glad to finally be with you, Father. I just want us to be happy."

"As do I. In fact, I have a surprise for you."

Laura pulled away just enough to look up into his face. "What is it?"

"I started the construction of our new house. The men broke ground two days ago. I wanted to show you the plans for it, but once again my work got in the way. I promise tomorrow at breakfast I'll show you what I have created. I think you're going to love it, and if you have any concerns, we can address those and make changes. I want you to feel that you have a say in it. It will be your home too . . . at least until you marry."

Laura didn't know quite what to say. She didn't want to contemplate marriage just now, and she didn't care about a palatial estate.

"The new house sounds quite interesting, but this place serves us well too. I'm in no hurry to move."

"We will have one of the finest houses in all of Cheyenne," her father declared. "Perhaps it shall even be the place to house the governor of the territory. Wouldn't that be something?"

"But President Grant appointed another. I'm sorry he didn't choose you."

Her father released her and shrugged. "I don't expect Campbell to stay long. He isn't from around here."

Laura laughed. "No one is really from around here, with exception to the Indians." That made her think once again of the necklace. She reached for her father's arm. "I know it's late, and we must go to bed, but I want to let you know one more thing. I think it's only right that I return the necklace to Will."

Her father studied her for a moment. His expression seemed one of concern. "Of course. I should have thought of it myself. Please do. And let him know that I will speak to the sheriff as soon as possible."

"Thank you, Father." Laura gave him a kiss on the cheek, then headed for the door. "I'll see you in the morning and look forward to seeing your plans for the new house."

She didn't really care about the plans but knew they were important to her father. She hated that she had managed once again to cause him such pain. But it dawned on her that she had done nothing wrong. She had confronted him about lying to her, and yet he didn't seem to understand nor care.

With each step she took, Laura began to see a pattern in her father's behavior. Whenever he was confronted with something he'd done wrong or asked questions that he didn't want to answer, her father had a way of creating a stir of emotions that caused her to pity him, to feel terrible for what he'd gone through. He always seemed so humbled by the confrontation and willing to admit his failings in the matter. But there was a lack of sincerity that Laura was only now coming to see.

She paused at the top of the stairs and frowned. Was it all just a game to distract her? Was Father still lying?

Granite sought the seclusion of his bedroom before allowing his anger to surface. He immediately went to where he kept the liquor and poured himself a tall glass of whiskey. With one gulp he downed the burning liquid and poured another.

How could he have been so stupid as to have given her the necklace? He knew where it had come from. But when she'd reminded him it was her birthday, the necklace was the only thing close at hand that he could offer to prove he was not only aware of her special day but had planned it out as well. At the time, he'd thought it fortunate that he'd found a small box for the piece. He'd hoped to sell it in Chicago and had been preparing it, along with the other jewelry and watches they'd collected from the stagecoach passengers. He'd known that it would be foolish to sell any of the pieces there in Cheyenne and planned to make arrangements with Gus for the stuff to be moved east.

His hand tensed on the glass. How could he have been so rash. Now there would be no end of questions about how he'd gotten the necklace. No end of questions regarding the supposed drifter from whom he'd purchased it.

Ire rose inside, and Granite couldn't contain his rage. He threw the glass into the fireplace and growled as the flames caught the alcohol on fire. What was he supposed to do now? He'd at least settled Laura. She was so easily calmed. All he had to do was pretend deep sorrow over the pain he'd caused. Then, by taking it one step further and making a scene of how much he'd failed . . . well, there wasn't anything Laura wouldn't do for him. She'd even gone along with his idea of arranging suitors.

Granite tore at his necktie and threw it across the room when it finally came loose. He'd been so careful, how could this be happening now? It was bad enough that he would have to deal with Grant's new appointment for the governorship. It offered little comfort that his friends in positions of power told him that his name had been a close second for the position.

Campbell, a bona fide Northerner, had served the Union army faithfully, while Granite could only boast the pretense of peacemaker between the two factions, while making a profit from both. While living in Virginia, close to the capitals, Granite had done his best to ingratiate himself to both sides, claiming that all he wanted was to see the severed nation brought back together. In truth, he couldn't have cared less. He was neither loyal to the South nor to the North. He was loyal to Granite Evans.

John Campbell's claim to fame of late had come in helping Virginia reestablish its political system. One of the casualties of war had been the politics of the South. Everything had to be made over, along with rebuilding businesses and agricultural endeavors. Campbell was apparently talented in this area, and Grant had likely presumed he could establish the political system for Wyoming's new territory.

The man was due to arrive the first part of May, and before then Granite had plans to see the unmarried thirty-three-year-old eliminated. Perhaps Indians could be responsible. Most likely, however, it would need to be some sort of accident, or maybe Granite could arrange a poisoning. That was always unexpected.

He grabbed up another glass and poured a third helping of whiskey. No matter what else happened, he needed to figure out how to handle this situation with the necklace. No doubt Porter would come to him with questions now that he knew Laura had the necklace. Perhaps it would be better still if Granite sent for Will. Yes, that might work well in Granite's favor. In fact, he could get word to the newspaper. Nathan Baker loved a heartwarming story. His "Wide Awake Journal for the People," as he called the *Daily Leader*, was full of local tales and stirring accounts. Granite would let word leak regarding the necklace, and Nathan would be after the story like a cat to a mouse, proclaiming how a lost memento had been returned to a grieving brother.

"It's all a matter of working the angles." Distracting on one point, focusing attention on another, and throughout the entirety, pulling on the heartstrings.

One way or another, Granite Evans would manage them all. He had worked too hard to see it all fall to pieces now.

# 18

Will was surprised when Mr. Cooper showed up at Bradley's Furniture Store with a message for him. He opened the piece of paper and saw that Granite Evans was summoning him to the house that morning, immediately if possible.

Will had tried to see Granite Evans at the store the day before, but he was gone, and his staff didn't know when he would return. The invitation to the house was more than Will had hoped for. After arranging with Mr. Bradley, he ran all the way to the Evans house, not even remembering that his leg had been broken. He was immediately ushered inside by Mrs. Duffy, who didn't seem the least bit surprised to see him.

"Mr. Evans is waiting for you in his office," she said, leading the way down the hall. She paused at the closed door and knocked.

"Enter!" Evans's strong voice called out.

Mrs. Duffy pushed open the door and stepped back. "Would you like me to bring coffee?" she asked Mr. Evans as Will crossed the room to where the older man sat at a desk.

"Would you like coffee, Mr. Porter?" Evans asked.

"No, thank you." Coffee was the last thing on his mind.

"No coffee, Mrs. Duffy. Just leave us."

"Yes, sir." She looked at Will. "May I take your hat, sir?"

He'd forgotten to even remove it but pulled the hat off now. "No, I'm fine, Mrs. Duffy." Having the hat gave him something to do with his hands.

"Take a seat, Will. I'm glad to see you up and about. You seem no worse for the accident."

"No, I'm completely healed. I even ran from Bradley's to your house." Will took a seat in a high-back leather chair and rested the hat on his lap.

Granite nodded. "Youth definitely has its advantages. Healing quickly is one of them."

Will said nothing. He was so anxious to hear what Evans had to say and then question him about the necklace.

"I'll get right to the point," Evans began. "I understand you were looking for me yesterday, and I know why. Laura told me that the necklace I gave her for her birthday belonged to your sister, and that it had been taken off her when she was killed in the Indian raid on the stagecoach."

"Yes." He had summed things up so succinctly that Will had nothing to add.

Granite Evans leaned back in his chair. "A stranger approached me and offered to sell it to me. He was an average man—nothing special at all. Dirty, unkempt, the roaming type. He had a worn-out horse and saddle and offered to sell me a few things that he had traded for. The necklace was one of those things. I did the sale with him for the necklace but had no interest in anything else. The man then went on his way, and I have no idea of where he went or what his name was."

"He didn't give you a name at all? You hadn't seen him before?"

"No on both counts."

"When did this happen?"

Granite shrugged. "I don't really remember."

"You don't remember!" Will barely held himself in check. "How can you not remember? It couldn't have been that long ago."

The older man looked at him with an expression that suggested he didn't care for Will's tone. "It wasn't of any great importance to me, Mr. Porter. Things like that happen all the time. I suppose it must have been around the time of the party I threw."

Will calmed. "Why did he seek you out?"

"As I said, things like that happen all the time. I often get fellas stopping by to sell me items. It just happens when you own a store. Folks figure you might buy goods similar to what you carry and then resell them. We have a section of jewelry in our store, and the man probably assumed I would be interested in seeing what he had."

"Besides the necklace, did he have other jewelry? Like rings? My sister would have been wearing a pearl ring. My mother would have worn two rings. Her wedding ring was an engraved gold band. The other ring was a large emerald, square cut. My mother might also have worn other jewelry."

"No, he didn't show me anything like that. Just the necklace. It reminded me of Laura and her love of Scripture, so I purchased it. The rest of the things were of no concern to me."

"And he said nothing about where he was headed? Are you sure he didn't stick around in town?"

Granite shook his head. "No, he told me specifically that

he was on his way out of town. Just needed to get some supplies, but first needed to make some money."

"So he would have gone to other stores. Maybe someone there learned more about him. What did he look like?" Will knew he was again sounding more demanding than curious.

"Very much like every other drifter in this town. Dirty, threadbare clothes. He wore a faded blue shirt, and I couldn't tell you what color the pants were. They were filthy. He smelled horrible, as most of those men do. I tell you, Will, I just wanted to get rid of him as soon as possible. I didn't even argue when he asked me to give him two dollars for the necklace."

"It was worth twenty," Will muttered.

"I know. I recognized the value of it. I'm certainly sorry I failed to pay the man much heed. He was just unremarkable, and like I said, I was focused on moving him along."

"He must have gone to at least one other place to get the supplies he needed. Did you happen to notice the direction he went?"

"He got on his horse and headed south. That was the last I saw him."

"Have you talked to the sheriff about this?" Will shifted and leaned forward. "They need to be able to find this man. We need to know how he came by the necklace." Will paused and fixed Evans with a look. "Did he say where he got it?"

The older man seemed to consider that. "I think he said he traded with some Indians." Evans thought a moment longer. "Yes. Yes, I'm sure that's what he said. Met up with some Sioux up north and traded them. He had food, and they were hungry. Yes, I remember him saying that."

"Where up north was he when he made the trade?"

"I can't tell you that. Honestly, Will, it's fortunate that I even remember that much. We didn't do a lot of talking. He was in a hurry, and so was I."

"Well, we need to go speak with the sheriff. The army needs to know all of this since they're out looking for the Indians."

"Yes, I understand, and as soon as I finish up here, I'll stop in to see him on my way to the store. I have just a few things that I must tend to first. I hope you know how sorry I am. I've already apologized to Laura. Pretending I had purchased the necklace and had it engraved for her was wrong, and I'm deeply ashamed."

"I appreciate that you care about getting this figured out," Will said, getting to his feet. He could see that Evans was anxious to get back to his work. "I'll let myself out."

"Just a moment, Mr. Porter. I had hoped to find out how you're doing. Have you given any thought to my offer of a job? I can always use industrious, honest men such as yourself."

"I haven't thought about it. I'm rather caught up with this and some other projects." But even as he spoke, Will knew he had little desire to work with Evans. There was something about the man and his ambitions that was off-putting to Will.

"Well, just know that the offer stands. Come see me if you need a good-paying job."

"Thank you. I appreciate the offer." Will walked to the open doorway and paused. "And thank you for your help."

Evans stopped fussing with the papers in front of him. "That's quite all right, Mr. Porter. I'm afraid it won't give you much to go on. Drifters show up here every day, especially now that the weather has warmed up. There's just no way of knowing who this fella was or where he's gone."

Will nodded. "I know the odds are against us, but I have to try to find him."

"Why?"

Evans's simple question caused a momentary sense of confusion in Will. Why was he looking for this man? What could he possibly offer Will? It wasn't like he was responsible for his mother's and sister's deaths, nor did he have any of their other items. At least not according to Evans.

Will met Mr. Evans's questioning gaze. "I don't exactly know. I just know I must do whatever I can to get justice for my mother and sister."

"Will, it won't change what's already happened. You can't bring them back by finding the things that were taken from them. That drifter can't help you with identifying the Indians responsible. One Indian looks pretty much like another, and if they're wearing war paint, it'd be even harder to separate them out. And if they know someone is trying to find them, they'll protect their own. I'm telling you, it would be better for you to just give this up."

"I can't give up. My mother and sister were killed only two months ago. Those Indians are around somewhere, and I intend to see the guilty parties brought to justice."

"Those Indians are long gone. They've been causing havoc all along the UP line. They've just been waiting for warmer weather to clear out and head up north to their hunting grounds. They're probably in Canada by now."

"Still, I must try, Mr. Evans. It's important to understand why they did what they did. Why did they attack and kill helpless men and women?"

"Why do the Indians do any of their killing? They hate the white man. They don't care if those men and women were helpless. Hate is a powerful force to reckon with, Mr. Porter. A powerful force."

Granite Evans immediately called for Curtis and sent him with a note for Gus. "He should be at the warehouse. But if not, find him. Don't leave it with anyone else."

"Yes, sir," Curtis said, hurrying out of the office.

Granite checked the clock, then poured himself a drink despite it not being noon yet. He slowly sipped the contents and wondered how long it would take Gus to get here.

As it turned out, Gus showed up much sooner than even Granite had expected. In fact, the man was so good at sneaking around that he had made entry into the house and into Granite's office without anyone raising the alarm to let Granite know someone had gotten into the house.

"You wanted to see me?" Gus asked, moving to stand near Granite's desk.

"Yeah, thanks for making it quick. I've had nothing but one problem after another."

"What do you want me to do?"

"Get the things from the stagecoach attack and send them to Chicago. I made a big mistake and gave Laura the necklace that was removed from one of the women. Told her I had it custom-made for her. The dead woman's brother recognized it as one he bought for his sister, and now he's all up in arms to find the man who sold it to me."

"Sold it to you, eh?" Gus shook his head. "Well, I can arrange for the stuff to leave Cheyenne tonight. No problems with that. There's not all that much to see to. The rings, the pocket watches, a couple of fancy-made wallets, and a few other things that were probably meant to be gifts. It won't be hard to get it out. My cousin Tilly has been hankerin' to see her ma, who lives near Chicago. I figured when you gave the word, we could send the stuff with her. Her ma has brothers who can get it sold. Won't cheat us. They're family, and there's a code."

"The more I hear about your family, the more I like them. In fact, why don't you crate up the other stuff we've collected from previous jobs. Take it all to Chicago. The real purpose of robbing that stage was the money box. The rest is just extra, and we need to get rid of the evidence. No sense in having someone find it and come after us. I'm not going to ruin my political ambitions on a handful of goods that might only bring in a few hundred dollars."

"That's a lot of money to some folks, Mr. Evans."

Granite was surprised at the comment. Gus wasn't one to share his thoughts unless directly asked for an opinion. Granite had always liked that about the man. He found it strange that now, out of the blue, Gus was worrying about money.

"You having financial troubles?"

Gus shrugged. "The family's got some problems. Nothing we won't work out."

Granite nodded. "I tell you what. Take that stuff and make sure it never sees the light of day around here, and you can keep the profits. All of it. You've earned it. You and those cousins of yours have been a tremendous help to me."

The look on Gus's face said it all. "Thank you, Mr. Evans. You won't regret it. My family knows how to be loyal. Ain't a one of them ever betrayed another. It wouldn't be tolerated. I'll send Tilly as soon as I can. Tonight if possible."

"Good. Then I'll consider the stuff no longer my concern. Now get out. I have other work to see to. We've got a governor to kill."

Gus smiled. "I'll be anxious to hear what you have in mind." With that, he exited as quietly as he'd entered.

Laura wasn't surprised to return home from visiting Mary-beth and Melody and find her father absent. She found him gone more and more these days. She had thought once the president made the gubernatorial appointment that Father would have more free time, but that didn't appear to be the case. It seemed his business was consuming all his time. She didn't know what he was doing but figured if he wasn't working toward finding her a husband, she could live with his absence.

She'd barely made it to her room when a knock came on her door. Laura opened it and found Rosey.

"I heard you come in, Miss Laura. I've come to lay the fire for your evening."

"Thank you, Rosey. I thought perhaps you were Etta coming to help me change my clothes." Laura began taking off her gloves.

Rosey shook her head. "Etta quit. She went home not long after you left this morning. She was terribly upset."

"About what?" Laura couldn't imagine the housekeeper just up and quitting without notice. She set her gloves aside.

"I don't know, Miss. She seemed afraid. But of what I couldn't say. She came into the kitchen and told Mrs. Murphy and me that she was leaving and not coming back. She said there were troubles all around, but I don't know what she meant by that."

"I don't either." Laura knew Etta Duffy to be levelheaded and of sound mind. What could have upset her so much that she felt she had to leave her job here? "She needs the work. Her family depends on her."

"I know, Miss." Rosey finished with the wood and kindling

and lit the fire. It wasn't long before the flames caught, and the dry wood began to burn.

Laura was deeply troubled by the news about Etta. They had gotten to be good friends and often confided in each other. It was hard to believe Etta didn't feel she could wait to talk first with Laura about whatever was behind this sudden action.

Rosey left, and Laura walked to the bedroom, shaking her head. What had happened that was so terrible Etta couldn't even wait to give notice and quit in a manner that would ensure she got good references for future jobs?

Laura heard the mantel clock chime the hour. It was only four. There was still plenty of time before supper. Laura hurried back to her sitting room. She grabbed her gloves and purse, then headed downstairs. She would go see Etta and find out what had caused her to leave her post so quickly. If there was a problem, Laura wanted to help.

She made her way to the carriage house. Etta's place was a bit far to walk, and Laura didn't want to risk walking back in the dark in case she was long at the Duffy house. Mr. Grayson was likely driving her father around, but Curtis would be able to hitch up the smaller carriage.

"Curtis, I need you to ready the carriage. I want you to drive me over to see Etta."

"I heard she quit."

"Yes, well, I think it was just a misunderstanding."

"I don't know where she lives, Miss Laura," the boy said, moving to get the horse.

"I have her address. Just please hurry."

He had the carriage ready for her in a very short time and thankfully knew the way to Etta Duffy's small house once Laura told him the address. When they arrived, Laura wasn't surprised to find the neighborhood much poorer than her own. There were several small wood-framed houses sitting side by side. They looked practically identical. All were painted with whitewash and had a door and one decent-sized window to designate the front of the house. The yards were quite small and unadorned for the most part. The Duffys' yard had a single very small tree.

Laura made her way to the door and knocked. It was only a moment before an older woman appeared. She smiled. "May I help you?"

"Yes, I'm Laura Evans. I've come to see Etta."

The woman frowned and bit her lower lip. She glanced over her shoulder as Etta moved up behind her.

"It's all right, Ma. I'll talk to Laura."

The old woman nodded and moved aside. Etta motioned Laura to come inside. "Welcome to my home."

Laura glanced around. It was a neat and homey place. The furnishings were modest, but clean and nicely arranged. Etta led her to an overstuffed chair by the fireplace.

"You might like to sit here. It's quite comfortable."

"Thank you, Etta." Laura settled in and continued. "I know I'm intruding, and I am sorry. However, when I came home and learned from Rosey that you had quit, I had to come and speak to you."

"I am sorry for the way I acted, Laura. I should have given notice."

"But why would you want to quit? I had no idea of anything being wrong. Were you unhappy with your duties?"

"No, there was no trouble with my duties." She looked away as if nervous.

Laura couldn't tell what was going on. Etta had always seemed willing to talk about most anything, but now she seemed quite tight-lipped.

"Please tell me what happened, Etta. I want to help, and I want you to come back to work."

Etta glanced over to where her mother still stood. "Ma, would you go see to the ham, please?" She waited until her mother left the room, then took a seat in the rocking chair not far from where Laura sat. "I'd rather not say what happened. It frightened me."

"Why can't you tell me about it?"

Etta looked down at her clenched hands. "It wouldn't be right to trouble you with it. Just allow me to say that I am sorry. I didn't want to leave in such a fashion. I thought perhaps I could send word that I wasn't well."

"You'd rather lie than be honest with me about what happened?"

She could see that Etta was more than a little upset by the matter, but it wasn't something Laura felt she could leave alone. "Did someone hurt you? Threaten you?"

"No." Etta looked away and shook her head. "Miss, I overheard your father say something. I don't want to speak ill of him, and maybe I misunderstood, although I feel certain I didn't."

Laura felt her stomach sour a bit. She was now the one to clench her hands. "I must admit there are things I've heard my father say and do that I don't understand. He lied to me recently. I didn't tell you about it yet because, frankly, I wasn't sure what to think.

"I can see how that would be the case. I was shocked by what I heard."

"About what, Etta?"

"The necklace that your father gave you for your birthday. It's part of what I heard your father talking about."

"What did he say? Who did he talk to?"

"First, he talked to Will. He sent for him, and Will came to the house while you were visiting. Your father told him that you revealed the necklace belonged to his dead sister. It seems a drifter had sold him the necklace."

"Yes, that's right. He told me that as well."

"He promised Will he'd speak to the sheriff about it, and then Will left." Etta stared at the dying fire and said nothing for a long moment.

Laura was just about to ask her why that should have distressed her enough to resign her position when Etta began again.

"After Will left, I went about my business, but then a little while later, I saw someone slip into your father's office. I knew it wasn't anyone I had let into the house, and Curtis and Rosey were in the kitchen helping Mrs. Murphy polish the silver, and Mr. Grayson had just left to ready the landau for your father. That meant someone had come into the house without the usual formalities. I figured it might be your father's man. A real bad character named Gus Snyder. Although you didn't hear his name from me."

"I think I know the man you're talking about."

"I went to the closed door of your father's study and heard the two men talking. I . . . I . . ."

"It's all right, Etta. Tell me what you heard. I'll believe you."

"Your father . . . he talked . . . to the man about the stagecoach attack. He told the man to take the stuff they'd taken off those people and get it to Chicago so that no one would know they had it. He wanted him to sell it." Once she started talking, Etta didn't seem able to stop.

"The man said he'd get his cousin to help. He would send her on the train tonight. Your father told him he could keep the money, but just make sure no one knew about the stuff. And it seems there were more things from other . . . jobs." She buried her face in her hands as tears came. "Oh, Miss Laura, I'm so sorry."

A tight band formed around Laura's chest, making it impossible to draw a breath. She struggled for a moment and sat up a little straighter. It didn't help much, but she managed to gasp in air.

"So they ransacked the dead after the Indians attacked and killed them?"

"Your father said the money box was what they were really after."

"I suppose Indians wouldn't have even known about the money box." Laura was feeling sicker by the minute. Had her father's men stood by watching when the Indians attacked and killed those poor people? Had they done nothing to help because they wanted to rob the stage?

"And that's not all," Etta said, raising her eyes to meet Laura's. "Your father said he's going to kill the governor."

# 19

In the days that followed, Laura wrestled with what to do. Should she go to the town marshal and tell them what she knew? Get her father in trouble for what might have been nothing more than him spouting off as he'd done so many times before? As time passed, Laura was more and more certain that her father wasn't going to commit murder. After all, she'd heard him say outrageous things herself, and he never meant it. At least he said he didn't.

But there was the matter of theft. If her father's men had truly taken the bank box and things belonging to the stage-coach travelers, what kind of legal ramifications would they face? Could she stand to be the one who sent Father to jail? What if Etta had misunderstood?

Laura could hardly bear to look her father in the eye. Thankfully, he didn't seem to notice or care. He told her more than once that he had a great deal of business to take care of but offered no other explanation. Laura couldn't help but wonder at the kind of business he'd gotten himself in-volved in. Frankly, she was glad he was gone and that she didn't need to make small talk with him. Everything had changed for her regarding the man she had once all but worshipped as a hero.

There was word around town that he was quite busy with the mayor and city council as they prepared for the new governor's arrival in Cheyenne. Laura wondered if her father was truly planning the poor man's death.

Finally, she knew she couldn't just keep this to herself. She didn't know exactly what to do but figured that Will would know. She hated to get him involved, but reminded herself he was already plenty involved. And as much as she didn't like the idea of telling him about her father's men ransacking the stagecoach, she felt she must. If Will ended up hating her because of it, then Laura would just have to face that when it came.

She waited until Thursday evening, knowing her father had plans that would keep him out late. The boardinghouse was only a few blocks away, so she decided to walk. She wasn't sure how she was going to tell Will about all that had happened, but she took the necklace with her and hoped that by giving it back to him, he would see she was on his side.

Although the air was a bit chilly, some of the other boarders were smoking at one end of the porch and laughing about something when Laura arrived. She asked about Will, and they told her he was at home.

"He's locked up in his room, as he is most evenings," one of the men told her.

Mr. Cooper agreed to see if Will would receive her while Laura waited in the foyer. It wasn't long before Will came downstairs.

"I need to talk to you." She hoped she wouldn't have to say anything more until they could be alone. "Could we maybe take a walk?"

"All right. Let me grab my hat." Will retrieved his hat. He followed her outside but said nothing more.

"I'm so sorry to bother you. I've needed to talk to you for some time now, but I didn't know how to go about it or what good it might do. However, it can't wait." She sighed and looked off down the road. Laura knew if she looked Will in the eyes, she would start to cry.

"What's so important?" The friendly familiarity between them was strained, and Will's tone reminded her of when she'd first met him.

Yet another thing that made her want to cry. She reached into her pocket and produced the necklace.

"First of all, I brought this for you. I should have done it before now, but I wasn't sure . . . I mean, I felt that . . ." She couldn't figure out what to say and handed the necklace to Will. "I'm sorry."

"Sorry about what?" he asked, pocketing the piece without looking at it.

Laura pulled her shawl closer to ward off the chilly air. "It belongs to you, and I should have been quicker to return it. I'm afraid a great many things have happened, however, since you first saw me with that necklace. Things that I'm not even sure how to tell you about. All I ask is that you please hear me out and try not to hate me."

Will frowned. "Why would I hate you? You didn't know. Your father lied to you about the necklace."

"And a lot of other things. He's not . . . he's not the man I thought him to be," she said, her voice breaking. She took a moment to regain her composure and continued to walk.

Fear gripped her like nothing ever had. She was terrified that Will would have nothing more to do with her once he knew the truth, and she was starting to realize that she was very afraid of her father. The night before, she'd heard someone walking in the hallway outside her bedroom door and worried that her father had learned what she knew and had come to silence her. That was the biggest reason she had decided she must speak to Will.

They moved away from the neighborhood and into the less populated edges of town. "Nothing is right in my life, and I'm afraid that what I have to say will cause you to hate the very sight of me. I just want you to know, I've had nothing to do with any of it, and I still don't even know everything that has happened."

Will touched her arm to stop her. Laura turned and found his expression much more compassionate. "Tell me what's happened."

"Etta quit the day you spoke to Father. After you left, someone else came. She wasn't sure but thought it was my father's man Gus Synder. He's the only one she knew who would be likely to sneak around the place."

"Sneak around?"

"Yes, Etta told me that he hadn't come to the door. He just showed up in father's office. No one let him in, so he must have snuck in."

"I see."

"Besides the department store staff, he's the only one of Father's men I've met, and when I did, Father didn't introduce him. He just dismissed me and . . . he was the one Father told to drown the kitten."

"Oh . . . him."

"It gets worse. Etta told me Father spoke to him about the stagecoach passengers. I can barely tell you what was said—it's so awful." She drew a deep breath. "Apparently, my father's men came upon the stagecoach after the attack and . . . and . . . they were the ones who ransacked the dead passengers. They're probably also the ones who took the money box." She forced herself to look up at Will.

His eyes narrowed as he frowned. "Are you certain?"

"Etta overheard the conversation. Father told his man to get the stuff they had taken, along with things they had collected from other jobs, and take it to Chicago. Etta said that Gus told Father he had a cousin who could take it that evening. This was a week ago."

His frown deepened. "Why didn't you come and tell me right away? Maybe I could have stopped them."

"There was something more, and . . . well, I can't explain why I delayed. I suppose because I'm afraid. I don't know what it all means or what's going to happen next, but Etta also overheard my father say something about killing the governor, and while I think he was probably just talking out of anger, I know the man is a friend of yours. Just in case he is really plotting something . . . I . . . well . . ." She shook her head. "I don't know what to do."

Will had never much liked Granite Evans. The man always seemed to be hiding something, and Will accounted it to spiritual discernment and avoided him. But now Laura was giving him proof that his suspicions were more than just odd feelings.

"He wants to kill John Campbell? You're sure?"

"Yes. Etta didn't know anything more than that. She heard footsteps and feared the man was coming to the door and fled. She was so afraid, she didn't even stick around. She told Mrs. Murphy that she was resigning her position and left immediately. I had to go to her house to find out why, and this is the story she told me."

They started walking again as Will tried to digest all that he'd heard. Evans's men and not Indians had ransacked the dead. Had they just happened upon them? Had they perhaps heard the attack and come to their rescue, then seeing they were too late decided to take what they wanted?

A horrible thought came to mind. Will tried to put it aside, but it wouldn't go. It was all that made sense.

"What if . . . your father's men attacked the stagecoach to begin with? What if there weren't any Indians at all?"

Laura stopped and shook her head. "No, that can't be. Surely not. There were arrows."

"How hard could it be to buy some and leave them around the stagecoach? People are always buying up Indian artifacts for museums. A white man who has the skill to make bows and arrows could easily paint them in the Sioux fashion and leave them around after the attack. The deaths were caused by bullets. A couple of people were shot with arrows, but anyone could have shot them if they had a bow. They might have even done so after the people were dead."

"But the men were scalped."

"A white man could do that as easily as a native."

Laura looked as if she might be sick. She glanced around as if to make certain no one could overhear her next words. "Then my father might be responsible for . . . all that happened?"

Will put an arm out to steady her as she swayed. He thought she might faint, but she straightened and looked at him. Her eyes were wide with fear. "Surely not. He can't be that ruthless and cruel."

But even as she spoke, Will could see in her expression that she already knew the answer to that question. Her eyes filled with tears.

"All of my life I've adored him. I thought he was the finest and best of men. He loved my mother so dearly, and when she died . . . our world fell apart. He was heartbroken." She sniffed back tears and used the edge of her shawl to wipe her face.

"I thought he was a good man. He always assured me of his love and kindness. People all around Cheyenne have told me what a wonderful man he is, but I know now for myself that he's not. He takes and sells stolen goods. He lies to cover up what he's done. And he . . . he may have been responsible for killing innocent people." She broke down, unable to hold back her emotions.

Will pulled her into his arms and held her while she cried, but the dreadful conclusion was playing out in his thoughts as well. Granite Evans very well may have staged the entire attack. There had been all sorts of Indian attacks along the stage routes. Both private and freight company wagons had been attacked, and it was thought Indians were responsible since they chased off the drivers and took the horses and wagons. The victims had fled for their lives, asserting that Indians had tried to kill them. What if all of it had been white men posing as Indians? Men who wanted the Indians to be blamed. But to what end?

Granite Evans was all about politics. He wanted the governorship for himself. He knew the Indians were a problem to the whites. They held reservation lands that might be good farm and ranch lands, and the whites were eager for homestead lands. Evans might have it in mind that he could turn everyone against the Indians and see them moved out of the territory altogether.

He put such thoughts aside and looked down at the woman in his arms. She was heartbroken. She had done nothing wrong, and he could not blame her for the deeds of her father. He cared too much about her.

As if hearing his thoughts, Laura looked up. "If my father is to blame . . . if he's responsible for the death of those people . . . then he's evil and must be made to pay for his actions. I will do whatever we have to do to see justice done."

"Justice . . ." Will murmured the word. "I have just been reading in Micah six as I've been trying to figure out what God wants of me."

She nodded. "'He hath shewed thee, O man, what is good; and what doth the LORD require of thee, but to do justly, and to love mercy, and to walk humbly with thy God?'"

Will nodded. "Exactly." He gently touched her cheek. "I know this is hard on you, Laura. For that I am so very sorry, but I agree that justice must be done. We must find the truth and see that whoever is responsible pays for what they've done. Too many people have suffered."

After dropping Laura off at her house, Will made his way to the city marshal's office. He shared the information Laura had given him with Edward Vogel and waited to see what his thoughts might be.

"And that's why I think it's possible that Granite Evans has a gang of cutthroats who has been pulling all of these attacks around Cheyenne."

From his expression, it looked like Edward was just as shocked as Will had been. "The man has a sterling reputation. He's liked by everyone and has helped a lot of the local charities. Even the army esteems him."

"I know. Laura thought him a hero as well, but she told me of things that have happened since she's arrived that have changed her thinking. This is just one more thing in a long line of discrepancies. She heard him threaten to kill a young employee, but he said he was just trying to drive home a point and scare the boy. Then she overheard him tell one of his men to drown a kitten she'd found—the one you have now."

"From what you've said, it sounds like he's power hungry."

"I haven't told you one other thing. It's something that you're going to have to take straight to the top of the law enforcement around here."

Edward cocked his head slightly, and his brows came together in a worried look. "There's more?"

"Unfortunately. Mrs. Duffy said she heard Granite Evans say that he plans to kill the new governor."

"The governor?" Disbelief was evident in Edward's tone, and Will gave a nod.

"Apparently Evans is making a plan to get the position for himself."

# 20

That night Will sat up thinking about all that Laura had told him and all that had happened over the last few months. His relationship with God was on better footing, but there were still times when Will prayed in a more accusing fashion than he should. He always sought God's forgiveness and knew his thoughts were already known to God before the words came out of his mouth, but sometimes he felt so ashamed.

God was good. Will knew that. He knew that God hadn't ceased to be good or loving just because his mother and sister had died. God hadn't stopped being in control just because bad things had happened and bad men were prevailing. They wouldn't prevail forever.

"But what am I supposed to do now? My mother and sister were murdered, possibly by white men seeking nothing more than money. My lifelong desire to serve You is in tatters, and my faith is shaken." He looked toward the ceiling as if he might glimpse God there. "What am I supposed to do now?"

He saw the letter he'd received sitting on the dresser. It was from the family lawyer. His mother's will had left everything to him with the instructions to take care of his sister. With her dead as well, the small fortune came to him alone. He wouldn't necessarily have to do anything for a while. But he'd never been one to sit idle.

Will pulled out his Bible and looked again at the sixth chapter of Micah.

> *He hath shewed thee, O man, what is good; and what doth the LORD require of thee, but to do justly, and to love mercy, and to walk humbly with thy God?*

Will let the words settle in his mind. Micah was a book of both tragedy and hope. The writer was a prophet filled with the Spirit of God, sent to speak out against the sins and false teachings of the day. He spoke this verse to make clear that God had showed them what was good and what He was asking of His people. Was this what God was also requiring of Will?

If Laura's father and his men were responsible for killing the people on the stagecoach, then he could hardly blame the Indians. But even if the Indians had done the horrible deed, they still needed forgiveness, and they needed to hear the Gospel message.

However, Will also wanted justice for his mother and sister. Maybe that was why Will hadn't received a position for ministering on a reservation. Maybe Will first needed to settle the matter of what happened during the stagecoach attack.

Another section of verse came to mind, and Will flipped over several books to Matthew twenty-two. Jesus was teaching, and the Pharisees and Sadducees were trying to ensnare Him with questions. They were hoping Jesus would answer in such a way that they could condemn Him, but Jesus was more than able to handle them. Then came the question from a lawyer. He wanted to know which was the greatest commandment.

> *Jesus said unto him, Thou shalt love the Lord thy God with all thy heart, and with all thy soul, and with all thy mind. This is the first and great commandment. And the second is like unto it, Thou shalt love thy neighbour as thyself. On these two commandments hang all the law and the prophets.*

The two passages were in complete agreement. After all, how could one do justly, love mercy, and walk humbly with God without adhering to the commands Jesus said were greatest? To love God with one's all, a person would have to walk with Him humbly, do justly, and love mercy. And to love a neighbor as one's self, a person would have to do justly and, again, love mercy. There was no contradiction, and the words settled on Will like a warm blanket. An encouragement to move forward in confidence that God was truly in control, and that despite the complications and disappointments Will had been made to face, his calling had not been altered.

*But Mr. Blevins assigned the work to someone else.*

He supposed there would be other opportunities . . . locations. People came and went from jobs all the time. If God truly wanted Will in a position of ministering to the Indians, He would make a way.

Will got up and went to the window. It was barely dawn. He heaved a heavy sigh. "Lord, I don't know what You have planned for me. I used to think it was all so simple, and now here I am."

Laura came to mind. He cared for her. In fact, he was confident that he'd lost his heart to her. She was quite an incredible woman, and in more than one way, she was the perfect woman for him.

Still, could he completely love someone whose father had been responsible for the deaths of his own mother and sister? As the years went by, would he fault her or hold it against her? He didn't want to be the kind of person who would make someone responsible for something via their association with the guilty party.

Then, too, there was his concern of losing her as he had the others he cared for. Was it better to guard his heart against love and admire her from afar? If he didn't allow himself to love her or anyone else, then he'd never again have to bear the pain he had endured over his lost family.

*But I already love her. Trying to stop now would be like trying to stop breathing.* He saw the sun edge up above the horizon.

Lastly, there was the complication of serving amongst the Indians. Would Laura have any interest in such a thing? It would be important that she also feel called to such a life-changing task. If he took her for a wife and she despised the ministry, Will would be stuck in a bad place.

"Father, I am trying so hard to understand and do what You have called me to do. I hadn't figured to take a wife, at least not right away, but if Laura is the one, please show me. Help me to see the truth of this entire situation. Let the truth be known, Lord, in every way."

At nine o'clock in the morning, Edward showed up just as they'd agreed. He and Will made their way to the jail, where they planned to meet with the city marshal and sheriff. Once they were assembled, Edward and Will explained all they knew.

"It seems to me," the city marshal finally said, "that the best hope we have of getting Evans as the responsible party would be if we could get one of his men to turn against him. Maybe one of the men who was involved in the stagecoach attack, if they indeed were the ones to do the job."

Will shook his head. "No one really seems to know who his men are. In all the time I stayed with them, I didn't see anyone but his household staff. He doesn't usually hold his meetings at home. Even his daughter hasn't met the men who work for him, except for that Gus Snyder."

"You ever hear of this guy, Vogel?" the sheriff asked.

"No, I can't say that I have. He hasn't been in trouble with the law. That's for sure."

"I'm not familiar with him either," the marshal threw in.

"Without knowing who his men are, it's going to be hard to get anyone to betray him." The sheriff seemed to consider this a moment. "What about his business associates and clerks at the store?"

"Could be someone there might know something, but I wouldn't bet on it. Evans is a very private individual. Between what I've observed and what Laura has told me, he seems to limit who knows about his business," Will replied. "Besides, it seems to me that since suspicions haven't come up before now, Evans's men must be extremely loyal. It's going to be hard to get anybody to talk."

"I agree, but what other choice do we have?" the sheriff asked.

"I might have an idea," Will said. "Granite Evans offered me a position. I don't know what he has in mind, but maybe if I convinced him that I was loyal and trustworthy, he'd hire me on to do some of his underhanded tasks. Then maybe I could stop whatever he has planned."

"What if we also convinced him that you were going to be working with the new governor?" the city marshal said. "Then Evans might see you as his inside man to Campbell. Maybe you could be his secretary or perhaps just his escort to Wyoming."

"As I said earlier, I know John Campell. We grew up together and went to war together. I'm sure he would cooperate with us and use me in whatever capacity will help."

"But would Evans trust you in a plot to kill Campbell if he knows you two are friends?" the marshal asked.

"And will Evans really believe that you'd do anything for him?" Edward asked. "He knows you're a preacher first and foremost. Is he going to believe you're willing to commit murder?"

"He knows I was angry at God and on the fence about issues of faith. I doubt Laura has told him of my progress toward repentance. And if she has, then I'll just have to assure him that it was nothing more than an act for her benefit." Will shifted and leaned forward. "I've got another reason to pretend loyalty to Evans. I'm in love with his daughter. Maybe I could wrap all of this up with a proposal of marriage. I don't have the powerful connections he wants, but with my mother's death, I've inherited a small fortune. That should be appealing to Mr. Evans. All of this could be just the right combination to pique his interest. Once he knows about my connection to John Campbell, I'm sure he'll see the value in hiring me. I can even make it sound like I have held a grudge against John all these years. That I'd just as soon see him not come to the territory."

"Sounds like a lot to coordinate," the sheriff replied.

"And a lot of lies to get straight and memorize," the marshal added.

"Can't say I would normally advocate lying," Edward began, "but it may be the only way to keep the governor from getting himself killed and put a stop to the supposed Indian attacks. I'm convinced the Indians aren't to blame."

The sheriff nodded. "I am too."

"This is an evil man with an evil plan. I am not one to advocate lies either," Will said, shaking his head. "But if it saves a life, I have to think that like Rahab in the Bible, it's more about the matter of heart than the deed itself."

"I told Father that you were ill," Laura said. "And in some ways, I know you are. You're sick of heart and worried about all that is going on."

Etta Duffy poured her another cup of tea as Laura glanced around Etta's small kitchen and continued with her thoughts.

"I think it's important that you come back to work. Otherwise, my father will wonder if something happened, and it might cause trouble in catching him in his horrid plots."

Etta's eyes widened, and the teapot shook in her hands. "I don't know if I can work in that house and not give myself away."

"I know you're afraid, but I need you there. I need you to help me. I promise you I'll do whatever I can to make sure you are safe. Etta, we must see justice done. If my father is responsible for the deaths of those people on the stage, then he must go to prison, perhaps even . . . hang." She had a hard time saying the word. It hadn't dawned on Laura when she'd been talking with Will that her father's guilt could cost him his life.

Etta put the pot back on the stove and returned to the small kitchen table. "Oh, Laura, I know this must be so hard for you. You love your father dearly, I know that much. I've watched you with him since you first arrived. You adore him."

"I did. Now I'm just so heartbroken to imagine him being the kind of man willing to end another person's life. He's not the man I built him up to be in my mind . . . and heart. I don't think I've ever really known him, and now it's too late."

The older woman huffed a breath. "I'll come back. I owe it to you. I'll do whatever I can. I've never been one to let fear rule my life."

"Oh, thank you, Etta. I know this is not an easy decision for you."

"I'll return tomorrow if that's soon enough."

"Yes. I'll inform Father tonight that I checked on you and you're much better and will be back on duty in the morning."

"Very well."

Laura leaned closer. "Etta, we're going to have to go through Father's things and see if we can find any incriminating evidence. I don't know just how we'll accomplish it, but it's important that you be thinking on the matter." Will had advised her to say and do nothing, but Laura felt she had to at least try to right this wrong.

"We'll have to search his office and his bedroom suite," Etta replied, looking thoughtful. "I have keys to those rooms. We'll have to find a time when he'll be out of the house and of no threat to us."

"I'll talk to him over breakfast each day and learn what his plans are. We usually discuss such things, so he won't find it strange." She reached out to cover Etta's hand with her own. Their eyes locked.

"I hate that it's come to this, but I can't live with a murderer." For a moment, Laura started at her own comment. Her father was a killer. Or at least, he had no trouble planning to kill. His words about the new governor were proof enough of that.

Will was just coming from the jail when he heard his name called. He turned and found Mr. Blevins rushing toward him. The little man seemed all excited about something.

"Mr. Porter, I had hoped to come see you later, but it's most fortuitous that God should cause our paths to cross just now."

"What seems to be the problem?" Will asked. Seeing the man gave him the slight sensation of being hit in the stomach.

Mr. Blevins gave him a glance from head to toe. "Now that you're back on your feet, have you reconsidered the idea of working on a reservation?"

"Why do you ask? I thought you already assigned the positions to others."

"That had indeed been the plan, but strangely enough, I have one opening left that no one else is interested in. Or they've moved on to another assignment."

Will's heart skipped a beat. "And now you wish to offer it to me?"

"I do. If you are willing to take it. I know your mother's and sister's deaths have no doubt sullied the vision you had of working with the natives, but not all Indians are bad."

"They weren't the cause—" Will had nearly said too much. "No. Not all Indians are bad."

"So does that mean you'll take the job?"

Will saw it as God's direction and answer to his prayers. "I will."

"Oh, glory be." The man put his hand to his chest. "I leave in the morning for Washington, D.C., and was hopeful I could tell them that the matter was arranged." He adjusted his wire-rimmed glasses. "I'll return in six weeks, and we'll finalize the paperwork. Be ready to leave for Fort Bridger on the first of June."

Will nodded. The first of June would give him plenty of time to resolve the issue of Granite Evans. The little man started to leave, but Will called out. "I have a question."

Mr. Blevins turned. "What?"

"Would there be a problem if I were to . . . say, bring a wife?"

"A wife?" The man looked momentarily confused, then shrugged. "I can't see any reason why not. I didn't realize you'd married."

"I haven't," Will said with grin. "But by then I plan to be."

Blevins shook his head and rolled his eyes skyward. "Bring a wife, bring a dog, bring whatever you like, so long as you bring yourself to fill that position."

With that Blevins disappeared around the corner. Will started walking down the street in a complete sense of wonder. So much had happened in just the course of twenty-four hours.

And then, as if preordained, he spied Laura down the block. She was putting something behind the seat of her carriage. The same horse and carriage that had struck him down back in January. As she turned to climb up, Will hurried forward to stop her.

"Laura!"

She turned in surprise. There was a look of questioning, as if she were worried about what he intended.

"I'm glad to see you appearing so well. I was concerned about you after last night."

A flicker of relief crossed her face. "I suppose I've been thinking that you would never speak to me again."

"Don't be ridiculous," he said, taking hold of her elbow. "Let me help you up, and then I can drive you home. I need to tell you something."

"What is it?"

"Something has developed, and I want to share it with you, but you must agree to keep quiet about it."

She nodded and took her seat in the carriage. Will quickly joined her. "You're still of a mind to get justice, aren't you?" He took up the lines and released the brake.

"Of course." Her response was immediate.

Their eyes met, and Will gave a nod. "Then I have a plan."

On the way to the Evans's house, Will explained their thoughts. "I'm going to ask your father for a job. He previously offered me one and even questioned me again about working for him when I came to see him about the necklace. Getting him to hire me will be step one. I'm also going to let him know that I know the governor, which will lead to step two. I'm going to pretend to be chosen to escort the new governor to Cheyenne. That news will come out in the *Leader* tomorrow morning to support my story. When I see your father, he will hopefully have already read about it and want to question me. If not, I'll bring it up. I'm also going to let it be known to your father that I hate John Campbell—that there was bad blood between us and that I don't want to be a part of anything to do with him. I think this will encourage your father to approach me to help him with setting the stage for killing the governor."

"Oh no!" Laura put her hand to her mouth.

"The authorities think your father will probably want the deed done prior to the governor's arrival so that the fair city of Cheyenne and its people here won't be associated with it. So your father, knowing that I'll be escorting the governor here, might decide to set up things en route."

"It will be very dangerous, and I would never forgive myself if something happened to you."

Will met her gaze and smiled. "Why, Laura Evans, are you breaking your vow?"

"What vow?" She looked confused.

He chuckled. "The one you made to never love another."

She bit her lower lip and looked away. "I might be."

He laughed all the more. "Could be I have done the same." He put the horse in motion.

Laura said nothing for a full block, then turned to him. Will could see the questioning in her eyes. "Then what are we going to do?"

Will sobered and flicked the lines to get the horse to pick up the pace. "First things first. We settle this mess, and then I have a feeling the rest will just fall into place." He looked at her a moment longer, then smiled again. "By the way, how would you feel about living on a reservation?"

Saturday morning, Granite read the front page of the *Leader*. There was an article about the new governor and his planned arrival in May. It also mentioned a group of men who had been called upon by the local city council to be part of the entourage to bring Governor Campell to Cheyenne. Wilson Porter was among the men listed.

He'd barely finished with the article when Mrs. Duffy appeared with a tray of coffee and his favorite cherry Danish.

She went to place it on a table in front of the fireplace. "Would you like me to serve, sir?"

"No, just leave it. I'll tend it myself." Granite got up from his desk and came around to the fireplace. "I'm glad to see that you're feeling better, Mrs. Duffy. I hope it wasn't anything too serious."

"No, and I'm fit as a fiddle now, Mr. Evans. Thank you for your patience." She straightened and gave him a hurried smile. "Now, if you'll excuse me, I told Mrs. Murphy I'd be right back to help her with something in the kitchen."

"Of course."

Granite had always liked the fact that she wasn't one to linger and draw out a conversation. Mrs. Duffy had proven to be quick to task and never all that interested in gossip.

He had just taken a seat beside the fire when a knock sounded on his office door.

"Enter," he called, pouring himself a cup of coffee.

"Mr. Evans, Mr. Porter is here to see you," Mrs. Duffy announced.

Granite couldn't believe his good fortune. "Show him in and bring another cup for him."

"Of course, sir."

She stepped back, and Will bounded into the room. He extended his hand to Granite. "Good morning, Mr. Evans."

"Good morning, Mr. Porter . . . Will." Granite smiled. "I was just reading about you in the paper."

"Me?" Will looked surprised.

"Yes, didn't you know? There's an article about the coming of the governor in May, and it says that you're among several men chosen to escort him here."

"Just from Omaha. John and I were boyhood friends and comrades-in-arms. Not that we're all that close. Truth is, I didn't want to go on the trip to escort him back, but I wasn't given much of a choice."

"And why would you not want to put yourself into the company of powerful men like Campbell?"

Will glanced up at the ceiling. "Well . . . let's just say there's some bad blood between us."

"Oh, really?" Granite wondered just how bad it might be. "Please sit." He motioned to the other leather chair in front of the hearth. "Mrs. Duffy has gone to get you a cup and saucer. Ah, see. Here she is."

The woman came into the room carrying the china set. She placed it on the silver tray. "Would you like me to pour?" she asked once again.

"No, I'll see to everything. Close the door on your way out so that Mr. Porter and I may speak without being disturbed."

"Yes, sir," she replied and quickly exited the room.

Once they were alone, Granite poured coffee into Will's cup. "Do you take cream or sugar?"

"Black is fine," Will said, reaching for the cup and saucer when Granite lifted it his way.

"There's cherry Danish, as you can see. The very best. Mrs. Murphy, as you know, is quite capable in the pastry department."

Will smiled. "I agree. I've had her Danish before."

"Well, help yourself," Granite said and took one for himself. "And then tell me to what I owe the pleasure of this visit." There'd be time enough to sort out the man's degree of feelings toward Campbell.

Will set the coffee aside and took up a Danish. "Sir, there are a couple of things on my mind. First, I've had a letter from my mother's lawyer. It seems I have inherited a great deal of money. Knowing you as one of the most successful men in Cheyenne, I am hoping you might offer me advice on management of the inheritance."

"Why, Will, I'm quite touched that you would think of me." This couldn't be going better if Granite had planned it out himself.

"Well, there's no rush. As I understand it, my mother's estate is still being settled, and it will most likely be summer before all is resolved."

"And the second?" Granite asked, eager to move the conversation along.

"Well, I wondered if your job offer is still available."

Granite wanted to shout an affirming response but forced himself to remain calm. "For a man of quality and intellect such as yourself, there is always a job available. I must say, however, I'm surprised. You seemed confident of continuing as you were."

"Things have changed considerably for me," Will replied before taking a long slow drink. He replaced the cup on the saucer. "And there's the other matter."

"What is it?"

Will smiled. "Your daughter."

# 21

The weekend had been stormy with threats of more thunder and rain on that Easter morning. Laura wasn't overly concerned. She had endured all manner of storms while living in Tennessee and wasn't all that alarmed to learn that Cheyenne was given to terrible thunderstorms from time to time and even the occasional tornado. She had never been one to worry overly much about such things and didn't intend to start now.

"Looks like another rain is moving in," Etta said, coming in to help Laura with her hair. "I'm glad you won't be attending a morning service."

"I'm glad for that as well."

"We don't usually have storms in the morning like this. I guess the world's just as upset with things as we are," Etta said in a hushed voice.

"I suppose so. You know"—Laura glanced around and lowered her voice—"Father told me that he'll be leaving right after breakfast and be gone until quite late tonight. That will give us all day to search his office and bedroom. I know it's dangerous, and Will would never want me to involve myself, but I can't help but think if we could find some proof of Father's activities it would help to settle the matter. And with the rest of the staff off for Easter, we won't have to worry about someone catching us in the act."

"That is a good idea. I see nothing wrong with searching for proof of what your father has been up to, but I thought you were going to have lunch with the Vogels?"

"We can probably still work it all out. It shouldn't take us all that long to go through things if we get right to it as soon as he leaves. He only keeps personal items in his bedroom and office, so we only need to look through those rooms."

"All right. Should we start up here or downstairs?"

"Up here. We'll take care of his bedroom first, then move downstairs to the office."

Etta braided Laura's long cinnamon-colored hair and pinned it up in a fashionable bun. She said nothing more, and Laura knew Etta was more than a little bit apprehensive about going through Father's things.

"It's going to be just fine, Etta. You'll see."

Laura went down to breakfast and tried to make polite conversation with her father. She had become quite guarded where he was concerned but fought to keep things as normal between them as possible. She still found it hard to believe he was such a corrupt and evil man, yet the signs were all there. She'd simply been ignoring them.

"It would be wonderful if you'd go with me to Easter services later. We're having them at four thirty instead of the regular time at seven. Couldn't you make an exception just this once?" She gave what she hoped was a look of expectation. Frankly, she didn't want him to be anywhere near her friends, but she did want him to repent and be saved.

"As I've said before, religion is all right for some, but not for me. You have your way of dealing with the disappointments of the world, and I have mine."

"I just thought it would be nice for us to be together."

"There will be plenty of other events where we'll be together. I've already heard of quite a few summer parties that are being given. But enough of that. We need to discuss something entirely different."

"And what is that, Father?"

He cut into the ham steak on his plate. "I have been lax on getting you settled with a husband, but I believe I have hit upon a solution."

"What about those summer parties we'd attend together?"

He chuckled. "I didn't mean that I would necessarily escort you, but we could attend together. If you have a husband, then you can be on his arm instead of mine."

Laura salted the quiche on her plate. "I don't need a husband at the moment."

"Hear me out. The young man I have in mind is none other than Wilson Porter."

"Will? You want me to marry Will?" She almost giggled. How strange that he should take this direction.

"He's a fine, upstanding young man, and he's recently come into an inheritance that can see you both settled with a very comfortable future."

Money. That was why Will had suddenly become acceptable. It would seem the plans Will hoped to lay were coming into play.

"What if he's not interested in such a settling?" Laura picked up a piece of toast. "He might have no desires for a wife. He did plan to go preach on a reservation."

"Not anymore. He's coming to work for me. Starting tomorrow."

"I must say all of this comes as a surprise." She tried to sound blasé about the entire matter.

"Get used to the idea. I believe you and Mr. Porter make the perfect match. You spent all that time caring for him and getting to know each other. I seem to recall you got along quite well. I think we should hold the wedding right away."

"Like this summer?" Laura asked, truly surprised by her father's desire to act quickly.

"No. Like next month."

"Next month?" Laura dropped the toast. "People will think we have to get married. That something untoward happened while Will and I were spending all that time together. I couldn't put that on him. He's to be a pastor and must live above reproach."

"Nonsense. Everyone knows you were heavily supervised while caring for Mr. Porter. I've spoken to him, and he's not opposed to marrying next month. This way when he leaves for his trip to escort the governor, he'll be doing so as a wedded man. That will make his social standing seem all the more important."

"You've talked to him about marrying me?" Laura considered all that Will had told her on Friday. He'd said nothing about asking her father for her hand. She supposed it was all just part of the pretense to catch him in the act of trying to kill the governor. Perhaps it had been a last-minute consideration, something Will felt would further gain her father's trust. That would make sense, but why was her father pushing so hard to make it happen right away?

Laura feared the only reason her father wanted them married in April was that Will's fortune would come to her should he die along with the governor on their trip to Cheyenne. She hated being so suspicious of her father, but it made sense.

The grandfather clock in the hall chimed the hour, and her father threw down his napkin and jumped up from his chair. He'd barely eaten any of his breakfast. "The time has gotten away from me, and I must go. I'll be back late tonight. Don't wait up. It will be after ten. If you have something you need to discuss with me, we can do it first thing tomorrow."

"Have a good Easter, Father," Laura called after him. "I'll be praying for you." He said nothing in reply.

She waited a good five minutes after hearing the front door close before getting to her feet and ringing for Etta. The housekeeper showed up in record time and quickly cleared away the dishes.

As the two women made their way upstairs, Laura commended her. "Breakfast was delicious, by the way, and your service impeccable. I had no idea you knew how to make quiche."

"I don't let my mother do all the cooking," Etta replied, laughing. "My boys are particularly fond of what they call egg pie. I learned to make it from an elderly French woman who lived in our building when I was first married. She taught me several wonderful recipes, but Mrs. Murphy is not of a mind to allow my inclusion in her kitchen unless it's for the purpose of giving her a holiday."

"Even so, I'm sure she'll criticize some poorly cleaned countertop, or a dish put in the wrong place." Laura shook her head. "But I do love that woman. She's quite gifted at cooking."

"That she is."

Laura led the way to her father's bedroom and tried the door. It was locked. Etta quickly produced the key and opened it.

The large suite with a fireplace at one end of the room and

a four-poster canopy bed at the other was quite masculine. The fireplace, like the head- and foot-board of the bed, was thickly carved dark mahogany. The walls were papered in a navy-and-gold pattern, and a thick Turkish rug had been situated in front of the fire beneath two upholstered throne chairs and a liquor cart. The other pieces of furniture included a massive wardrobe, dressing table, desk, chair, and nightstands. All were heavy, dark pieces that again suggested male ownership. Everything appeared quite imposing . . . almost threatening. Laura chided herself for being silly. A room couldn't be threatening. She was just nervous because of why they had come and the things she had learned about her father.

"I'll look in his desk," Laura said. "You go through the armoire."

"What am I looking for?"

"Anything that suggests a connection with robbing stages or travelers on the road. Maybe a ledger or a diary? Perhaps a collection of jewelry—you know, odds and ends that might have been taken off people. I have no idea, really. You've been here this past year, so if you see anything that seems strange or out of order, or if it's something that you don't recognize, tell me."

Etta nodded and got right to work. Laura opened the top right-hand drawer of her father's desk and began to search. There was nothing out of the ordinary. She found expensive letterhead and a blotter, along with a few invoices and correspondences. Laura looked through the letters thinking perhaps one might reveal her father's secret life, but so far, the topics she found were political in nature, except one from a hospital in Alabama.

She scanned the lines long enough to get the general

point. Her father had apparently promised an endowment but withdrew it at the last minute due to some scandal with members of the hospital board. The man who had written the missive begged her father not to deny those in need of the facilities and help that could be had at their hospital. He pleaded with him to reinstate the endowment, as thousands of people were counting on the improvements.

Yet another mark against her father's character.

She searched on through the next few drawers, and nothing seemed out of place. Laura had just closed the last drawer when there was a loud crash from downstairs, quickly followed by a stream of expletives.

"Father is home!" Laura said, looking to Etta.

Etta waved her to the door. "Go to your room. I'll take care of things here."

Laura didn't question the housekeeper and made a mad rush for her bedroom, knowing she'd have to cross the top of the stairs. If her father was coming up, he'd easily spot her.

Thankfully, she heard him head off down the hall, evidently going to his office. Laura hurried to her room and stood just inside her open door. She had already decided she would step out as her father came upstairs. If he came up.

He did.

"Why, Father, what are you doing home? I thought you'd be gone until this evening." Laura came down the hall toward him from her room.

"I forgot something, and now I'm going to be late," he all but growled. He stomped off to his room with Laura following close on his heel.

"Can I help you find it?"

He stopped with a frown at his open bedroom door. "What's going on here?"

Laura could see that Etta had knelt down in front of the fireplace. "Looks like Etta is cleaning."

"You don't ever clean on Sundays. I had a hard time getting you to even work Sundays," he said, moving toward the housekeeper. "What are you doing?"

"It was quite chilly last night, sir. I presumed, correctly, that you had kept a fire going. I had to clear the ash because tonight might be just as bad, and you would have a mess on your hands if you went to lay a fire. However, it is true that I hate to work on the Sabbath."

"Bah!" he huffed and went to his desk. He threw open one of the drawers and then another. Finally, he took up one of the small ledgers Laura had seen. It was a book full of numbers, and she had wondered what the figures represented.

"Is that what you came for, Father?" Laura asked, trying to sound cheery.

"Yes." He headed back for the door and paused. Looking back at the two women, he frowned. "Lock the door when you're done, Mrs. Duffy."

"Yes, sir. I will." Etta stood and then picked up the ash bucket. "I'll just go dump this and bring back some wood."

Laura's father gave a curt nod and headed back downstairs. The front door slammed shut, and Laura hurried to the window. Father climbed into the landau, and Mr. Grayson drove him away. It wasn't until the carriage was out of sight that Laura and Etta both fell back against the nearest wall. The bucket was still in Etta's hands.

"That was too close. If he'd come upstairs first instead of going to his office, I would have been hard-pressed to explain why I was in his room."

"I know," Etta replied. She seemed out of breath and pale.

"Are you all right?" Laura asked, coming to where the housekeeper stood.

"Yes, but he frightened me so. If you hadn't been here, I'm sure I would have fallen to pieces."

Laura gave her a one-armed hug, then hurried to the door. "Let's go. I'm no good at this game, and I won't see you in jeopardy again."

The heavy storm clouds passed just in time for the Easter service. As the sun came out, the afternoon took on a glorious glow, cheering Laura considerably. She was anxious to speak to Will but waited until after the service. The pastor had already been speaking for some time, and she found it impossible to pay attention. When he spoke of concluding, she straightened and forced herself to listen.

"This is the day we celebrate the risen Lord," the pastor told the congregants. "We celebrate the defeat of sin and death."

Granny Taylor, by whom Laura was sitting, gave a resounding "amen," as did others. Laura couldn't help but smile. Despite the terrible things going on in her life, she had complete confidence in God. Her earthly father might be guilty of all manner of sin, but her heavenly Father was steadfast and faithful. He was unchanging. She hadn't misjudged His character.

"You've heard the teaching over and over from the pulpit. A world full of sin was in desperate need of a Savior. A Savior who could bring man into an acceptable accord with God Almighty. A Savior who would become the ultimate sacrifice for all sin. Once for all.

"How precious is the sound of that. Once for all. Each and

every soul has only to come to Jesus for salvation from their sins. I urge you today to repent of your sins. Repent and be saved. Come up from the grave of sin. Be raised from death and be victorious with Christ."

They joined together in singing a hymn, then closed in prayer. Laura felt so happy to be a part of this wonderful congregation of believers. She was here with friends that she knew she could trust. Friends who loved God as much as she did and would stand beside her no matter what was learned about her father's activities.

Still, it hurt to know that she would never have the father that she longed for. She had endured all of her years away because she was confident they would one day be together and all would be right once again. Now that would never happen. If her father had done all of those terrible things, he would go to prison at the very least, and she might never see him again. The aching deepened. Only God could see her through this second loss of the man she had loved so dearly.

"Well, that was certainly a wonderful service," Granny said, turning to Laura. "Sometimes I get so overwhelmed when I remind myself that as good as this is, heaven will be even better."

"That's a very hopeful way to think of it." Laura fought to corral her emotions.

"It's so glorious that we cannot even begin to imagine it."

Laura drew a deep breath and finally looked up to meet Granny's gaze. "I don't know. I can imagine a lot."

Granny patted her arm. "Child, just remember, these are light and momentary troubles." She raised a brow as her expression grew most serious. "Troubles that God has already seen and provided for. Rest in Him and find your joy again."

"Oh, Granny, thank you. You always know the right things

to say." Laura gave her a hug. "I just know it will be so wonderful to have the world set to rights . . . to have no more sickness or heartbreak, wrongdoing, or evil. There will just be peace and goodness all around because God will be all around."

"Granny, would you please come talk to my wife and remind her that she's supposed to be taking these last few days easy?" Edward Vogel asked as he joined them. "I can't get her to stop working. I even hired a woman to come clean up and cook."

"My, I wish I could have had that kind of help when I gave birth. When I had my first baby, we were fifty miles from the nearest town. I was completely reliant on a friend who lived about three miles to the south to help me deliver the baby. I'd helped deliver hers, and it was only fair." Granny laughed. "I waited until Jed finished breakfast, then told him he'd best ride and get her because I'd been having pains for most of the night."

Laura was fascinated and horrified all at once. "Oh goodness, Granny. That must have been hard to cook breakfast and wait while being in such misery."

"It's just the way it had to be. When you're a rancher's wife, things are done in a different way."

"So what happened?" Edward asked, looking at Jed. "Did you get back in time?"

"Barely," the old man replied. "Granny was in the bed bearing down when we got back. She'd already set up everything that needed to be there. Had her hot water and blankets, baby clothes, and diapers. She probably could have taken care of everything by herself, but I was mighty glad she had someone there besides me." He chuckled. "I think she was too."

"I was," Granny admitted, "but I knew the good Lord was watching over me."

Edward shook his head. "I need you folks to pray for me. You know what I'm up against, given the past."

Granny took hold of him. "We do know, and we've been offering up powerful prayers for you every time we pray for Marybeth and this child. Trust in the Lord, Edward."

"I trusted Him last time," Edward replied, "and the worst happened."

Laura felt terrible for him. She had heard Marybeth speak of his fears and had often prayed for them both.

"The worst would be to face it without Him," Granny said. "Son, you need to remember that no matter what, God will never leave you. He didn't abandon you then, and He won't abandon you now. Marybeth belongs to Him too, just as your first wife did. We don't know what will happen tomorrow or the next day. I've seen good people collapse and be gone when their heart gave out. My own pa went that way. We just don't know how much time we have on earth, but we know the character of the God we serve."

"And even when we don't understand why He allows the things He does," Jed said, "we can trust in Him. We don't have to understand. We just need to put our hope in Him and hold on to the love He's given us."

Edward nodded. "I know you're right. I'm doing all I can."

"Maybe it's time to let Him do all He can," Jed said, grinning. "I've never known my best to be better than His."

Laura felt Will's presence before he even spoke. She turned and saw him joining their little group.

"May I talk to you for a moment?" he whispered in her ear.

Laura nodded and excused herself, giving Granny a kiss on the cheek before following Will outside. "What is it?"

"I wanted to tell you how things went with your father on Saturday."

"You don't need to. He told me that you're going to start working for him tomorrow." Her smile faded. "Will, I am afraid. Etta and I were searching his bedroom this morning—trying to find anything that might give you evidence against him. We didn't find anything, but he came back unexpectedly, and we were both sure that he'd catch us at it. Thankfully, he didn't."

"Don't put yourself in danger. We have this under control." He touched her cheek. "Please just stay out of it. I don't want to lose another person. I don't think I could bear it."

Laura knew he was right. Will and the others were more than capable of doing whatever needed to be done.

"I'll stay out of it," she whispered, knowing that if Will asked her to sprout wings and fly to the moon, she'd give it her best try. She had fallen in love with this man.

# 22

"Will, this is Gus Snyder," Evans introduced in the dimly lit warehouse.

Will couldn't make out much of the man's facial features. It was too dark, and he wore a wide-brimmed hat low to further shadow his face.

"Pleased to meet you," Will said, extending his hand. Gus didn't reach out, and so Will gave a shrug and pretended to be caught up in the warehouse. "Is this where you keep things for the store?"

"Yes, along with other pieces I come to own," Evans replied. "I wanted to bring you here so you could become familiar with the business from the ground up. If you're to be a part of this family, then you'll need to know it all."

Will was surprised at how casually Evans had included him. He was even more surprised at how easily Snyder could disappear into the background.

"Gus handles a lot of things for me. Most importantly, he manages the men who work here. I want you to spend time with him and get to know the warehouse and the more physical side of my investments."

"All right."

Evans turned to Gus and motioned him forward. "Take him with you to oversee off-loading at the train yard. Show him how things are done, but he doesn't need to actually do anything. Will is going to be working in more of an office job given his education, but as I said, I want him to understand how things are done."

"Yes, sir," Gus replied.

Will wondered if he harbored any jealousy over a new man showing up and laying claim to an important role that might overlap some of Gus's own work.

"I'm going back to the store, Will. When Gus finishes with you, come and find me there."

"Sounds good, Mr. Evans." Will watched him leave through the same door they'd entered before turning to face Snyder. "So what now?"

"Now we go to the depot." Gus moved across the warehouse to an entirely different set of doors. These were large double doors big enough to allow a wagon entry. Several men were working just outside. Will didn't know if they were employed by Evans, so he asked. After all, finding someone willing to speak against the man was why he was there.

"Are these fellas working for Mr. Evans?"

Gus pulled down on the brim of his hat. "They're nobody so don't concern yourself with them. If you need to know who someone is, I'll introduce you."

He kept walking down the long alleyway toward the depot. Will wasn't surprised to find Snyder a man of few words. He also wasn't surprised that the man kept to the shadows, avoiding wide-open spaces—hugging the walls whenever possible. Synder reminded him of a wild cat stalking its prey.

He blended in so neatly with the various wagons, equipment, and shipping crates that Will found himself forced to keep his gaze fixed on him at all times.

They were soon on the back side of the train depot. There, Will found a lot more activity, what with the railroad workers, the freight drivers with their teams, and laborers to load the dozen or more wagons.

"Stay here," Gus instructed, leaving Will near a wooden platform.

Gus wove his way around to where two men were straining to lift a wooden box into the back of an already heavily loaded freight wagon. He waited until they'd finished before motioning the larger of the two men over to the side. Will watched as Gus and the big man talked. He couldn't hear any of the conversation, but the big man glanced over at Will. A deep frown etched his features.

Will did his best to memorize how the men looked. The larger man had massive shoulders, a bearded face, and a large nose. Will turned his attention to the smaller man as Gus concluded his discussion and came back to where he'd left Will. The smaller man was nothing notable. Medium build and height, no distinguishing marks.

"Come with me," Gus instructed.

"Where are we going now?"

"We're going to drive that wagon to where Mr. Evans wants it."

"Why aren't the men who loaded it going to drive it?"

Will saw Gus clench his hand into a fist, then release it. The man did not like being asked questions. It was something to use to his advantage, and when Gus wasn't forthright with the answer, Will pressed the matter.

"I just want to understand the process and how Mr. Evans

wants things run. He told me I could ask you any questions I had."

Gus grunted. "They have another wagon to load."

When they reached the wagon, the men had already finished securing the load and had walked off to tend to something else. Will climbed up beside Gus on the wagon seat.

"So where are we off to?"

"Just another warehouse," Gus said.

"Not the same one, eh? How many warehouses does Mr. Evans have."

"Three."

Will could hear the irritation in the man's voice. Gus snapped the lines, and the two draft horses pulled forward.

"For someone who's only been here a little over a year, Mr. Evans has certainly done well for himself. I admire that kind of ability in a man, don't you?"

Gus said nothing, and Will didn't press him this time because he saw another curious thing. The bigger of the two men Gus had been talking to was now mounting a large strawberry-roan gelding. Will watched as the man made his way in the opposite direction as they were going. He did his best to act as though he was just gawking around the area so that he could see where the man was headed. He thought about mentioning it since Gus said they were to load another wagon, but Will realized that might draw attention to the fact that he was watching the man.

"I've never been down here. At least not since I arrived," Will said instead. "It's impressive the way Cheyenne has built up. Seems there are more people coming in every day. Say, did you hear that I'll be part of the escort bringing the governor to Cheyenne?"

He decided to stir things up a bit. "Not that I can much

stomach the guy. I'd just as soon he'd have died in the war. We have some hard feelings between us. Maybe I'll get a chance to teach him a lesson while he's here."

Gus said nothing, but Will knew he heard every word.

Later that day after Evans sent him home, Will made a roundabout trip to the Vogels' house. Edward met him at the door and welcomed him in.

"Would you like to stay for supper?" he asked Will.

"No, just wanted to report in and let you know what I learned today, which isn't much. There are a couple of ware-houses, one over between Fifteenth and Sixteenth off O'Neil and the other south of the tracks. Supposedly there's a third warehouse, but no one said where it was.

"I went with Gus Snyder to pick up a load of stuff at the depot. There were two men who loaded the wagon, but Sny-der didn't introduce me to them or even let me get near them."

"What'd they look like? Would you know them if you saw them again?"

"I would the first guy. He was a big man—tall, broad shoul-ders, and a bit of a belly. He wore a beard and had scraggly hair down to the shoulder. Wore a faded felt hat. He rides a strawberry roan with a white face."

"I know that man. His name is Bigs. Bigs Brixton. He's hasn't been in Cheyenne all that long. He's been in trouble more than once. You know, we could probably use him. He hates to be in jail and will go out of his way to avoid it. I might be able to set up something. Maybe set it up so that he gets in trouble and then bring him into the jail. Of course, if we can wait long enough, Bigs will probably get himself sent there." Edward grew thoughtful. "It makes sense that he works for Evans. Anytime he gets himself in jail, he doesn't seem to have any trouble paying his fines and getting back out. And the times he's been accused of more serious crimes, the witnesses disappear, or new ones come forward to say he wasn't the man."

"Yeah, it would make sense if he had a wealthy benefactor."

An older woman appeared with a pail of water. She gave Edward a nod. "Your supper is on the stove, and the cleanup is done. I'll be headin' home now."

"Thank you, Mrs. Knudson," Edward said. He looked to Will. "This is the woman I hired to help Marybeth. Her husband, Ollie, owns the livery stable on Fifteenth. Mrs. Knudson, this is Will Porter. He'll be around a lot, so you might as well get to know him."

"Mr. Porter," she said with a nod.

"Glad to meet you, Mrs. Knudson." Will gave her a smile.

Edward continued. "She made Swedish meatballs and noodles, and they're really good. I sampled them." He grinned. "Are you sure you won't stay?"

Will laughed. "No, I can't, but invite me another time."

There was a knock on the front door, and Mrs. Knudson moved toward the stove. "I'll answer it on my way out." She poured water into the stove's reservoir, then put the bucket on the floor. "See you tomorrow."

"Thank you, Mrs. Knudson."

"I'll head out the back," Will said. "No sense in making my presence too well-known."

"Why, hello, Miss Evans," the men heard Mrs. Knudson say. "Mr. Vogel is in the kitchen."

"I just brought a few things by to drop off," Laura replied.

Edward and Will both headed for the front room. Edward chuckled as they tried to go through the arched entryway at the same time.

"A little eager?" he murmured to Will.

Will grinned, but his focus was on Laura. She was holding a large basket and smiled when she caught sight of him.

"I didn't know you'd be here," she said, holding up the basket as Mrs. Knudson headed out the front door. "I brought a dozen diapers that I finished hemming for Marybeth. There's also a couple of flannel gowns."

"Marybeth is resting, and Carrie is over at the neighbor's playing," Edward told her. "But you're welcome to stay. I'll let Marybeth know you're here."

"No, that's all right. Just let her rest. I'll leave these things and get the basket tomorrow."

"Have you plans for supper?" Will asked. "I thought if not, you might be willing to go with me."

"I have no plans, and Father is out for the evening. Mrs. Murphy has already fixed a meal, so why don't you come on over to the house? The staff will be there so there won't be any improprieties."

"Sounds good to me. It's hard to turn down supper with a beautiful lady." He turned to Edward. "Beauty trumps Swedish meatballs." They laughed.

As they walked back to her house, Laura asked Will about his day. She knew her father had instructed him to come to the store first thing.

"Did you have a good day with Father?"

"It was interesting to say the least. I spent some time with him and then some time with Snyder. He is as dark and brooding as you described."

"I don't care for him at all. Ever since Mrs. Duffy said he

snuck into the house to see Father, I've taken to locking my bedroom door when I'm at the house alone."

"I would too." Will frowned. "I don't know why your father would allow that now that you're in residence."

"As far as he knows, I've no knowledge of it, and he's told the staff to completely ignore Mr. Snyder. It terrifies poor Etta. She said she's never seen him on the second floor, but there could always be a first time."

"How did you get Etta to come back to work for your father?"

"It wasn't easy, but I told her that we had to keep things as normal as possible so Father wouldn't be suspicious. I also told her that I needed her and would do everything in my power to keep her safe. She spends a lot of time with me now. When she's working, I try to be near her, and when she doesn't have much to do, we just sew and visit. Sometimes, I accompany her when she does the shopping, and if I can't be there, I make sure Mrs. Murphy and Rosey are around."

"I was just seeing Edward to tell him about one of your father's workers. We're hoping to find a man who would be willing to turn against your father and testify to his illegal dealings."

"I'm praying it works," Laura said, shaking her head. "But I worry that you could be found out. If Father is as ruthless as we think, then he won't hesitate to kill you if you get in his way." She felt a band tighten around her chest. It would be so unbearable if Will were to die.

She glanced up at him, and Will met her gaze. "I care for you, Will."

"And I care for you, but I think you already know that."

She looked away as her cheeks warmed. She wanted to ask him about what her father had said of Will asking for her hand. She wanted very much to know if it was just a pretense—part of the game. But she held back for fear that it was nothing more than that. If only for the moment, she'd like to believe it was more. It was then that she realized they were holding hands. She drew their hands upward and smiled back at him. "Looks like a good fit, eh?"

"A very good fit."

# 23

Laura was still at the table when her father came home that evening. It was the earliest she'd seen him home in weeks. He had apparently been drinking, since he staggered and swayed with each step.

"Missssssussss Duffy," he said, falling back against the archway. "Get me . . . get me a whisss . . . key." The housekeeper nodded and hurried away.

Father stumbled into one of the dining room chairs and pointed his right index finger at Laura. "You're the talk of the town, you know." He waggled his finger and smirked. "I think folks . . . folks are surprised that I have a daughter. Even more . . . sus . . . shurprised that she's . . . so . . . so beautiful. I've had all sorts of offers for you . . . your hand."

"Goodness, I hope you didn't take them up on it. I'm not of a mind to marry anytime soon."

"You're gettin' married!" He pounded his fist on the table, making the dishes dance. "I told you."

"Father, you're drunk. I think it's best we discuss this another time."

For some reason, that seemed to sober him a bit. "You're already going to marry Wilson Porter."

TRACIE PETERSON

Mrs. Duffy appeared with the glass and a decanter of whiskey. She poured the drink and brought it to Laura's father. "Here you are, sir."

He grabbed the glass, sloshing amber liquid on the tablecloth. "I'm making all the arrangements."

Laura waited until Etta left the room. She cleared her throat as her father drank. "And what does Will have to say? He's not talked to me about a wedding date. Don't you think a couple should arrange their own wedding?"

"That's not how it's done in upper . . . society. You know that. Most of your friends were engaged even before . . . coming to that . . . fancy finishing college of yours."

"That college offered a much more detailed education than merely finishing young ladies to marry. I believe I could match most of the men in this town in any political conversation or discussion about the sciences or humanities."

"You don't usually boast," he replied and took another drink. He glanced at the food left on Laura's plate. "What is that?"

"It's a little of this and that. Mrs. Murphy was baking bread and other things this afternoon, and I told her I'd just eat whatever we had left over from other meals. I figured since you had no plans to join me for supper, we didn't need to have her making anything new."

He frowned. "We aren't poor. We have money! That should have been thrown out."

"Oh, Father, you needn't worry about anyone finding out. I won't say a word." Laura found his drunken state appalling.

His frown deepened. "I know . . . know this is all a joke to you." He waved the mostly empty glass. "You've never suffered from a lack of money like I have . . . like your mother did."

265

"I wasn't trying to offend you, Father." She could hear the anger in his tone.

"I don't think you appreciate all that I've done for you." He finished his drink and got up to pour himself another. Mrs. Duffy had left the decanter on the sideboard, so Laura's father staggered over and brought it back to the table. "You don't know what I've had to do in order to see you be so . . . so comfortable."

"I didn't ask you to do it. I would have much rather stayed poor if it meant we could be together. It wasn't easy to lose you and Mother."

He poured the whiskey and swayed. Laura held her breath, wondering if he'd crash to the floor. She felt a huge sense of relief when he finally sank onto the chair.

"I never wanted children," he said, staring at the glass.

Laura felt as if he'd slapped her. She bit her lip to keep from commenting as he continued.

"Your mother . . . wanted children. I just wanted her." He shook his head. "I knew I'd be no good at being a father. I didn't want the responsibility." He met her gaze. "That offends you, doesn't it? Insults your sense . . . sense of well-being . . . your love for me."

"At least you're being honest." Laura fought back tears. "I'll start immediately to find a place of my own. I don't need to impose myself upon you any longer. I'm quite capable."

"You aren't going anywhere." He slammed the glass down, and it broke. Shards of glass splayed out on the once-beautiful tablecloth.

Father frowned and studied the mess for a moment before looking up and shaking his head. "You've benefited from me all these years, and now you're going to benefit me. I will arrange your . . . marriage. Your Mr. Porter knows the new governor. Knows him quite well." He gave a hollow laugh. "With any luck at all, we can kill two birds with one stone."

"What are you saying?" Laura wondered if he might share his plans with her since he was clearly freer with his thoughts in his current state. If he would just tell her, she could in turn share the information with Will and Edward.

"What are your plans, Father?"

He got to his feet and looked at her as though she were the one responsible for the mess he'd made. "It doesn't matter. . . . You don't matter."

She felt the breath catch in the back of her throat and prayed for strength as he left the room.

After that evening with her father, Laura had given a lot of thought as to what she should do. She had a small savings, but nothing all that great. It wasn't like she could set up housekeeping for herself. Not unless she was able to get a job, but employment for women was very limited. Besides, her father had made it clear that he wouldn't allow her to leave.

Her heart had been completely shattered by their conversation, and yet her father had not tried to speak to her and sent no note of apology. She wondered if he'd been too drunk to remember what he'd said. He hadn't been at breakfast since that night, and so they'd shared no meals at all. They did encounter each other once several days later. It had been late, and Laura was getting ready to go upstairs for the night. Father looked her way but said nothing. Offered no apologies. Perhaps he truly didn't remember anything at all.

At church, she had quickly told Will what transpired. He offered her comfort and sympathy, but before she could ask him about the plans for marrying, they were interrupted, and then she had to leave for home.

Laura supposed it wasn't all that important. After all, he had told her that he was pretending to want to work for her father and pretending to be on the list of men to escort the governor. It really was all right that he was also pretending to want to marry her. Even still, she worried incessantly that he would get caught trying to find evidence against her father. She no longer trusted her father to be fair or in the least way kind.

Will had asked if she'd join him for supper on Tuesday, and that was what she was now preparing to do. She had gotten up early and planned to tell her father about it, but he hadn't been around long enough for her to share the news. In fact, when he saw that she was awake, he rose and headed for the door. She supposed it was possible that he was embarrassed by what had happened, perhaps even sorry for what he'd said. Then again, maybe now that the truth had been told, he no longer had to make a pretense of loving her.

"Don't let the things he said hurt you," Etta told her as she helped Laura into her gown. "It was the alcohol talking."

"They say alcohol forces a man to speak the truth."

Etta shook her head. "Men often lie and boast when they're well into their cups. He was angry at something else, and that anger made him cruel."

"Anger from the past has kept him cruel in life. I know that now." Laura waited as Etta did up the buttons. "Sadly, I can hardly bear the sight of him. I hope things get settled soon." She looked into the cheval mirror and frowned. "Yet settling them will probably see him hanged. How can I live with that?"

"None of it is your fault, Laura. Besides, Will loves you. I'm sure of that. Just as I'm sure you love him."

"I do. But I fear it as much as I rejoice over it. There's so much wrong."

"But not between you and Will." Etta turned Laura to face her. It was totally out of character for the older woman but seemed quite motherly. "You are a good woman of God, Laura Evans. Do not let the devil whisper lies in your ears." They heard the knocker on the front door downstairs. "That will be Will," Etta said, dropping her arms. "Now, calm your heart, and go have a wonderful evening and tell that young man how much you love him."

Will greeted her warmly and came to offer his hand as Laura walked down the last few steps.

"You look beautiful." Admiration filled his expression.

Laura had dressed carefully in one of her finer dinner gowns. The cream-and-emerald dress complemented her auburn hair and pale complexion.

"Thank you for saying so." She took up her wrap, and Will helped her drape it on her shoulders.

Etta Duffy stood to the side of the door. "Laura, I will most likely be gone when you get back," she explained. "So just let me say good night to you both."

Laura nodded. "You should just go now. I don't want you to be here in case Mr. Snyder shows up sneaking around. Tell Mrs. Murphy I said she could also leave. Father won't be back anytime soon. I heard him tell Mr. Grayson not to pick him up from the club until nine."

"Thank you," Etta said. "I hope you have a wonderful time together."

Laura glanced at Will, determined to be joyful. "We usually do. It's something I've come to count on."

Will took hold of her arm once they were outside. "Are you all right?"

"It's been hard," she admitted. "I've hardly seen Father."

"A couple of the clerks at the store were commenting on the change in his demeanor. I think the new developments have made him feel threatened." Will drew her closer to his side.

"Not receiving the appointment for governor was an irritation to him to be sure," Laura said, remembering things her father had said. "I feel certain that he thinks he can use you to get rid of the man. I don't know what he has planned, but from what he said when he was drunk, I fear it won't bode well for either of you. Will, I think he means to get us married so that I will inherit your fortune when he kills you."

"You're probably right, but try not to fret. We have a plan in place. We've wired Governor Campbell as well as the president himself. They're working with us to get this resolved."

"But Father has so many men working for him, and we don't even know who they are."

He smiled down at her. "Don't worry. Edward and I have already considered that. We're not going to let him get the best of me. Have no fear."

"Father is cunning, and he doesn't care who he hurts as long as he gets his way." Laura's voice broke, and she fought for control. "It would devastate me if something happened to you."

He slowed their walk, then stopped altogether. "I don't want anything to happen to you either. I wish you could stay with the Vogels for your safety, but we can't raise your father's suspicions."

"I don't think he'll hurt me, Will. He has plans for how I can repay him. Until that is done, he'll leave me alone."

"I pray so. I pray for you constantly. You've become the

most important person in the world to me." He drew her hand to his lips and kissed her fingers.

Laura was awash in emotion. "After my first encounter with love and deception in Paris, I never thought I would want to fall in love again. I prayed for years, asking God to guard my heart and keep me from feeling those things again. But now . . ."

"Now you're feeling them again?" he asked.

"Yes."

"And you're glad it's that way?"

Laura was amazed that he so easily read her heart. She gave a nod. "I am. It's not the same at all. Before, I was a child, and my thoughts were very immature. I don't think I understood anything about truly loving someone."

"So did you give any consideration to what I asked before?"

She frowned. "What was that?"

"I wondered how you might feel about living on a reservation. I've scarcely had a chance to tell anyone, but Mr. Blevins said if I still wanted to go and preach on a reservation, the job was mine. I'd have other responsibilities as well. Oh, and he did say that it was fine for me to bring a wife. Given your nursing skills and education, you would be a valuable addition for the government, and a precious and vital one for me. I don't know that I could face each day without you by my side."

"Is this your way of proposing marriage to me?" Laura asked, her heart racing at the very thought.

He chuckled and kissed her hand again. "I suppose it is. I love you, Laura."

She pulled away, shaking her head. "But my father may have killed your mother and sister, or at least have been responsible for it. How can there be a future for us with that between us?"

"It's not between us. I've considered that question, and the answer is simple. You had nothing to do with it. If your father is guilty of the deed, then he and his men bear the responsibility. I will never blame you for what happened, nor hold it against you.

"I've lost a lot this year, and it did cause me to guard my heart as well. Why let myself get hurt again? Why risk loving someone? But you know, life is a risk. Every day presents new challenges and heartache. But it also allows for happiness and good gifts. And no matter which come our way, God is there to help us through. I'd like it very much if you were there too."

"I do love you, Will Porter. But . . . I'm worried about this entire matter. My father is not easily cast aside. He has his plans, and the men to make those plans come together. If he wants you dead, I fear you will be. I can't bear the thought of you risking your life this way."

"Life will be full of risks, Laura. We have no way of knowing what will happen tomorrow, but God admonishes us to not be afraid—to seek His kingdom, His righteousness." He pulled her close and gave her a light kiss. "I'm willing to take whatever risk allows us to be together for the rest of our lives. Are you willing to take it too?"

She had thought she would say yes immediately should Will truly propose, but now she hesitated. "Let me pray about it," she said, hating the puzzled look on his face. "I want to say yes, you know that. At least I think you do."

"I do, that's why you should say yes." Will put his arms around her again. "I'm afraid we may get talked about. It seems I'm always embracing you in the middle of the street."

She shook her head. "I don't care. I'm not worried about my reputation, although I do worry about yours. You're a preacher. You must live above reproach, and this isn't exactly the way to do it."

"Speaking of which, I'm to leave for Fort Bridger on the first of June. I love you, Laura, and I want you to be my wife. I want us to have a future together and to share the Gospel with the Indians. Do you feel that you might be called to this as well?"

Laura knew she would cherish a life sharing God's Word with the native people. The very idea had appealed to her since she first heard Will speak of it. It didn't frighten her to imagine living with Indians, at least not like the last few days of living with her father did. She supposed there would be a great deal of adjustment, and daily life would certainly be harder.

"As I said, I will pray about it. I think I know the answer, but I want to make sure."

Will nodded. "I respect that and agree. I will pray too."

"So we'll set it in place. I'll have Will and Laura marry on the twentieth of April," Granite said, looking at the calendar. "The committee intends for Will to leave for Omaha on the twenty-fifth. I'll make sure that he puts all his affairs in legal order before he leaves by calling him to a meeting with my lawyer. I'll explain that I am setting things up so that he and Laura will inherit all my money should anything happen to me. I'll have a new will written out that shows all the transfers of ownership upon my death.

"Will can see for himself how much I believe in him, and when I mention casually that he should put his affairs in order as well, leaving everything to Laura, then we will be ready for him to go."

Granite sat back and picked up his whiskey and fixed his right-hand man with a stern look. "I want you to go with whichever men you choose. We can't afford any mistakes on this job. You'll leave for Omaha the week before to scout things out and make the final decision about how to kill them both. Either poison in the governor's food or a shot in the head. Whichever you choose is fine, just make sure Wilson Porter gets the blame and is killed in the process."

Gus nodded. "It won't be hard to manage."

It was glorious to imagine resolving everything in one fell swoop. Laura would inherit a vast fortune from her dead husband, and the governorship would come to Granite as President Grant's number two choice. His poor widowed daughter, in time, would then be married off to another rich and powerful man, and who knew what might happen. Perhaps the presidency could come even sooner than Granite had hoped.

"Everything I've worked for is about to come together."

Will stepped inside the city marshal's office. Edward had sent for him, saying it was of the utmost importance. Thankfully, it was before he was due to report to Granite.

The marshal, sheriff, and Edward Vogel stood just a few feet away, interrogating someone. Edward waved him toward the group, then turned back to the man sitting in front of them. "So you're willing to testify, to tell everything you know?"

The man pulled at the brim of his hat. "That's what I signed on for. I haven't put in all this time to watch a man like

Granite Evans go free. Up until this last stagecoach robbery, it had been possible to keep people from being killed. That time one of the new men got spooked. He was one of ours, but he'd been through too much in the war, and something just broke inside him. Once he started firing, that was it. The men who weren't a part of my group started firing as well, and then everyone was dead." The man looked up at Will. "I sure did what I could to keep it from happening."

Will's eyes widened as he caught sight of the man's face. "So you knew about Evans and the things he was doing?"

"We did, and the president intends to see him prosecuted. We were sent to get in close—earn his trust and then expose him for the criminal he was. I'm truly sorry I couldn't save your ma and sister."

"Thank you. I'm confident you did what you could. I wish we'd known the government already had a fix on Granite Evans," Will replied. "It would have been nice to know someone in power is on to him."

"President Grant has known about his double-dealings since the war, but Evans always managed to slip out of the grasp of the law. He even used an alias at times. We could never get anyone close enough to take direct orders from him. Until now. He's ordered the death of the governor, and I have all the details needed to see Evans put behind bars for the rest of his life."

Edward gave the man a smile. "Well, he wasn't counting on someone like you, Gus Snyder."

Gus gave an uncharacteristic grin. "Nor the Pinkertons."

Will looked at the others. "So how does this alter the plan we've made?"

Getting to his feet, Gus straightened. "I was just about to fill them in on how I think this should move forward."

# 24

**Y**ou ready for this?" Edward asked Will as they headed up the walkway to the Evans house.

"I am. I told Laura to go shopping with Mrs. Duffy and get the rest of the staff out of the house. I don't want anyone at risk when you fellas arrest Evans."

"Good idea. And I like that we waited for him to call the meeting with his lawyer. Now there will be no suspicion when I show up as your witness."

"Good morning, Wilson," Granite said, opening the door before they could even knock. "I was watching for you. My lawyer has already arrived and is waiting for us in my office." He looked at Edward. "I know you, don't I?"

"I'm Edward Vogel, a good friend of Will's. You've seen me on many occasions," Edward said, offering his hand.

Granite shook it and gave a nod before looking to Will for an explanation.

"Edward is going to be my witness. You said you'd had the lawyer draw up a standard will for me, leaving everything to Laura."

"Yes, that's right. I'm glad you thought of bringing a witness. I asked Grayson to stand with me. Come to my office."

They followed him into the house and down the hall. Inside his office, Will noted Mr. Grayson standing by the bookcase while the lawyer sat behind Granite's desk. It seemed odd that Granite Evans would have allowed the man that position of authority.

"Gentlemen," the man said, getting to his feet.

"This is my lawyer, Herbert Damarus," Granite said. "Herbert, this is my future son-in-law, Wilson Porter, and his witness."

"Glad to meet you both," Damarus said, reclaiming his chair. "Let's get right to work. Mr. Evans has arranged a new testament for the distribution of his properties upon his death. He is leaving the entirety of his estate to his daughter, Laura Elizabeth Evans."

Will smiled. "I didn't know her middle name was Elizabeth."

The lawyer frowned. "Hmm, yes. Well, it's written here on the document."

"It's of no consequence at the moment," Granite interrupted. "Please continue."

"Mr. Evans has reviewed the will and agrees to the contents herein and will now sign the document before these witnesses." The lawyer presented Granite with a pen and turned the paper to face him.

Granite signed the copies and turned with a smile to Will. "Now it's your turn."

Will stepped up, knowing what was expected of him. The lawyer handed him a single piece of paper to read over. It was a very simple document stating that upon his death, all of Will's earthly goods would go to Laura Elizabeth Evans.

He took up the pen and signed it quite willingly. No matter what, he wanted Laura taken care of.

"And sign this copy as well. One will be kept in your possession and one in mine."

Will nodded and signed the additional page. He would take care of getting his own lawyer to manage it later.

"Now we will have the witnesses sign," the lawyer instructed.

Once the signing was complete, Granite looked more than a little satisfied with the way things were going. He motioned Grayson to leave. The lawyer handed Will his copy of the will and then left Granite's on the desk.

Evans ushered out the lawyer while Will folded the signed paper and put it in his pocket. He glanced over at Edward as the grandfather clock in the hall chimed the top of the hour.

Granite returned to the office all smiles. He went to his liquor cabinet and drew out three glasses. "I know it's early, but we need to drink a toast."

"I think we can forgo that," Edward said.

There was a sound of someone in the hallway outside the door. Will hoped it was the Pinkertons as planned.

Granite gave it no notice. "It's a celebration, Mr. Vogel. I'm welcoming Will into our family. Surely you can take a drink in support of such a wonderful occasion."

"I'm afraid not, Mr. Evans. You see, I'm on the job, and you're under arrest."

Evans turned to look at Edward. "I don't know what you're playing at, but it's an inappropriate joke."

"I'm afraid it's no joke, Mr. Evans. You're under arrest for a long list of offenses, including a plot to assassinate Governor John A. Campbell."

Just then, Gus and Bigs entered the room. Granite lost the

look of concern. He turned back to the decanter of whiskey. "Well, I'm afraid that my offenses will have to wait. You see, my men here won't allow you to drag me off to jail."

"He's right, you know," Gus said, looking at Evans.

Granite took his glass and started to walk back to his desk. "Stop," Edward demanded. "Don't move."

The order froze Granite temporarily. Will watched the situation play out as he stepped back against the bookcase. He had promised Edward and Gus that he'd get himself out of the way.

Granite motioned to his men. "Gus, Bigs, take this man out of here."

"I'm afraid I can't do that," Gus replied.

"You work for me. You'll do what I say," Evans commanded in a growl. He slammed his glass down on the desk. It shattered, spilling whiskey everywhere.

Gus stepped forward. "No, sir, I only pretended to work for you. Same with Bigs here. We're actually employed by the Pinkerton Agency. We were sent to get the goods on you and see you arrested. President Grant has long had his eye on you, given your traitorous offenses against the government as well as numerous individuals."

Granite's mouth dropped open in stunned silence. He slowly shook his head, then fixed Will with a glaring look. "Are you in on this as well?"

"I'm not a lawman, if that's what you mean," Will replied. "But when I found out you arranged the stagecoach attack and were responsible for my mother and sister being killed, I asked to be around for your arrest."

Evans looked back at Gus and Bigs. "And you . . . you're both Pinkertons? How in the world did I fail to know that?" He began to pace. "Wait a minute. You've both done things for me that were illegal. You're just as guilty as I am. You've killed for me."

"Never have," Gus said. "We let you think we did. Those other stage and freight attacks we made were arranged with the people involved. As you know, by your own instruction, we were careful not to kill unless absolutely necessary. It was never necessary."

Evans stopped and pointed a finger. "But your men killed. You ordered it done. Your cousins were involved."

Gus chuckled. "My Pinkerton 'cousins.' There is a team of Pinkertons working with me, and while I call them cousins, we're not related. We are like a brotherhood, however. And loyal to the end. Bigs and I served in the war. He saved my life, and I saved his. You don't turn on a fellow when that's in your history."

Granite stood in silence. Will could see that he knew he'd been defeated. His gaze darted around the room as he shoved his hands into the pockets of his coat.

"I've seen trapped animals with the same look on their faces as you have now," Gus said, moving toward him. "You're trying to figure out how to get out of this fix, but you might as well give up. You're gonna stand trial for a great many wrongs."

Without warning, Granite pulled a small revolver from his pocket. A single shot rang out as Evans leveled his gun at the closest man, who just so happened to be Edward.

Granite stood for a moment, then clutched his chest where a crimson stain was spreading on his gray wool suit. He hadn't even been able to get a shot off. Snyder was much too fast for him.

"I-I . . . it was . . . mine."

Gus kept his gun trained on Evans as Edward went forward to take the man's revolver. When he did so, Granite Evans sank to the floor.

"It was mine," Evans murmured again and fell over. He stared up at the ceiling. "God owed it to me. It was all . . . mine."

"I'll carry him over to the hospital," Bigs said.

"No need," Gus replied. "He's gone."

Granite's eyes were still open, but there was no life in them. Will thought of Laura and wondered how she would take the news. She had so wanted a close relationship with her father, and now that was impossible.

Will knew he had to find her and tell her what had happened. "I'm going to get Laura." No one said a word to stop him.

He tried to remember if Laura had mentioned where she and Mrs. Duffy planned to go, but nothing came to mind. He went to a couple of the stores he'd seen Laura go to, but she wasn't there. Then it dawned on him that perhaps she'd gone to Mrs. Duffy's house. Laura had told him roughly where the place was, and since she'd driven them in her carriage, Will figured he'd be able to find her. It took some doing, but after about thirty minutes he found the place.

Mrs. Duffy came to the door. "Is it over?" she asked.

"In more ways than one," Will replied in a hushed voice. "I need to see Laura."

She pulled back quickly. "She's right here."

He came in and immediately spotted Laura. She had been sitting in a rocking chair and got to her feet. They locked gazes, and she bit her lower lip. Tears filled her eyes. She seemed to know without him saying a word that things had not gone well.

"He's . . . dead?" she asked.

Will nodded. "Yes. He pulled a gun on Edward, and Gus had to shoot him."

She sat back down. "I feared that would be the outcome."

Will came and knelt beside her. "I know. Your father wasn't the kind of man to be hauled off to jail. I'm so sorry, Laura. I know what he meant to you and how much you loved him."

"The man I loved . . . didn't exist." She looked at Will. "I didn't even know Granite Evans."

Will pulled her into his arms, and she began to weep.

# 25

Laura closed the door to her father's office and refused to set foot inside. She told Will that if any of the law officials needed entry there or elsewhere in the house, they were welcome, but she'd rather he handle their visits. She couldn't bear to see where her father had died even though Etta had cleaned up the blood. Will promised her that either he or Edward would take care of everything.

It seemed like a bad dream to know that just a few months ago, Father had been her whole world. He had welcomed her home and seemed happy to have her close by. Now Laura realized it had all been lies. He hadn't loved her. Hadn't wanted her.

Now she understood why he truly sent her to boarding school and visited so seldom. At least he had loved her mother. Of that, there was no question. Laura tried to find comfort in that, but her pain refused to abate. Why couldn't he have loved them both? After all, Laura was a part of her mother and the love they shared.

On Sunday, Will showed up to drive Laura to church.

Curtis brought the carriage around while Will greeted her at the door.

"I really don't want to go. Father was just killed yesterday. I'm sure folks are talking about it and will have so many questions."

"Probably, but I'll keep them away and protect you. That's the job I have taken on—the one I want for the rest of my life." He touched her cheek gently. "And you have friends there who love you. They'll want to help you carry this burden."

At church, they learned that Melody and Marybeth had both gone into labor. Faith Cooper delivered this news, as Granny Taylor was helping to attend Melody and Marybeth. The pastor led the congregation in prayers for both women, then gave a sermon on the rich man and Lazarus from the sixteenth chapter of Luke. By the time services ended, Laura was more than ready to return home. She didn't want to answer questions about what had happened to her father, and she didn't want to deal with the curious looks she got from those who didn't know her well.

Will stayed at her side the entire time, shooing people away when they approached with questions. Faith Cooper came and embraced Laura. She had no questions, just words of love, and it touched Laura so much to know she cared.

"If you need me, you have only to send word. I'll come and just sit with you if you'd like. I've hired a woman to help me at the boardinghouse, and she's so capable I could leave her to manage the entire thing for a time."

"Thank you, Faith. You are so kind, and I have no words for how much that means to me." Laura felt her eyes dampen and did her best to fight back the tears.

"I know Granny feels the same way, although she's a bit

busy at the moment." Faith smiled. "I can just see her running back and forth from each house to make sure those girls are well cared for."

"Do you suppose I could be of any help to them?" Laura was surprised by her own question but pressed on. It was the right thing to do. "I have had some nursing training, and at college we had classes in midwifery."

"You know, I would imagine you could be of service. Why don't you go home and change, then make your way over? Seems to me having a trained nurse would be most useful."

Laura nodded and looked to Will. "Let's go, so I can help."

He smiled. "Of course."

Will had her back at the house in a matter of minutes. They hurried inside, and Laura was quick to take off her gloves and hat and leave them by the door.

"I'll be down in just a minute."

She hiked her skirt and raced up the steps in a most unladylike fashion, wondering if she'd shocked Will with her actions. She didn't think that would even be possible. Will seemed to know her better than she did herself.

Etta appeared just as Laura was undoing the buttons of her jacket. Laura motioned her to come help. "I'm going to see if I can help at the Vogels' or Deckers'. Both women are in labor."

"How wonderful." Etta helped her out of the jacket. "I'd be happy to come too, if you think I'd be needed."

"Yes, that would be good. I have no idea if they have anyone besides Granny Taylor. I need my old black skirt and the dark green calico blouse."

Etta had her dressed in a flash. Laura hurried back down the main stairs while Etta raced down the back staircase to collect supplies.

"We need to wait for Etta," Laura told Will. "She's going along to see if she can help as well."

❧

They found Granny upstairs at the Vogel residence. "Granny, we're here to help," Laura announced. "Etta and I both have midwife experience."

"Praise God! Jed's been driving me back and forth to see to Melody and Marybeth, but Edward doesn't fare as well as Charlie. When I leave Marybeth, he just about wears a hole in the rug by their bed. Poor Marybeth can hardly rest for his questions about whether she's all right. If you'd stay here, Laura, I'll take Etta and go check on Melody," the older woman suggested. "That way both women will have a woman with them who knows what to do."

"I'd be happy to do that," Laura replied, and Etta nodded her approval.

Laura looked at Edward, who seemed fit to be tied. "Will can even keep Edward occupied." She smiled at Will. "Maybe you two could play a game of checkers or something."

"Granny, are you sure she's doing all right?" Edward asked, not seeming to hear the mention of checkers.

"She's doing very well. Better than many women I've tended," Granny replied, giving Edward a pat on the shoulder. "Now, you go keep Will company, and, Laura, come with me."

They went to the bedroom where Marybeth was laboring. "She's still got a ways to go. Melody is progressing a little faster, and I need to get back to her," Granny told Laura. She went to check Marybeth and show Laura the progress.

"I know exactly what to do. I helped attend a delivery when I was back at the college."

Granny nodded and looked to Marybeth. "How are the pains?"

"Persistent. How's Edward doing?"

"As expected. He's terrified, and I've not been able to calm him much."

"Poor man," Marybeth said, shaking her head. "I know this is his worst nightmare, whereas it's my happiest dream. I'm glad you suggested we send Carrie to play with the neighbors. Mrs. Greeley said she'd keep Carrie all night if need be. I know Carrie won't mind that. They have a new litter of puppies to play with."

Laura admired the woman for her concern about everyone else, even while enduring labor. She hoped one day the same could be said of her if she had a child.

"I'm going to go see Melody, but Laura is going to stay with you. She's fully trained and probably better at this than I am," Granny said. "She knows all the new and modern ways of dealing with childbirth."

Laura moved closer to the head of the bed while Etta stayed by the door. "I think your old tried-and-true methods are perfect, Granny."

The older woman covered Marybeth and nodded. "Well, they've served me well in over fifty deliveries through all these years. Now, you keep doing what you're supposed to, Marybeth, and I'll get back as soon as possible. Try to rest as much as you can in between contractions."

"I will, Granny. Why don't you send Edward in to see me? I want to reassure him as best I can."

"I'll do that." Granny took up her bag and headed out the door. Etta followed after her.

It was only a matter of seconds before Edward was in the open doorway. "Are you all right?"

"I'm doing fine, my love. Please try not to fret so much. I know you're worried, but my delivery is nothing like Janey's, and everything is going very well."

Edward moved to the bedside and took hold of her hand. "I can't help my fears. I keep praying and asking the Lord to help me through, but I prayed when it was Janey in the bed too."

Marybeth smiled. "All we can do is trust that God has this, Edward. Worrying won't change a thing. Just know that I love you and am happier than I've ever been. I wouldn't change a single thing."

His worried expression softened. "I know. I love you too. I just don't think I could bear losing you."

"You aren't going to lose me." She grimaced and let go of his hand to grab her swollen abdomen. "Contraction."

Edward frowned and looked to Laura. Laura smiled. "Everything is fine. Why don't you go back out and keep Will company? He knows very little about these things and probably wonders what's happening. We'll be just fine here."

"Go on," Marybeth managed to say between clenched teeth.

Edward headed for the door. He paused only a moment to give her one more glance. "I'll be here if you need me."

Laura went to the door. "She'll be just fine. Try to rest. Once this baby gets here, you're both going to be busy."

Edward left, and Laura returned to Marybeth, who was still breathing heavily. "When I helped with one of the deliveries, the mother said the Lord's Prayer with each contraction. She said it helped with the pain. I don't know if it really does, but I figure anything is worth trying."

Perspiration beaded on Marybeth's forehead, and Laura took up a wet cloth to wipe it away.

"I was . . . with . . . my stepmother . . . when she had Carrie." Marybeth writhed as if trying to escape the pain.

"I remember you telling me that Carrie was actually your little sister but had only ever known you as mother."

"Yes . . . my stepmother died shortly . . . after her . . . birth." A moan escaped her lips. "I'm trying so hard . . . to be . . . quiet. Edward . . ."

"That's all right, Marybeth. I understand. I know he's very worried."

Marybeth met Laura's gaze and nodded. From her expression, Laura could tell the pain was worse than ever.

"Something is happening," Marybeth said. "I feel like I must push."

"Let me check and see." Laura moved the covers away. The baby had indeed progressed much quicker than she or Granny had expected. "Yes, you are very close to delivering. Did Granny explain what we're going to do?"

"Yes, she told me a great deal." Another moan rose up, and Marybeth clasped her hands over her mouth.

"It's all right. You moan or cry out if need be. Edward will be just fine."

Thirty minutes later, no one was hearing anything but the cries of a healthy baby boy. Laura worked quickly to clear his mouth and nose before plopping him in Marybeth's arms. She tied off the umbilical cord near the boy's belly and put another tight tie a few inches from that before taking scissors to cut the cord.

With the baby free, Laura brought a towel to wrap him and took him to where Granny had pitchers of water waiting and a basin for washing the infant. Laura marveled at the way the water seemed to calm the child. He looked up at her with wide blue eyes.

Behind her, someone knocked on the door. No doubt it was Edward. "Give us a few minutes, and you can come in," she called.

She hurried to finish the baby's bath, then wrapped him up without bothering to dress him.

"You've a fine little son," she told Marybeth. "You hold him while I get you finished up. I have a feeling Edward isn't going to wait for long."

Marybeth laughed and cried at the same time. "No. I think he's more than ready to greet his boy."

With everything done for Marybeth that could be done, Laura asked Will to take her to Melody and Charlie's house. They arrived to the sound of a baby's cries, and Laura realized she was too late to help with this infant's delivery.

They were ushered inside by Charlie, who looked rather pale and uncertain. "I don't know what the baby is, but the lungs sound good."

Laura laughed. "We've just come from Edward and Marybeth's, where I helped her deliver a fine son."

"A boy for Edward?" Charlie's mouth broke into a huge grin. "Well, isn't that grand?"

Laura moved past Charlie. "I'll see if I can be of help with the babe. Where are they?"

"Upstairs and to the right," Charlie instructed.

Laura followed the sound of Granny's voice as she went on and on about the size of the baby compared to Melody's petite frame.

"Why, he's half grown," Granny said as Laura entered the room.

"Another boy, Granny?" Laura asked, looking to where Etta was gathering up towels.

Granny looked surprised to see her. "Another?"

Laura couldn't help but chuckle again. It was such a happy day. "Yes, Marybeth just delivered a healthy baby boy. They're both resting well." She moved closer and gazed down at the tiny woman holding her firstborn.

Melody looked up in wonder. "I told Marybeth we were having boys."

"Yes, you did," Granny agreed. "And you were obviously right. But none of us was expecting your baby to be this size. He must be at least ten pounds."

"I'm guessing maybe even eleven or twelve." Laura gently touched his cheek. "It is a wonder, what with you being so tiny."

Granny nodded. "I was worried for a moment, but you know Melody. That girl is determined to do whatever she puts her mind to."

Melody was so lost in examining her son that she didn't even seem to hear. Granny nudged Laura. "I'm gonna have to put in a few stitches. Have you had experience with that?"

"No, but I'm happy to learn."

Will brought Etta home, then drove Laura back to the house. They stood at the front door, still in awe of all that had happened that evening.

"Thank you for helping us. I wish I could invite you in, but it's just me now. Everyone has gone home except Curtis. He lives in the carriage house, of course."

"I don't like you being all alone."

"I hadn't realized it until just now. Last night Etta stayed, and I was still so overwhelmed with all that had happened I didn't even think of it. It's hard to believe my father is dead."

"I know." Will touched her cheek. "It'll be hard for a long time. At least it's been that way for me."

"I suppose I could ask Rosey to stay here at night." Laura found it impossible to think clearly with him rubbing his thumb along her jawline.

"That would be good for at least a few days," he said, taking Laura into his arms. "Look, I know so much has happened, but I was hoping you might have an answer to my proposal."

"I think you already know the answer."

"I think we should marry right away . . . if that's all right with you."

She wrapped her arms around his neck. "Yes. Yes, I will marry you right away and go to the reservation and help you in whatever way I can. I was feeling sorry for myself that my father never loved me, but although he never cared, God has always been there and has always provided the love I longed for. Now He's given me you as well. I don't want to think about the past and what I didn't have. Instead, I want to focus on the here and now and all that God has given to bless me."

"I'm so glad to hear you say that. I feel the same way. In fact, I told myself the same thing. I don't want to think about the past and the things I've lost. I just want to keep my attention on what God has for me right now, and that's you." He bent down until their lips were just inches apart. "May I kiss you?"

Laura nodded, and Will pressed his lips to hers.

# Epilogue

On April thirtieth, Laura and Will were joined together in holy matrimony. It was a beautiful Friday evening, and since the weather had been so nice, they decided to hold the affair outside in a new park area the city was working to put together. It wasn't all that much to look at, but they had cultivated an area of grass that, due to the warm spring, was already coming in nicely.

Laura's father had been dead less than three weeks, but she had no regret in marrying Will so quickly. Her father had been laid to rest without a funeral. Laura knew he would have been appalled to be so quietly disregarded, but she felt the sooner they were able to forget the man, the better. Will helped her to arrange it all with the undertaker, who sent a brief note when everything was completed.

She only thought of her father once that day, and it was when the pastor asked who was giving the bride in marriage. Laura had forgotten about that part of the ceremony. It had never dawned on her to arrange for that, but Will hadn't forgotten.

To Laura's pleasant surprise, a chorus of voices sounded from behind her. "We do," they said in unison.

She turned to find Granny and Jed Taylor, Faith and Gerald Cooper, Marybeth and Edward and their children, Melody and Charlie Decker and their new babe, and Etta Duffy all standing together. They gave her broad smiles, and Laura couldn't help but giggle. Their love made her happier than she'd ever been.

The ceremony continued, and Laura found herself swept up in the vows she made to Will. She had no idea what their future would hold, but it was sure to never lack adventure.

"Will you promise to love this man, Wilson Allen Porter, for the rest of your life?" their pastor asked.

She smiled. "I didn't know your middle name was Allen," she whispered, then spoke louder. "I will."

Will chuckled, and when it was his turn to pledge his life, he leaned close. "I only recently learned your middle name is Elizabeth." He looked up at the pastor and gave a nod. "I will."

"Then by the powers vested in me, I declare that you are husband and wife. Wilson, you may kiss your bride."

There was no time lost in accomplishing that deed. Will pulled her into his arms and gave her a gentle, but firm kiss that lasted perhaps a few seconds longer than expected. Laura opened her eyes to find him smiling.

"Are you ready to begin our lives together, Mrs. Porter?"

"Quite ready, Mr. Porter."

"It's my turn to kiss the bride," Marybeth Vogel said, coming forward with the others in congratulations. She kissed Laura's cheek, then handed her the baby. "Little Robbie wanted to see his honorary aunt."

Laura looked down at the little one. "Hello, Robbie. How

you have grown." Despite seeing him several times since she'd helped to deliver him, Laura was in awe of how much he'd changed.

"It seems every day he's just a bit different," Marybeth declared. "I had worried he would never grow into a name such as Robert Klaus Vogel, but I believe he's well on his way."

Melody Decker edged in and handed Laura her wrapped bundle. Laura balanced a baby in each arm and laughed. The Decker boy outweighed the Vogel child by at least two pounds.

"Goodness, just look at them both. Except for the size difference, they're like twins."

Like the Vogels, the Deckers had named their son after their fathers. When he began to fuss, his mother admonished him to quiet. "Michael Bertram Decker, you hush now. Your aunty is holding you and loves you very much."

"I thought you named the baby after your father," one of the church ladies said. "But his name was Clancy."

"Yes, but his middle name was Michael," Melody replied. "We preferred it to Clancy and knew Da would approve. He was never all that fond of his name but said that a man could hardly put such things aside."

"Well, I think they are properly and most adequately named," Laura said, turning to Will. "Would you care to hold one of them?"

He waved her off. "No, no. You're doing a wonderful job."

"Are you afraid of holding a baby, Will?" Marybeth asked in a teasing tone. "I think the practice might do you good. You never know when the Lord might bless you with your own."

Will looked a little pale at that, and Laura laughed as she handed the babies back to their mothers. "Come along, husband. It's been a hard day for you. I wouldn't want you fainting dead away at our wedding."

"No, indeed," Granny declared. "You'd never live that one down in all your days."

Will chuckled. "Granny, don't be silly. I have no intention of fainting. I just find the idea of fatherhood a little daunting. After all, I've only just taken on the job of husband."

Laura looped her arm with Will's. "I do hope everyone will pray for us daily. I think we're both going to need as much help as we can get for the months to come. There's still so much to be settled. The government has put a hold on all of my father's assets, so the store and house—even the new house—are all under their jurisdiction, and I have no idea where it will all lead."

"But we have my inheritance, and that gives us plenty to live on as we prepare for our trip west. We're trying to figure out what to pack for the reservation," Will added. "There are all sorts of things we'll need. When Mr. Blevins gets back from Washington, he plans to go over all of it with us, but we're trying to prepare ourselves as best we can before then."

Granny gave each of their hands a squeeze. "You're in the service of the Lord, and when you are seeking His kingdom and righteousness, all the rest will be added unto you. The very best God has to offer."

"The best has already been given, Granny," Will said, looking at Laura with so much love she thought she might well cry.

"The best," she whispered. "The very best."

If you enjoyed
*A Truth Revealed,*
read on for an excerpt from

# *With*
# EACH
# TOMORROW

By TRACIE PETERSON
*and* KIM WOODHOUSE

AVAILABLE NOW
WHEREVER BOOKS
ARE SOLD.

# 1

TUESDAY, MAY 10, 1904—MONTANA

Every last bit of patience Eleanor Briggs once claimed as her own had disappeared about two hundred miles ago. This train trip used it all.

But why? It wasn't like this was any different from any of the last hundred journeys with her father. This was her life.

She flipped through the pages of *Century* magazine, trying to find something that would occupy her mind.

*When* would they arrive at their destination?

Mile after mile of endless prairie had left her feeling rather empty and—dare she say it?—lonely. Thank goodness they had finally reached the mountainous region with its magnificent scenery, but even the views out the windows couldn't change the fact that she was bored. And tired.

Of trains.

Of living out of luggage.

Of the same conversations, articles, and lectures on conservation.

Horrid thoughts really, but as long as no one else heard them, she could be honest. She used to love traveling with her father. His work in assisting his dear friend George Grinnell in seeing to the formation of a new national park in Montana was a worthy cause. Still, there was a restlessness inside her that, at twenty-four years of age, she couldn't quite explain.

Patience was hard to come by, but she couldn't allow others to see her inner turmoil. Especially not her father.

No matter what, she couldn't damage his work or reputation.

So here she sat. On a train. Bored out of her mind.

The train took a steep incline, and it jerked and tilted on the tracks. Oh, she did not like the looks of the curve ahead. Several passengers gasped, and another woman squeaked and gripped the man's arm next to her.

Never in her life had Eleanor been on such a ride. Heavens, if this was how the railroads were built in Montana, perhaps Father and Mr. Grinnell should address that before attempting to bring scads of people out for a national park.

Her heart jumped at the screech of the train's wheels.

The conductor walked through the car, speaking with a calming voice. "We're going over Marias Pass. Don't worry. This is all normal and the train is perfectly safe."

Forcing herself to look down in her lap, she blew out her breath slowly. Normal. Sure. Hadn't her father said that the rail lines *west* of Kalispell were the worst? Over Haskell Pass? With tight curves and bridges the railroad had a headache keeping maintained?

She closed her eyes against the turmoil in her stomach. Haskell Pass was worse. This was Marias Pass. They were fine.

They were fine.

They were fine.

All she had to do was think about something else.

Anything.

The train jerked again, and a small child whimpered and then cried.

Eleanor turned the pages in the magazine and found the article her father had encouraged her to read. It was written by Mr. Grinnell and spoke of the great beauty held by Montana's mountainous regions. He referenced it as the "Crown of the Continent," and given his vast travels all over North America, she supposed he could be trusted as the expert.

The views so far were lovely, even if the journey here might kill them all.

Wincing, she pushed the dreadful thought aside and made herself read the article.

By the time she reached the end, the tracks were straight and level again.

With a sigh, she laid the magazine back in her lap and allowed her gaze to roam the landscape. For years she had listened to her father and George Bird Grinnell speak of Montana and the grandeur of its mountains and the unspoiled wildness of its vast forests. Grinnell had been instrumental in the creation of the Lewis and Clark Forest Reserve. As was his usual approach, he sought Congress to set aside lands in a forest reserve and then went to work convincing them to do more. In the case of Montana, he wanted a great national park to be created. Her father wanted that too.

So did she.

As a conservationist, Stewart Briggs was well known for his belief that the vast, majestic lands of the United States should be preserved for everyone to enjoy. For years, her father had touted the perils of farmers and ranchers owning thousands and thousands of acres of land, especially when it encompassed large areas of land best preserved by the federal government. She'd heard him speak to more than one group about the unjust practice, and the idea made sense to her. Although—she smiled—every once in a while her mind liked to argue the other side. Even though she didn't understand it and hadn't researched it. What would it be like to own a large ranch or farm? What if the land was passed down from generation to generation? Questions flourished. But it was best to agree with her father. He'd done plenty of research over the years.

Of course, he was violently opposed to the Homestead Act of 1862 that gave millions of acres of land to settlers who were willing to improve it. *"Why improve what Nature has perfected?"* was Father's motto.

This also made sense to her.

Still, in their travels through the country she'd seen many family farms. That was a piece of the puzzle she wished to understand. Obviously, they needed food to eat, but did one family need so much? It was not a topic she could bring up with her father.

Grinnell often used Father to raise money for his causes, and the two were determined to see land ownership limited in America.

"Did you see George's article?"

She glanced up to see her father return to his seat from the smoking car.

At least some conversation would pass the time. "I did. I must say he intrigued me with his comment that this area is the Crown of the Continent." She glanced out the window. "It is impressive, but I could compare it to the Colorado Rockies . . . say, Estes Park. Surely that place could also be called a Crown of the Continent. And what about some of the scenery we've seen in photographs of Alaska? Photos never do justice to an area, but it is easy to see that Alaska holds many great views. Perhaps it could also hold the title." Not that she necessarily *wanted* to argue with her father about the same things they'd already discussed at length, but something inside egged her on.

"You are simply in a disagreeable mood. If Grinnell says it's the Crown of the Continent, then I doubt we shall be disappointed. Already the scenery has changed from prairie to mountains."

As if she couldn't see that for hersel—

*Stop it, Eleanor.* She blinked away the disrespectful thought.

Her father took out his pocket watch and frowned. "This thing isn't keeping proper time at all. I just inquired of the porter, and it was completely off." He shook the watch a bit. "Remind me when we're in Kalispell to seek a repair shop."

"I will." Eleanor set aside the magazine and picked up her journal. Just like Father to change the subject and shut down a conversation when he didn't like where it was headed.

Oh my. She *was* in a disagreeable mood.

She dug a pencil out of her pocket and made a note to herself: *Watch repair in Kalispell.*

She put the pencil back and closed the journal. "How much longer for this trip?"

"Not all that far. Four hours at the most. The mountainous terrain will slow us considerably, but hopefully we'll soon be able to glimpse the full glory of Montana."

After days on the train, four hours wasn't all that much. So why did it seem an eternity? She picked up the magazine again but tossed it aside almost instantly. There was nothing in it to hold her attention.

Why was she so . . . restless? Unsatisfied?

Every bit of this feeling was unsettling. She and Father had gotten into a comfortable pattern. Why couldn't she just go on with the way things had been?

She released a sigh.

"I hesitate to mention it"—Father brushed lint off his trousers—"but before we left Chicago, I had a letter from New York."

She turned to him and schooled her features. Father expected her to listen—no matter how mundane the topic. No need to react until he said exactly what the letter was about. Since New York had once been their home state, it was anyone's guess what information the letter might contain.

"It was from the Brewsters."

She tipped her head ever so slightly, keeping her eyes on her lap. The mention of the family threatened to twist her insides. But she willed her heart to slow and kept her mask of indifference. "And how are they?"

"They offered a bit of news. It seems their eldest son, Andrew, is marrying in August. They invited us to attend. A formal invitation will be sent later, but they know how busy I am and wanted to give some warning."

"And do you plan for us to attend?" Every bit of her hoped against hope Father would say no. A long time ago, when she and Andrew were still young, they had been considered a couple. She found him compatible enough, handsome, and even intelligent, but he was also self-focused and rather greedy. She'd put an end to their relationship long before anything official was declared. It didn't seem prudent to attend with such a history.

Still, Eleanor knew the family meant a great deal to her father. If he wanted to go, she would travel with him. Just as she always did.

TRACY PETERSON and KIM WOODHOUSE

"Are *you* of a mind to attend?" He rubbed his bearded chin. "I am not opposed if that is your desire."

"Not at all. I have no interest in his wedding." She smoothed her hands over the cover of her journal. "Seems rather senseless to go all the way back to the East Coast when our summer plans clearly have pointed us west." She had no desire to go anywhere back east after this horrid train ride.

Her father relaxed a bit in his seat. Had he been concerned about her reaction? "I'd rather hoped that would be your conclusion on the matter."

"Would you like for me to send a gift when the time is right?" She picked up her journal.

Her father's expression grew thoughtful. "I suppose that would be a kind gesture. What would be appropriate, Ellie?"

Her chest tightened. Why couldn't he remember she wasn't Ellie any longer? Not for ten years. Mother always called her that . . .

And the nickname died with her.

Over the years, Eleanor insisted Father call her by her full name. But every once in a while, he forgot.

Best not to make an issue of it. She smiled at him. "Knowing them as we do, I might suggest crystal. Waterford, of course."

"That sounds sensible. Pick out a piece and let me know when it's ready. I'll pen a letter to send when the time is right."

Eleanor jotted a note, then glanced at him. "Anything else?"

"Nothing of importance." He settled back and closed his eyes. "Your mother would tell me to use this time for a nap despite the growing beauty outside. I believe I'll heed her advice and try for a bit of rest before we arrive in Kalispell."

Mother.

The band around Eleanor's heart tightened even more. They had mentioned her less and less as the years passed, but for some reason Father had mentioned her more and more since heading out west this trip.

Was Mother on his mind that much? Even after all these years? Perhaps in his older age, he was simply recalling fond memories of her.

Father's soft snores filled the space. Didn't take him long, did it?

Eleanor turned back to the window. Although, instead of Montana, she saw the last few weeks of her mother's life. Heard Mama praying for death to come quickly . . .

Even now, it ripped Eleanor's heart in two.

That had been her first experience with death. It was horrible. How could Mama say that if this was the will of God, they would bear it with grace?

The will of God? For a woman to bear such wretched pain that she could scarcely draw breath? The will of God for a fourteen-year-old child and her father to watch their dearest on earth suffer for weeks on end? Where was *grace* in that?

Mama's words washed over Eleanor until she couldn't bear it. She closed her eyes and squeezed them against the barrage.

*Pray for understanding and peace of mind.*

*God will provide comfort.*

*He's a good and loving Father who watches faithfully over His children.*

*Trust Him. Trust Him. Trust Him . . .*

Rebel tears slipped out from underneath her lashes no matter how much she commanded them to stop.

No.

Eleanor blinked and swiped at her cheeks. No more. She couldn't deal with it.

She frowned and cast a glance at her father. He was still asleep. What would he think of her rambling thoughts?

While Mother was alive, Father had been by her side, at church every time the doors were open. But after her death, he lost himself in his conservation work and the new scientific discoveries of the day, and bit by bit, little was ever mentioned about spiritual matters. That suited Eleanor just fine.

Every once in a while, her mother's teachings drifted through her mind, and a great swell of the faith she'd felt as a child would overwhelm her. But it was easily pushed away.

They traveled so much that their friends and family had no idea if they attended church or not. What did it matter anyway? Most people assumed someone was a Christian if they acted with kindness and bowed their head for the meal-time prayer.

Eleanor propped her chin in her hand, watching trees and mountains swim together in a dizzying palette of grays, browns, and greens. This was what really mattered, wasn't it? Conserving the land. Making sure generations after them could enjoy the splendor and beauty the western frontier had to offer.

There was enough to do without worrying about faith.

Besides, Father's work and writing had garnered him a small measure of notoriety. People didn't seem to care what he believed since he was making the world a better place. As far as she was concerned, the less said about God, the easier it was to ignore His existence.

Plain and simple.

He'd taken away her mother. He deserved no better.

"We'll reach Kalispell in about twenty minutes." The conductor's voice reached the fuzzy edges of Eleanor's brain.

Opening her eyes, she straightened and looked across the way to where her father sat, his gaze fixed out the window. When had she fallen asleep?

"This is amazing country, Ellie."

She shook the haze from her mind, smoothed her traveling suit, patted her hair, and leaned toward the window. Now that the train had slowed, she could make out the complex details of the landscape. Majestic mountains rose in snow-covered glory against a brilliant blue sky. Forests of pines, thick and lush, pointed ever upward across the green valley floor, scaling the mountainsides like Alpine climbers.

"It's most impressive."

"I can see why George wants part of this state set aside as a national park. We shall have a wonderful time on this trip." He clasped his hands together and grinned like a schoolboy. "Already I have a feeling of great consequence. It's almost as if I'm meeting my destiny head on."

Eleanor stared at him, a chill washing over her. Pulling her gaze away, she shifted it to the window. What had Father meant by that? She had no desire for this trip to be one of great consequence. Normalcy and peace were all that she longed for. Putting aside a momentary sense of panic, she drew a deep steadying breath.

"Maybe we should think of settling down this way, Ellie."

Ah. So there it was. *And* another use of her nickname. What was going on with him? "But why here? I've never heard you *once* speak of settling down. You said there was too much work to do." She hated that she sounded accusatory, but at least it was honest. They'd promised to always be honest with each other.

"Yes, but I am fifty-five years old. I won't be able to continue this life indefinitely."

Since when did Stewart Briggs talk of retiring from his conservationist work? Why would he start now? He was still young and able-bodied. Fifty-five wasn't all that old. She'd seen him climb mountains and raft rivers with the strength of a man half his age.

"We no longer call New York City home, and I truly have no desire to return there. The only thing we left behind was your mother's grave, and certainly she would admonish us to disregard that matter. As much as I loved her with my whole heart, I know that she never wanted us to spend our days at the cemetery mourning her passing."

Panic rose further in her chest. She wasn't attached to Mother's grave, and what Father said was true. Still, the direction of this conversation was unnerving. "No. Indeed not. Mother was clear about that."

"It seems we should probably give some thought to where we might like to settle." He leaned back in his seat. "You're at the age where you should take a husband, not continue traipsing around behind your father."

*What?* Eleanor turned and faced him, placing her hand on his sleeve. "Where is this coming from?" She shook her head. "You've never been one to push me to marry."

Father's face tightened and he refused to meet her gaze. "I suppose it was that news about young Andrew. Sometimes I think about your sacrifice to work at my side and wonder if it was the wisest choice I might have made to allow it."

Eleanor stiffened. "Have I disappointed you? Have I failed in assisting you?"

"Of course not." As the train slowed, Father leaned closer and covered her hand with his, giving it a pat. "My thoughts were only that I may have kept you from the life you should have had. You might have married and had children by now. Most of your friends have done so."

That last sentence sliced through her middle like a knife. "I do not regret my choice to work at your side, Father. I hope you don't regret it either." She slipped her hand from his grasp and lifted her chin, giving him a pointed look. If ever there was a time to change the subject, it was now.

He didn't take the hint. "I don't. I just think perhaps it's time for an . . . adjustment. For now, however, let us explore the area around us and see what George has to say about his strides toward getting the president's ear on this matter. President Roosevelt is a tremendous supporter of preserving the lands. It would be the perfect end to my career if I should share in the creation of a national park."

Eleanor clenched the arm of the seat as if she might suddenly be thrown to the floor if she loosened her grip. She forced her hand to relax. Everything would be all right. Father was just having a moment of reflection. He hadn't really had time to think things through. He wasn't going to give up his conservation work. He wasn't going to insist they settle down in one place.

But . . . why did that bother her so? Hadn't she just been abhorring the length of yet another journey?

She was simply tired. Not herself. She squared her shoulders and glanced at her reflection in the window. Her hat was on straight, and her coat lapels lay perfectly flat against the simple collar of her blouse. She was ready for Kalispell and whatever fate it had in store.

The train came to a stop. She stood and collected her bag.

If she was feeling addled and stressed from the treacherous trip the last few hours, then Father might be as well. Maybe that's where all the retirement conversation was coming from. Too much time to think on the train ride.

But then to bring up marriage! He just *had* to remind her that she was a spinster.

Tingles ran up and down her right leg. Then her hat took that moment to come undone, and it flopped down over her eyes.

Reaching a hand up to right it, she fiddled with the cantankerous object until her hand came back full of feathers and ribbon. She took a long, deep breath and refrained from stomping her foot.

All right, so she wasn't ready for this. Not in the least little bit. In truth, she was a frustrated, overtired spinster with a numb backside and leg, and a hat that was no longer decent or presentable.

**Tracie Peterson** is the award-winning author of over one hundred novels, both historical and contemporary. She has won the ACFW Lifetime Achievement Award and the Romantic Times Career Achievement Award. She is often referred to as the "Queen of Historical Christian Fiction," and her avid research resonates in her stories, as seen in her bestselling HEIRS OF MONTANA and ALASKAN QUEST series. Tracie considers her writing a ministry for God to share the Gospel and biblical application. She and her family make their home in Montana. Visit her website at TraciePeterson.com or on Facebook at Facebook.com/AuthorTraciePeterson.

# Sign Up for Tracie's Newsletter

Keep up to date with Tracie's latest news on book releases and events by signing up for her email list at the link below.

TraciePeterson.com

FOLLOW TRACIE ON SOCIAL MEDIA

Tracie Peterson

@AuthorTraciePeterson

# More from Tracie Peterson

Marybeth and Edward are compelled by their circumstances to marry as they trek west to the newly formed railroad town of Cheyenne. But life in Cheyenne is fraught with danger, and they find that they need each other more than ever. Despite the trials they face, will happiness await them in this arrangement of convenience?

*A Love Discovered*
THE HEART OF CHEYENNE #1

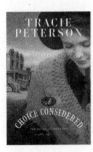

Melody Doyle has spent years following her father as the transcontinental railroad is built. Now she's determined to stay in Cheyenne, but her father will only allow her if she marries. As the men in town vie for her hand, she gets to know the new banker, Charles Decker, who upends all her plans—and steals her heart along the way.

*A Choice Considered*
THE HEART OF CHEYENNE #2

Eleanor Briggs travels to Kalispell, Montana, with her conservationist father to discuss the formation of Glacier National Park, and sparks fly when she meets Carter Brunswick, despite their differences. As the town fights to keep the railroad, the dangers Eleanor and Carter face will change the course of their lives.

*With Each Tomorrow*
THE JEWELS OF KALISPELL #2

## ◊ BETHANYHOUSE